Ryan,

Still with me for the 2nd volume maybe I'll see you for Volume 3.

enjoy!

White Noise Stories

Volume Two

By
Tammy Vreeland

E-BookTime, LLC
Montgomery, Alabama

White Noise Stories
Volume Two

Library of Congress Control Number: 2017943430

ISBN: 978-1-60862-730-1

First Edition
Published June 2018
E-BookTime, LLC
6598 Pumpkin Road
Montgomery, AL 36108
www.e-booktime.com

Dedication

To the ones whose life travels are the hardest but know it's not about the destination it's the journey they traveled! When you begin your journey in life sometimes you form friendships that can withstand time and distance. In my case, Jodi and Teresa not only succeeded but brought light into my darkest hour and for that I will be eternally grateful.

Contents

Contents

White Noise Stories

Lauren checks out her room one last time for any items she may have missed while packing. Pausing, she tries to make a mental image of her room. Lauren had come to think of this room as her safe zone!

After her "incident" at her first apartment, a term her mother came up with, Lauren had spent a couple of months recovering at her parent's home. When the incident happened, her parents whisked her home without question and made her feel safe.

Unfortunately, Lauren lost the job opportunity in the city, but on the upside, it had not hurt her resume since she had never started the job. As a career standpoint, it is only a couple of months after her graduation and with the economy the way it is, it simply looks like Lauren has been looking for a job during the couple of months she was actually off for her recovery.

Fortunately for her, things had a way of working out! Her friend, Roxy, had landed a job in California. Roxy's current work had an opening where she could not only move up but transfer to what Roxy thought would be paradise.

The downside would be moving on her own to an area where she would have no family or friends. Determined, Roxy started looking into other positions in the company. She was surprised to see another opening in the same area and instantly thought of Lauren. Knowing that Lauren's incident had taken a toll on her, Roxy thought perhaps a move would be exactly what Lauren needed to get back into the game. Plus, what better way to move clear across the country to the unknown than with at least one of your friends in tow?

When Roxy first pitched the idea to Lauren, Lauren was a little hesitant. Being that far from her parents, Lauren knew if something happened there would be no safety net for her. And yet, having a safety net came with its own costs. While in her parent's house she had to follow their rules. Once you've been on your own, it's tough going back. Even though she appreciated their help, there were times she wished she could run away and this may be her chance. Plus, the idea of Roxy living on the West Coast while Lauren remained on the East Coast made her sad.

Lauren had met Roxy when she first moved here with her family. For some reason, Roxy had latched onto Lauren. Even though Roxy was self-centered and uncompromising, not at all like her friends back home, she was still better than nothing. Lauren had become accustomed to Roxy being around, almost dependent on her.

With a determination Lauren did not think she would ever have again, she applied for the position Roxy had found for her. After the interview, Roxy's company was more than happy to offer her the job. Of course, Roxy's determination and enthusiasm had to have been part of the equation. Whatever the case, Roxy and Lauren found themselves planning a road trip to their new jobs.

Surprisingly, Lauren's parents had been supportive of the idea. Although her mom was sad to see her leave, she was happy that Lauren was not going to let her incident get the best of her.

Lauren can't help but think back to her incident. Sometimes she wonders if it really happened. Honestly, there was much Lauren did not remember. If it had not been for her recording her meltdown in the lobby, more than likely, Lauren would not have remembered any of it.

The hospital had kept her a couple of days; rehydrating her and making sure she started eating again. While there, Lauren talked to a psychiatrist only a couple of times. He had listened to her recording and discussed it with her. They both came to the conclusion that the stress of the move, the anxiousness of starting a career, along with the change from college life to real life may have hit her too hard. Combined with sleeping too much, aggravated with all the noise and not eating, Lauren was bound to have a break!

Her parents agreed with her and the psychiatrist. They even took it a step further and arranged for her apartment to be cleaned out so that Lauren would never have to see the place that had made her break.

Lauren had followed through on her part. She had notified her new job that a personal situation had arisen and, although she appreciated the opportunity, she felt that she could not take the job at this time.

It was almost as if nothing had happened! Almost. However, deep inside, Lauren knew something major had happened. She was just not sure if she believed it! How had she known so many stories? Were they only her dreams? Perhaps she had heard the stories in the apartment complex and her subconscious had turned them into dreams?

Lauren wanted to immediately research all of the stories/ dreams, but her psychiatrist and her parents did not think it was a good idea. She needed time to recover first. There would be plenty of time for research later.

While Lauren was recovering she had little contact with Roxy. Roxy had hooked back up with her ex-boyfriend and never seemed to have time for her. She didn't mind because her other friends were more than happy to listen and be there for her. Imagine her surprise though, when Roxy presented the idea of moving to California together. Granted, it happened to be after yet another break up with her ex. Lauren was tempted since she really had nothing planned for the future and it was a perfect opportunity to break away from her parents' hold.

Once Lauren agreed, everything became a whirlwind of activity. No longer was there time to investigate the stories/dreams from the apartment complex.

And here she is today… standing in the middle of her room wondering when the next time will be that she will see it again. Feeling a bit anxious and a little sad, Lauren takes a deep breath and tries to be strong for the goodbyes she will have to say to her parents.

After the long tearful goodbyes, Lauren finds herself driving away with Roxy gleefully beside her. "For a second there, I didn't think your mom was going to let you go!"

Lauren agrees, "I know, though I have to give her a lot of credit. As bad as she wants me to stay, she still wants to be supportive of my decision."

Roxy sighs, "You are lucky. Although my mom says she will miss me, I think in a way she is relieved and anxious to get on with her own life!"

Lauren thinks about it. "Must be tough being a parent. Devoting your life to raising a child, only for them to grow up and go away."

Roxy tries to bring the conversation around to being more upbeat, "Fortunately, you and I are not going to have to worry about that for a long time! We have too much partying and single life to enjoy!"

Lauren smiles and starts to get her mind settled in for the long drive, "Unfortunately, we have to make it through this long-ass drive ahead of us first!"

Roxy is not deterred, "What do you mean? A lot of people would kill to go on this road trip!"

Lauren teases her, "This coming from a girl who will not be driving at all, since she never bothered to get her driver's license!"

Roxy tries to defend herself, "Hey, I always lived and worked in the city! Never had a need for a car, especially when my bestie already has one!"

Lauren is curious, "What about when we get to California?"

Roxy smiles, "From what I hear, walking and biking is the best way to get around in Long Beach." She looks over at Lauren and winks, "And my bestie, will still have a car!"

Lauren laughs, "You have it all figured out, don't you?"

Roxy's smile fades a little, "Not all of it, I am a little worried about car sickness!"

Concerned, Lauren asks, "Did you get what you need from the doctor?"

Roxy sighs, "I did, but he warned me it will more than likely knock me out."

Lauren is not worried. "Don't worry about me, believe it or not, I enjoy driving long distances. I used to do most of the driving when my parents and I would visit family out in Oregon. I just listen to the radio and get in the zone."

Roxy can't help but tease her, "And I bet this was the car you drove!"

Lauren smiles, "Are you trying to knock my grandmother's car again?"

Roxy looks around, "Girl, I just can't understand why you didn't trade this old thing in for a different, trendier car!"

Lauren shrugs her shoulders, "What can I say? The car has low mileage on it and it is easy to fix. My grandmother took excellent care of it. Plus, bottom line, it really isn't worth anything. I wouldn't have gotten much money for it."

Roxy is not convinced. "Honey, surely there would have been some cute used car out there that had your name all over it!"

Lauren shakes her head, "No thank you, I promised myself I would never buy a used car! The next car I own will be brand new!"

Roxy is surprised. Lauren is usually not one to be bothered about having the nicer things. "Really? Look at you, all high and mighty!"

Lauren blushes, "Oh, it is not for the reason you are thinking! Actually, it's kind of a stupid one."

Roxy is intrigued, "Do tell!"

Lauren, still blushing, replies, "It has to do with a book I read once called the Transporter of Souls."

Roxy laughs, "You and your scary books! Why do you torture yourself? Was it fact or fiction?"

Lauren knows she should have never brought it up but tries to defend herself. "Fiction, but the basis was dead on! Did you know you can buy a used car that someone has died in and they don't have to tell you?"

Roxy giggles, "Honestly, just between you and me, let people think you are high and mighty! It is easier to think of you as a princess than a kook!"

Lauren briefly thinks about the book and finds chills coming over her. No one ever thinks twice about who the previous owner of a used car was or what may have happened in the car. And yet, so many people worry about houses they buy being haunted, or worse, apartments. Lauren quickly chases that thought out of her mind. That is something she promised herself she would not dwell on.

Lauren focuses back on what Roxy had said and answers, "I understand. I would have never told anyone else the real reason. Anyway, I love this car! It makes me feel closer to Grandma."

Roxy thinks back, "And yet, didn't your grandmother die in this car?"

Lauren nods sadly, "Yes, she did. After shopping at the market, she got in the car and her heart just gave out."

Lauren reassures herself that the premise of the book, Transporter of Souls, was nothing more than made up. Although there may be cars that are haunted, Lauren doesn't like the idea of her grandmother being trapped in the car due to an old gypsy curse. No, sometimes even Lauren's imagination stops her and tries to be reasonable.

Roxy regrets bringing it up, "I'm sorry, I shouldn't have mentioned it."

Lauren doesn't let it bother her, "It's ok. I think she planned it that way. My grandmother never wanted people to see her weak. I am sure she was determined to make it to the car so as not to let anyone see her fall!"

Roxy remembers her, "She was a sweet old lady."

Lauren pats the dashboard, "Yes she was and I think she will be riding along with us on our road trip looking over us." Lauren has to add in her mind, if Grandma is with them, it is only because she wants to, not because she is trapped in the car... stupid book!

Roxy sighs, "Ok, but I really wished she had invested in a decent radio! I don't see how, with an antique like that, you will be able to listen to anything! I'm telling you, I might be able to figure out how to pipe your music from your phone through your car stereo."

Lauren looks at her phone in disgust. "You know how I hate my phone! Give me the basics any day! Besides, I like listening to old stations with hometown DJ's. Gives you a peek into what small towns are doing."

Roxy shakes her head, "I swear girlfriend, you have such an old soul!"

Lauren cringes a little at hearing the word "soul". A quick flash of Mr. Akeru comes to her mind. An even stranger thought occurs, what if "old souls" were even more of a prize to Mr. Akeru? If that is the case, perhaps it was a good thing she was moving. She doubted Mr. Akeru, if he existed, would pursue her clear across the country.

Roxy yawns, "I think those pills are already beginning to work. This sucks! Not much of a road trip if I'm sleeping the whole time!"

Lauren smiles, "Don't worry, I promise to wake you up if I see something cool!"

Roxy looks out the window, "You better! I want this to be not just about the destination, but about the journey as well."

Lauren agrees, "Fine by me, beats the hell out of the way my parents used to travel! Granted, we never had a lot of time; however, my dad would not stop for anything! When we got gas, we got food, and took a bathroom break. You would hope that the gas station may have some cool souvenirs because it was the only way you would see something of the state we were driving through!"

Roxy, always having to one up her, sighs, "At least your parents took you on vacations! We never took a family vacation, how sad is that? Both my mother and father worked constantly; there was no time or money for such luxury!"

Lauren feels bad, "You are right, I was lucky that they took vacations. We didn't have much money either. To be able to take a vacation, we would camp and take food from home. However, we did get away and enjoy the area we were in."

Roxy becomes a little snarky, "Well, at least we know the first two days you'll enjoy no matter what! With seeing Teresa in Indy and Jodi in Oklahoma, the road trip will completely center on you and your old friends."

Lauren is surprised to hear the jealousy in Roxy's voice, "Don't blame me! When I suggested we could see them on the way, you were all for it. If you didn't want to see them, you should have spoken up."

Roxy shrugs her shoulders, "How could I, when I know you really want to see them?"

Lauren admits, "I do want to see them and I want you to meet them. You've already met Teresa at Christmas time. I thought we all had a great time then."

Roxy sighs, "We did."

Lauren continues to make her point, "And we will again! Plus, we'll be driving right past them; it will not take any time away from us. You have to admit, I let you decide where and when you wanted to stop after that."

Roxy agrees as she yawns again, "Taking Route 66 most of the way and stopping at the Grand Canyon should be fun!"

Lauren teases her, "Ok then grumpy, why don't you get comfortable and take a nap already?"

Roxy blushes, "Maybe that would be a good idea!"

Lauren turns the radio on and starts trying to find a station. She settles for a talk radio station.

Roxy grabs her purse and pulls out her ear phones, "If you don't mind, while you listen to that crap, I am going to listen to the good stuff!"

Lauren watches the road and listens to her radio while Roxy begins to doze off listening to her music.

After driving a while, the radio station begins to fade out. Suddenly, a blast of white noise comes over the radio. Annoyed, Lauren reaches to change the station, but before she does, a clear signal comes through. It sounds as if it may be a caller calling into a station about a story she has. Intrigued, Lauren listens.

Dime

Dime

Chelsea reads over her notes. Sam, her best friend, leans over her shoulder to take a peek. Sighing, Sam asks, "Still working on the whole urban legend assignment I see?"

Chelsea shrugs her shoulders, "I can't help it, it fascinates me! Anyway, didn't you once say it is easier to write about something you find interesting?"

Sam smiles as she takes a seat in front of Chelsea, "I did, but I can't take full credit. I heard it somewhere."

Chelsea's eyes sparkle, "Hmmm, almost like an urban legend?"

Sam rolls her eyes, "A bit of a stretch, but I guess. What have you come up with so far, more of the same chanting some poor dead girl's name in front of a mirror crap?"

Chelsea looks wide eyed as she shakes her head, "No, nothing like that! This is way better and some of it may even be local!"

Sam looks at her watch, "Alright, I have fifteen minutes before I have to catch the bus. I am all ears!"

Chelsea looks at her own watch and nods, "That works for me, since Todd will be coming to pick me up after his detention."

Sam rolls her eyes, "What did he do now? Wait! Let me guess! Another fight?"

Chelsea becomes defensive, "It wasn't his fault!"

Sam sighs, "It never is. Chelsea, the guy is bad news! We've already seen it first-hand. That night he hit you, I thought for sure that would be the last you would see of him."

Chelsea lowers her eyes, "You have no idea how many times he has apologized for that. It was just after losing the big game; it was nothing more than a perfect storm. He promised he would change."

Sam disagrees, "And yet, he is in detention over a fight right now. Chelsea, people like that never change! He is toxic! He does not deserve you!"

Chelsea sighs, "There is something about him that attracts me to him. I can't help it!"

Sam realizes there is no way of her convincing Chelsea so instead she tries to joke, "I guess it is no different than your fascination with this stupid assignment, right?"

Chelsea is relieved in the change of topic. "Exactly! Let me ask you, have you ever wondered how an item becomes cursed or even haunted? And if so, what sort of images pop into your mind when you think of such an item?"

Skeptical, Sam answers, "If you believe in those types of things, I would venture to say a child's toy. A doll or some sort of toy that was special to a deceased child."

Chelsea nods, "Very good! Hey, did you see the special on TV about the haunted doll in Florida named Robert?"

Sam shivers a little, "Yes, which was the reason for my answer."

Chelsea smiles, "I figured as much. It was such a cool show!"

Sam laughs, "Leave it to you to think it was cool! Mind you, most people would have found it disturbing, to say the least!"

Chelsea agrees, "Oh, it was disturbing! However, let me ask you why you thought it was disturbing."

Sam thinks about it, "I guess because they made it seem so real. That Robert really is a haunted doll!"

Chelsea smiles, "Ok, if you can think a doll could be haunted, what about other items like a music box or a piece of jewelry?" Before Sam can answer, Chelsea quickly answers for her, "If those items are plausible, do you think money can be haunted or cursed?"

Without thinking Sam agrees, "Of course, we have all heard the term "blood money," but I'm not sure what that really means?"

Chelsea agrees, "Honestly, I didn't either so I looked it up."

Chelsea looks down at her notes and reads, "The true definition of blood money is money paid in compensation to the family of someone who has been killed. It can also mean money paid to a hired killer or even money paid by the police for information on a killer or killing."

Sam is not impressed, "Doesn't seem like any of that would mean the money is actually cursed or haunted!"

Chelsea loves that Sam is making her defend her research, it is exactly the perspective she needs to make her paper convincing to a non-believer.

Chelsea smiles, "Patience dear, there's more. First of all, let's go back to the most well-known and classic tale of blood money. That would be the thirty pieces of silver paid to Judas for betraying Jesus which is described in the New Testament."

Sam rolls her eyes, "The bible, really?"

Chelsea sighs, "Yea, yea, I know your take on the religion stuff but it is still interesting! The story goes that after Jesus was arrested a remorseful Judas returned to the temple and tried to give back the silver he received for the betrayal. Judas admitted that he had sinned and betrayed an innocent."

Chelsea is encouraged that Sam is still listening intently and goes on, "When the priests denied him, Judas threw the coins into the temple and fled to hang himself. Not wanting to keep the coins in the temple, the priests purchased a plot of land to bury foreigners."

Sam raises her eyebrow, "Ok, I admit it's getting interesting."

Chelsea chuckles as she proceeds, "The story says that the coins were kept together in a small brown sack. In fact, the coins could not be separated from each other for very long. The individual coins had a strange way of finding their way back to the owner within a week, due to a strange set of circumstances."

Sam is intrigued, "What kind of circumstances?"

Chelsea answers, "Month after month the coins would have an adverse effect on the particular owner at the time with different degrees of severity. The only way to be rid of the coins was when they were willingly accepted by someone else."

Sam thinks about it, "Wouldn't that action in itself be not very 'Christian' like? You know, giving someone else your problem knowingly?"

Chelsea agrees, "I know, right? Although, in another version of the story it was told that the coins had to be spent in seven days through charitable acts."

Sam smiles, "I like that version better!"

Chelsea adds, "And there is yet another version which states the curse could be lifted if buried in the original plot of land for foreigners."

Sam sighs, "Well, at least they had options!"

Chelsea laughs, "You're too much! Let's move on to the next famous example of blood money. The money of Cortes, also known as the treasure of the Isla de Muerta. This treasure consisted of 882 identical pieces of Aztec gold placed in a stone chest supposedly buried on an island in the Caribbean."

Sam lights up, "Now we're talking! Treasure of the Caribbean kind of stuff! I love Johnny Depp!"

Chelsea agrees, "Oh, I do too! Anyway, according to the legend, the Aztecs delivered the chest to Cortes as blood money paid to stem the slaughter he wreaked upon them with his armies."

Sam listens intently, definitely caught up in the story. Chelsea continues, "However, because the gold fueled Cortes' greed, the Heathen Gods placed a curse over the gold. Any mortal that removed a piece from the chest would be damned. The curse could only be lifted if the money was returned along with a blood debt repaid."

Sam can't resist, "See, no need for reading! We pretty much knew that from the movies!"

Chelsea disagrees, "Reading gives you so much more information."

Sam shrugs her shoulders, "I guess, but what does all of this have to do with your assignment on urban legends? I am sure those two examples may be legends, but I don't really think they are urban!"

Chelsea frowns, "I know. My research sort of took me down that path when I was trying to find history on cursed or haunted money. I'm not sure if I am going to use them in my paper."

Sam realizes how hard Chelsea has been working on her assignment and softens her tone. "I don't know, maybe you should use it. It is interesting and it will help you with the word count!"

Chelsea smiles, "That it does! Ok, so now we fast forward to the modern day. Have you ever heard of the curse of the lottery?

Many lottery winners have felt the wrath of the curse, ranging from broken marriages, greed, destitution, and even death."

Sam nods, "Yea, now that line of thinking is definitely urban legend!"

Chelsea agrees, "I know and I have a lot of examples I can use."

Sam is curious, "When we started you asked me about money being cursed or haunted. Is there a difference?"

Chelsea is surprised, "Damn! We do think alike! I wondered the same thing and had to look it up. A curse is an utterance to invoke a supernatural power to inflict harm or punishment on someone or something."

Chelsea quickly looks down at her notes, "A haunting is to visit or appear in the form of a ghost; or, to come to the mind continually; obsess."

Chelsea looks perplexed, "I am not sure whether my theory about the dime is cursed or haunted."

Sam is confused, "The dime? What are you talking about?"

Chelsea gets excited, "Remember, I mentioned earlier there may even be local urban legends?"

Sam nods and Chelsea continues, "Strangely enough, I was talking to Karen about this assignment and she told me her cousin Annie had heard about a story involving a returning dime at the toll plaza."

Sam teases her, "Well, coming from such a reliable source, I am sure it must be true!"

Chelsea laughs, "Alright smart ass, laugh all you want but that is how urban legends spread! One person knows someone that passed the story along; it's very rare you get to hear it from the person it actually happened to!"

Sam is curious, "Why is that?"

Chelsea shrugs her shoulders, "Probably because they are dead! Anyway, I found the story fascinating and went to the library to look up anything that may involve the toll booth."

Sam is impressed, "That was smart."

Chelsea blushes, "Thanks! The first story was this girl telling her story about a weird accident involving a dime after the toll plaza."

Chelsea looks down at her notes, "I will read you what she wrote: "My boyfriend and I were heading out for a long road trip. The first toll plaza we reach, he looks over to me for the money. Not surprised, I pull the money out of my pocket."

"The toll attendant gives him back the change. Not wanting to mess up his precious car, he hands the change back to me. I then shove it into my pocket."

"I soon realized that while shoving the coins into my pocket, I had also pushed my shirt into the pocket. Sighing, I pulled my shirt out of the pocket which of course made the coins come out and they fell out onto the seat and floor."

"Knowing my boyfriend was quick with his temper, I hastily tried to scoop up the coins but it was too hard with my seat belt on. I carefully told him I would pick them up when we stopped for gas. He, of course, made a curt answer along the lines of 'you better!'"

"We stopped at the gas station right after the toll plaza. I undid my seat belt and quickly gathered the change up before getting out and going to the restroom."

"After leaving the restroom, I bought him a Coke, hoping this would put him in a better mood."

"When I got back in the car, I tried to put my seat belt on. Of course, he didn't wait for me to get it on. We were back on the highway going pretty fast with me not having my seat belt on. I began to get scared!"

"Time after time, I tried to click my seat belt on but for some reason it wasn't allowing me. After several attempts, my boyfriend looks over at me annoyed and asks 'what is the problem?'"

"A bit nervous about what his reaction would be, I told him I could not fasten my seatbelt. Without stopping, he tries to click it himself as the car swerves from one side of the road to the other, but he couldn't get it to fasten either."

"Beyond frustrated, he abruptly pulled off to the side of the road so he could see how "I" damaged his seat belt. Meanwhile, I could not understand what could have possibly happened from the time I had it on, to the time I went to the restroom."

"Shocked, he yells out as he is looking at it, 'No wonder you can't click it, there's a damn dime lodged in it!'"

"A dime? How was that possible? Then I remembered the change coming out of my pocket when I pulled my shirt out. However, how in the world did the dime go into the mechanism if my seat belt was on at that time?"

"The only thing we could think of was that it balanced on there until I unfastened the seat belt and then fell into the mechanism when I got out. What are the odds?"

"Fumbling around trying to get it out, neither he nor I were able to. Pissed, he tells me to sit my ass on the guard rail while he got in the trunk to get his multi-purpose tool."

"As he tried to get the dime out with the tool, he told me that he couldn't do this anymore and that he was going to leave me there alongside of the road."

"Crying, I told him I needed my phone to be able to call someone to come and get me."

"Suddenly, he stood up smiling, holding the dime in his tool like a trophy. He then threw the dime at me and laughed, 'Here's a dime, now go and call someone.' Right after he said that a car slammed into the back of his car and killed him instantly."

Chills come over Sam, "Sounds like something Todd would do to you!"

Annoyed, Chelsea says, "Whatever! At least the girl was safe!"

Sam realizes she should have kept her mouth shut about Todd. "What else do you have?"

Still aggravated about the Todd comment, Chelsea becomes curt with her answers, "There was a couple fighting coming from the toll booth. The husband said the wife had reached over to pick up a dime that had fallen on the floor when they hit the divider."

Sam is curious, "Did anyone die?"

Chelsea nods, "Yes, the wife. This time it seems as if the wife was the abuser in the relationship."

Sam perks up, "So you are seeing a pattern? Where the dime seems to target someone that abuses another? Perhaps someone haunting the dime died under similar circumstances and is now targeting the abusers as payback?"

Chelsea nods, "Yea, that's my thinking too! There was another story, although there was no mention of a dime, about two friends on a road trip. One friend said after they received their change, they continued a fight they were having."

Chills begin to rise up on Chelsea as she continues, "The survivor said the sun shone in so brightly the driver could not see and drove right into an oncoming car."

Sam smiles as she subconsciously rubs her own arms due to chills, "There you go, I tell you it's a haunting!"

Chelsea laughs, "Wait a minute! You haven't heard all of the evidence!"

Before Chelsea goes on with the evidence, "Mind you, the statistics for accidents after this toll plaza are unusually high. So high in fact, they have had several engineers evaluate what the reason is for that many accidents but no one can come to a conclusive theory."

Sam can't help but smile, "Let me guess, your theory is the haunted dime?"

Chelsea shrugs her shoulders, "Or cursed dime. So far the examples I have given you are ones of couples fighting; therefore, it stands to reason that perhaps there is a haunted dime out there causing these accidents, but then again, there is another story."

Chelsea fumbles through her notes and retrieves the paper she is looking for, "Here it is! They interviewed a young boy who had hidden away in his sister's car."

Chelsea quickly skims the paper, "The boy said his sister was running away from home. He had overheard her fight with their mom and hid in the car so he could go with her."

Chelsea proceeds, "He told the police his sister must have dropped the change at the toll plaza because he remembered her saying that yes she needed another dime. Now that she was on her own, every dime counts."

Chelsea looks up wide eyed at Sam, "Right after leaving the toll plaza, his sister hits a deer. The poor deer is half in the car and proceeds to kick his sister to death."

Shocked, Sam shakes her head, "That poor kid! I can only imagine the nightmares he's had!"

Chelsea nods, "I know, right?"

Sam looks confused, "So, how does one story lead you to think the dime could be cursed?"

Chelsea smiles, "That is where the urban legend kicks in. I have only given you true examples that are recorded. Now, I will tell you what the urban legend warns about."

Sam is all ears, completely losing all track of time, "Do tell!"

Just as she is about to tell her, Chelsea sees Todd walking in and lowers her voice, "Be nice, Todd is here."

Sam quickly looks down at her watch, "Damn! I missed the bus!"

Todd walks over smiling and kisses Chelsea full on the lips, "Hi beautiful!"

He looks over at Sam and smirks, "Hi, Sam."

Sam, annoyed, barely gets out a response. Chelsea quickly speaks up, "Don't mind her, she just missed her bus. Hey, you wouldn't mind dropping her off, would you Todd?"

Todd shrugs his shoulders, "Anything for you beautiful."

Sam is not so sure that is a good idea, "I don't know, Chelsea."

Chelsea refuses to take no for an answer, "It'll be fine, plus I can finish telling you about the urban legend!"

Sam sighs, "Ok, if you are sure you don't mind?"

Todd helps Chelsea gather her books, "Not at all, my pleasure."

Chelsea leans over and whispers to Sam, "See, I told you he has changed!"

Sam is not buying into Todd's little act, but at least she does not have to call her mom to come and get her. Once they are all in Todd's car, Todd looks over at Chelsea in the passenger seat and asks, "What urban legend are you talking about?"

Chelsea buckles up and answers, "The toll plaza."

Todd nods, "I've heard about that one!"

Chelsea turns in her seat and looks at Sam in the back seat, "Legend has it that a girl and her boyfriend were running away from home. The girl's mother tried to convince her not to go. As the girl leaves, her mother throws a dime at her and yells she better hope she never has to use it."

Chelsea continues, "Although the girl was convinced her boyfriend was going to marry her and provide her with everything she would need, she still picked the dime up because it was the only money she had."

She explains, "Back in the day, a dime was all you needed to make a call. Everyone carried at least a dime with them so they could use the payphone."

Chelsea becomes a little embarrassed with the next part, especially in front of Todd. "Apparently, before he even got on the main road, he convinced the girl to have sex. He told her it was not a big deal; they would be married soon anyway."

Todd mumbles, "Man had a point."

Chelsea blushes and tries to ignore him as she goes on, "After the incident with her mother, the girl became ashamed and started having doubts. She sat in the passenger seat rubbing the dime her mother had thrown at her."

Sam can't resist, "The girl had a point."

Todd glares at her in the rear view mirror. Chelsea is not sure she should go on, but does, "Her boyfriend noticed the dime and when they came up to the newly opened toll plaza demanded the girl give him the dime to help pay the toll."

Sam understands, "Knowing that was the only way for her to escape."

Chelsea wishes she had never brought this story up, especially in front of Todd with Sam. Not knowing anyway around it, Chelsea finishes the story. "The boyfriend over paid the attendant and the attendant ended up giving him back the same dime."

Todd laughs, "At this point the boyfriend says something along the lines of, like a bad penny, this dime is going to keep showing up."

Chelsea becomes somber, "Not paying attention to the road the boyfriend throws the dime back at the girl. They wreck and the girl dies holding the dime tightly."

Chelsea adds one last detail, "When the mother found out about the girl holding the dime she asked for the dime as a keepsake, but the dime had mysteriously disappeared."

Todd can't help being stupid, he makes a scary sound, "Wooooo, careful or the dime will get you!"

Chelsea turns in her seat looking forward. Todd puts his arm around her and tries to cuddle, "You know Sam, Chelsea and I have talked about running away together."

Sam looks disgusted and blurts out, "Why? So you can get laid like the guy in the story?"

Todd yanks his arm away from Chelsea and angrily replies, "No! I don't know why you think so little of me, Sam!"

Sam stares him down in the rear view mirror, "Maybe it's because I don't approve of guys hitting girls! From what I've seen, once a guy goes down that path he never stops!"

Todd rolls his eyes, "Oh my God! This one has been watching too many afternoon specials! Give it a break Sam! I've already apologized to Chelsea and I will never let it happen again!"

Sam is curious, "Do you two know which toll plaza this urban legend happens?"

Todd nods, "Yea, around exit 117."

Sam's eyes sparkle, "Then I suggest we put this urban legend to the test."

Chelsea becomes a little concerned, "I don't know if that is such a good idea."

Sam shrugs her shoulders, "Why not? Seems to me the perfect storm. An abusive boyfriend and a girl who has contemplated running away with him. This could be your proof the urban legend is not just a legend!"

Todd laughs, "You are on!"

Chelsea looks worried, "You are kidding, right?"

Todd shakes his head, "No, what is the worst that could happen? It is in the middle of the day."

Chelsea explains, "It can happen any time of the day or night!"

Todd is still up for the challenge, "If I see we are getting a dime, I'll just refuse it. No big deal. It'll be fun."

Todd turns the car around and gets on the highway. Chelsea looks back at Sam, "Why are you encouraging him?"

Sam tries to look innocent, "Chelsea, if you honestly don't want to go, tell him no!"

Chelsea nods, "Todd, I'm serious! I really don't want to go. Just take the next exit off and take us home."

Todd's anger quickly comes over him, "Screw that, we're going! I'm not going to let your girlfriend decide on what we want to do!"

Chelsea looks shocked, "It's what you want to do! I don't! C'mon, just take us home."

Todd flies by the last exit before the toll plaza, "I will after the toll plaza!"

Chelsea and Sam sit in anticipation as Todd rolls up to the toll attendant. Todd pulls his money out and jokes with the attendant, "The girls here are terrified of the stupid urban legend crap about this toll plaza. Think you could give me nickels instead of a dime?"

The toll attendant laughs, "Sorry dude, all out of nickels just for that reason. A dime it is or not, your call."

Not wanting to look bad in front of the attendant, Todd laughs, "Just give me the dime, who believes in that crap anyway?"

The attendant hesitantly hands him the dime, "You would be surprised!"

Todd shakes his head as he takes the dime, "Oh, please!" He gives the dime to Chelsea, "See, nothing but an ordinary dime!"

Chelsea looks closely at the dime and shivers. Sam becomes concerned, "What is it, Chelsea?"

Chelsea looks fearfully back at Sam, "The other interesting thing about the urban legend is the dime itself. Apparently, the father collected unusual coins. The mother had it in her apron to clean it. Some say the mother didn't want it back for a keepsake, it was the abusive father demanding to get it back for his collection."

Sam is afraid to ask, "What was so special about it?"

Chelsea shows her the dime, "The head was upside down just like this one."

Todd laughs, "That was a good one Chelsea, showing her the dime upside down. You even had me going!"

Todd looks in his mirror as he sees a big rig bearing down on them, "What the hell is that trucker doing? Isn't he going to stop for the toll?"

Unfortunately, the trucker couldn't stop. His brakes that had worked only minutes before were now not working! He slams into the back of Todd's car.

After the wreck, right before passing out, Chelsea sees a shadowy girl come up to her and take the dime she was holding. As she does, she looks sadly down at Chelsea and mumbles, "Sometimes an item can be both cursed and haunted!"

White Noise Stories Continued

Roxy abruptly turns off the car radio, "Oh my God! How can you listen to that noise?"

Seeing how her outburst startled Lauren, Roxy quickly apologizes, "I'm sorry. I was fast asleep and my earphones must have cut out. Suddenly, I was hearing what you were listening to on the radio and it freaked me out!"

Realizing Roxy meant no harm, Lauren brushes it off easily, "It's ok, how are you feeling?"

Roxy yawns, "Still very groggy. I see the toll plaza is coming up, do you have EZ-pass?"

Lauren shakes her head, "No, I cancelled it before we left. I put toll money in the ashtray."

Roxy reaches over and pulls the money out for the toll. "Look at you, all prepared! Keep track of this so we can get refunded for our moving expenses."

Lauren smiles, "I will."

Lauren rolls up to the attendant and hands her the money. The attendant smiles nicely and hands her the change back. Lauren suddenly realizes it is a dime and quickly drops it!

The attendant gasps, "I'm sorry, here let me get you another one!"

The story from the radio about the dime comes crashing down on Lauren. What if the dime thinks she is running away from her parents, not appreciating all they had done for her? Or perhaps, the haunted part may think Roxy is the abusive part of this relationship! Lauren has to admit there are times she lets Roxy have her way just so she will not have to deal with her wrath!

Lauren shakes her head and feebly smiles at the attendant, "No, that is ok, it was my fault! Have a nice day."

Before the attendant can answer, Lauren pulls away. A little confused, Roxy decides to let it go. Roxy had tried to prepare herself for small incidents along the way involving Lauren.

Roxy looks happily at the next exit, "Wow! We are already at exit 117, you are making great time!"

Lauren had been so involved in the radio she didn't have a clue to where they actually were! Uncontrollable chills come over her as she vaguely remembers the story saying something about the toll plaza being around exit 117!

Roxy notices huge goose bumps on Lauren and reaches over to turn the AC down. "Honey, you look like you are freezing! I hope you are not keeping it cold just for me. Remember, the driver has full control over all devices."

Lauren, clearly distracted, simply replies, "Let's stop here for gas."

Roxy goes to the restroom while Lauren pumps the gas. As Lauren is finishing, she notices a young girl on the other side of the pump. Being friendly, Lauren smiles and says, "Hi."

The girl returns the smile and points to the ground beside Lauren, "Hi. I think you dropped a dime."

Lauren looks down at the ground and sees a shiny dime beckoning her. She looks closer and is shocked to see the head is upside down on the dime! Just like the one in the story!

The girl whispers, "I think it's time I left it here."

Fear washes over Lauren. "No! It can't be!" Suddenly the gas nozzle pops out of the tank, spilling gas. Lauren picks it up quickly and clicks it off.

The gas attendant comes around the tanks, "Is there something I can help you with ma'am?"

Frightened, Lauren turns to look at him. "I'm sorry, I was talking to this girl and the nozzle popped out."

The attendant looks around, "What girl?"

Lauren looks back to where the girl was standing and realizes she is gone! Lauren mumbles, "I guess I was mistaken."

Quickly finishing up, Lauren gets in the car and pulls it up to the building. Before going in to use the restroom herself, Lauren tries to calm down.

What was going on with her? Did she really see the dime from the story on the radio? Lauren rubs her temples as she whispers harshly, "No! That's not possible!" And that girl! Where did she go and what did she say at the end? Lauren is not sure. Feeling foolish, Lauren decides to shake it off and not dwell on it.

After going in to use the restroom, Roxy and she are back out on the road.

Roxy, a little bored, decides to ask, "Lauren, you really never told me… exactly what happened in your apartment?"

Lauren sighs, "I figured this was going to come up. I suppose you do have a right to know since you are going to be my new roommate."

Roxy leans over and pats her on the knee, "You do know nothing you say is going to change my mind! I'm curious, that's all."

Lauren nods appreciatively, "I understand. I would be curious as hell too if all of sudden you broke and became a raving lunatic!"

Roxy brings her hand back a bit guilty, "I should have been a better friend. The last time I saw you, you were obviously sick; however, I had my stupid sister's wedding and I just overlooked the obvious."

Lauren agrees, "How do you think I felt? I remember day after day looking in the mirror and seeing myself go down, but I kept reassuring myself it was nothing to worry about!"

Roxy is curious, "Do you think if you had started work immediately after moving in, you would have had the same result?"

Lauren shrugs her shoulders, "Maybe not, but I still would have had to sleep. Sleep turned out to be the problem!"

This time Lauren does not get chills, but a cold sweat comes over her at the thought of the apartment complex. Not that she can remember much, but the recording of her breakdown plays over and over in her mind.

Lauren casually mentions, "Did you know someone had died in my apartment?"

Shocked, Roxy gasps, "You have got to be kidding me!"

Lauren shakes her head, "No, a young artist committed suicide. He was the tenant before me."

Roxy is curious, "How did you find out?"

Lauren tries to remember, "I think through a dream, but I'm not sure. I do remember there was a crack in the bedroom window in the dream. The same crack was in my bedroom window!"

Lauren continues, "When my parents heard the recording of my meltdown, they investigated on their own. Sure enough, it had happened! Actually, that was how my parents were able to break the lease. The apartment complex had not disclosed that information to me."

Roxy's voice is barely above a whisper, "Do you think your apartment was haunted?"

Lauren thinks hard about it, "I think the whole complex might have been!"

Roxy is shocked, "What do you mean?"

Lauren tries to explain, "I think the dreams I was having were dreams from people that had died in the complex!"

Roxy shakes her head, "Seriously? You can't honestly think the dead can dream!"

Embarrassed, Lauren simply mumbles, "Maybe I do."

Roxy is confused, "How did you tap into their dreams? Do you have a physic grandmother in your family, or were you touched at an earlier age?"

Lauren has to laugh, "Touched at an earlier age? What does that mean? Like in the head?"

Roxy smiles, "No, like had you ever had any encounters with anything supernatural when you were younger?"

Lauren thinks back, "No, nothing like that, in fact, I always stayed away from anything related to such things. What about you?"

Roxy's manner changes, "There was this one time my cousins and I did something stupid with a mirror late at night. Not sure if what happened really happened or if it simply was our imaginations!"

At the mention of mirrors, Lauren vaguely remembers a dream about mirrors. "I had a dream about a mirror and twins! The one twin was a doppelgänger who could actually use the mirror late at night to try and scare their twin to death!"

Roxy is not surprised, "My family is very superstitious when it comes to mirrors. To this day, if anyone dies we cover the mirrors in the house for seven days."

Now it is Lauren's turn to be curious, "Why is that?"

Roxy explains, "I was told that evil spirits and demons come to visit a family in mourning. When a soul leaves this world it leaves a void which can be filled by dark forces. When there is a vacuum, negativity can creep in."

Another vague memory pops up for Lauren. A dream about riding a train and demons trying to take her over! Lauren tries to focus on the memory but it suddenly disappears.

Roxy continues, "Where loss is felt the most seems to be a magnet for evil spirits." She looks over at Lauren, "The evil spirits or demons can't be seen by the naked eye, but when looking in a mirror you may be able to see their reflection in the background."

Roxy thinks back to when her cousins had come to visit during her grandmother's funeral. As a dare, they decided late one night to take the covering off one of the mirrors to see if there really were evil spirits or demons lurking in the mirror!

Three little girls timidly pulled the sheet down off the large mirror in the living room. The room was dark as they gazed up into the mirror with wide eyes. Two red eyes proceeded to stare back at them menacingly! Their screaming woke up both their parents and grandpa.

Roxy's father had logically explained it had to be parking lights from a car across the street. This made the girls feel better; however, old grandpa was not hearing it! He grumbled that certain things can't be explained away so easily and the girls were lucky to still have their souls intact!

Roxy continues without going into details, "In college I ran across a study about it. They said that maybe the ghosts that visit a mourner are nothing but regret, guilt and anger. When people are grieving they tend to take a hard look at themselves in the mirror. They often feel like they didn't do enough for the departed; they didn't get to say all they wanted to say. Maybe they had loose ends or unfinished business with the deceased."

Roxy continues, "So, we cover the mirrors. When the heart hurts the most there is no room for harsh self-judgment! If we have unresolved issues, there will be time to deal with them later. We give ourselves a week to focus only on the loss itself."

Lauren admits, "I like that version much better than the demons coming to get you!"

Suddenly Roxy's pills that she had taken back at the gas station begin to kick in. Yawning, she can feel her body begging to go back to sleep.

Lauren notices Roxy's yawn, "You're ready for sleep again, aren't you?"

Roxy nods tiredly, "I'm sorry. I really want to carry on our conversation, but I'm afraid I will fall asleep at the worst time possible!"

Lauren understands, "That's quite alright, we still have most of the trip ahead of us. There will be plenty of time for us to talk later."

As Roxy gets her earphones out and is about to put them in Lauren has to ask, "If you don't mind, will you tell me what you saw in the mirror with your cousins?"

Roxy did not want to feed Lauren's own fears, but not knowing a way around it, she answers honestly, "When we pulled the sheet off during the week of mourning for my grandmother I thought I saw two red eyes staring back at me."

Lauren is curious, "What do you think now?"

Roxy shrugs her shoulders, "I think we were young and caught up in the idea of being afraid. Your mind can play weird tricks on you when you are afraid."

Roxy puts her earphones on and snuggles down in her seat, falling asleep in no time.

Lauren can't help but think about what Roxy said. Perhaps she had been afraid in her apartment, causing her mind to play tricks on her? None of that makes sense though; wouldn't she know she was afraid? Lauren tries to think back to while she was in the apartment, but it is all still so foggy!

Perhaps, after having the dreams Lauren was having in the apartment, she subconsciously identified with them throughout the day? They say when we dream we are subconsciously thinking of things we have seen or done while awake. What if the same happens after we dream? A lot of times we don't remember the dreams we've had. Isn't it possible our subconscious would identify with the forgotten dreams throughout the day without us knowing it? Sounds plausible.

Lauren then thinks about what happened at the gas station. Perhaps after hearing a scary story her mind was trying to identify with the story. Look at how she reacted when she saw the dime at the toll plaza! Then seeing another dime on the ground at the gas station made her mind play tricks on her! Lauren starts feeling better. That had to be the answer! She just has to remind herself that it is simply all in her mind!

Lauren turns the radio on and tries to find a station. Surprised, she is able to find another station that seems to be having callers call in with scary stories. Lauren is tempted to change the channel, but seriously? What could be the harm now that she knows how to identify the fear? Anyway, for some reason she is addicted to hearing more of these stories!

Road

Kill

Road Kill

Johnny goes back into the house to get his gun. Ma calls out from the kitchen, "That you Johnny?"

Johnny yells out, "Yea Ma, forgot my gun."

Ma comes out with her hands on her hips, "How many times have I told you that I don't want to clean buckshot out of those varmin?"

Johnny sighs, "I know Ma, just gettin' it for protection!"

Ma has to laugh, "Protection? When was the last time you shot something that wasn't half dead already?"

Johnny tries to defend himself, "Why waste money on ammo when the road provides us with plenty?"

Ma can't complain too much, at least Johnny did bring food home. Unlike the good ole days where her husband would go out drinking and hunting all day and the only thing he would bring home was a hangover!

Ma grumbles as she walks back to the kitchen, "Just try and get all the metal and rubber off them before you bring it home! Hard enough to cut out the bad pieces without having to deal with that other crap!"

With gun in hand, Johnny happily walks out the door yelling back, "Will do, Ma."

As Johnny gets into his Pa's beat up old truck he thinks to himself how good of a job he has been doing. When Pa had the hunting accident, Johnny suddenly found himself the man of the house.

Johnny slowly backs out the long dirt driveway. Sure, Ma and he really had to buckle down since Pa's accident, but life had always been hard for them. Pa only worked when the beer funds got low.

Johnny could barely remember when life had been normal. Back when they all lived closer to town in a normal house, and Pa and his brother went to work every day at the coal mine. Then the coal mining industry became a political target. After tough restrictions, the company had no choice but to close their doors.

It was a mighty blow to the small town. The mine had provided life to the town's occupants for generations. Now families found themselves suddenly unemployed. Proud families that refused to take help from a government that took away their means for providing for their families in the first place.

The town had little to offer to the starving families. Not knowing what else to do, the families began to move back into the hills. The old hunting shacks everyone had for recreation suddenly became their new homes. The two things the town did provide were ammo and beer. Two things that still cost money and were vital for a decent life.

Johnny looks down at his gas gauge a little concerned. He realizes he needs to be more observant of how much gas he was using. The end of the month was still a couple days off.

The only windfall most of the people in the hills had was fuel rights. A long time before the mine closed, the fuel industry came in asking for rights to the land. In return for the rights, a small check would be given along with free fuel at the end of the month.

Never did the people in town think that would become their main means of income. It had always been pocket money and a nice benefit. Now it was their life line. The free fuel ran their generators and cars. The small checks provided them barely enough for essentials. If an emergency came up, like beer funds running low, the fuel company would let you work off the books clearing the land a couple of days.

Many of the coal miners would have loved to have started working for the fuel company when the mine closed; however, they were a different union. The fuel union was terrified of the coal union coming in and taking jobs.

Keeping the peace with its own union, the fuel company agreed to not hire any previous coal miners. However, not completely heartless, it was an open secret the fuel company would let some work for cash. The work was hard and not what the fuel union members would do anyway, so there was a peaceful coexistence.

Out of habit, Johnny turns his radio on but the familiar hiss of white noise is the only thing that comes through this high up in the hills. Sighing, Johnny turns the radio off and thinks about where he will be going for the day.

There are three good spots down on the highway. With it being the summer season and more people traveling, there has to be at least a couple of road kill today! Deer rut season had passed and now the does and fawns are out exploring. Johnny's mouth begins to water at the thought of Ma's dinners involving deer meat.

However, doubt begins to set in. For some reason, road kill had begun to get sparse. It didn't make sense to Johnny. Ever since he could remember there were animals lined up for miles along the highway. In fact, that is how Johnny came up with the idea.

When his Pa died, Johnny took up hunting. He had to admit he never was any good at it. Pa always said Johnny was too kind hearted, a hunter's biggest downfall. Pa told him one day he'd get over that when he got hungry enough.

Within days after the funeral, Johnny took up hunting due to him and Ma beginning to run out of Pa's latest kill. Sure, Ma had the garden and the chickens, but winter would be on them soon and Ma needed meat to cure.

Day after day, Johnny would come home empty handed. He didn't know which was worse, the hunger in his belly or the disappointment in his Ma's eyes.

Not wanting to, Johnny decided to go see his Uncle Rodney. Not a pleasant thought, for Uncle Rodney was nothing more than a mean drunk. Pa had watched after Uncle Rodney when Aunt Sue had left with the kids. Uncle Rodney had always fueled Pa's own drinking habits.

Uncle Rodney had been with Pa that fateful day, coming back to the house so drunk he could barely walk, blubbering some wild story about the animals and large raccoons. Somehow he shot Pa by accident. Hunting accidents were not uncommon in the hills. Ma and he knew it was only a matter of time before one of those two would get themselves killed! Of course they desperately wanted Uncle Rodney to be the one, not Pa.

Yet, Uncle Rodney knew how to hunt and maybe he could tell Johnny where to go and what he was doing wrong. On the way to Uncle Rodney's for advice, Johnny came across a big doe lying beside the road. He had quickly pulled over to check it out. Although there were no cars around, the doe had recently died. In fact, the blood still felt warm to the touch.

Johnny looks around and sure enough there was broken glass from the car that must have hit it. The owner of the car had kept going. Johnny flipped the doe over to see how much damage was done. Surprisingly, the doe was fully intact. Only one leg was really messed up. The poor thing must not have been able to get up and died of exhaustion or heart failure. Of course there could be internal damage, but Johnny wouldn't know that until he opened her up.

Not wanting to waste the opportunity, Johnny begins to think of a plan. He could tell his Ma he had shot at the deer but had only hit the leg. After finally tracking her down, the doe was dead by the time he found her. He would clean the doe for Ma, thus hiding any evidence of internal damage. Excited, he had gone back to the truck and retrieved his gun. He shot the doe in the leg and then took it home for dinner that night.

His plan worked! What a feast it was! Ma was so proud of him and they were able to eat off that doe for quite some time.

As time went by, with more failure at hunting, Johnny decided to investigate the idea of picking up road kill. He had to be careful, after all, it was summer and there was a high chance of parasites. That was one of the main reasons people only hunted during certain times of the year.

Unfortunately though, when you are hungry you take your chances. Plenty of the hill folk had started hunting year round. The warden didn't even bother checking on them; who was he to take food from a family simply trying to survive?

Not only did Johnny have to worry about parasites, but also other animals that had picked off the animal before he got there. But Johnny was smarter than them. He started going to the spots where there was a lot of road kill at different times of the day. That was when he discovered the traffic pattern and the best times to be there for a fresh kill. Johnny soon realized that the road would be the one to provide for him and Ma.

Eventually Ma figured it out and word got out. Sure, many of the hill folk made fun of him. Said he was nothing but a lazy hunter looking for the easy way out. But Johnny, he paid them no mind. He was kind hearted and killing an unarmed animal never seemed fair. This solved that problem. The animals were already dead and could provide for him and Ma. He just had to find them.

Just like hunting, Johnny had his good and bad days. Strangely though, there had been more and more bad days recently. In fact, never had Johnny seen such a dry spell, especially his favorite three spots! They were notorious for heavy road kill. In fact, the road crew had such a hard time keeping up with the cleanup that the transportation crew was looking into re-shaping the road to cut down on the road kill.

As Johnny nears one of his spots, he can't help but wonder if someone else was cleaning up road kill too. Sure, the hill folk loved making fun of him, but hunting had become sparse. Maybe they had to lower their standards too. Johnny is not too fond of that idea. Sure, they have a right to eat just like him and Ma, but this was his territory. His hunting spot. No different than someone coming in at your fishing hole. It was simply not done! There still is a code, if you staked it, you kept it!

Johnny sees red flashing lights ahead of him and slows down. It was early in the morning and he hadn't seen anyone else on the road. Recognizing the police officer from town, Johnny decides to pull over and offer his help.

Timidly, Johnny walks up to the wreck. "Morning Joe, every-thing ok?"

The officer looks a bit shaken up. "Oh, hi Johnny. No, I'm afraid it's not."

Walking closer, Johnny is a little unnerved to see Joe is not his usual happy self, "Anything I can do to help?"

Joe wipes subconsciously at his mouth, relieved that Johnny hadn't arrived sooner or he would have seen him throwing up. "Just be careful where you walk. When there is a traffic death, forensics has to check the area."

Johnny peers over at the bodies lying on the ground by the car, "What happened?"

Joe forces himself to try and look at the bodies objectively, "Not real sure, I only came across them a few moments ago. I have a call in for the State Troopers."

Curious, Johnny looks at them closer and blurts out, "Good Lord, they look like road kill!"

Johnny is just what Joe needs to put him in the right frame of mind before the troopers arrive. "I know, it's exactly what I thought when I first saw them."

Joe clears his throat a little and begins to get a hold of his emotions. Hell, if this kid can look at this mess so calmly so can he! "Maybe they stopped to change their tire and were attacked? You're a hunter, what do you think could have done this?"

Joe knew all too well the talk about Johnny and giving him credit for being a hunter was a little over the top. However, being with the Road Kill King, as they call him in town and in the hills, was much better than being alone with two dead corpses out in the middle of nowhere!

Johnny feels important and steps closer to the bodies. Making sure not to touch anything, he squats down for a closer look. "They've been here for a while; the blood is thick and not moving. Looks like every animal out here had a taste! Look at all those different teeth marks!"

Joe looks back at the highway when he hears the sirens. Before the troopers roll up, Joe for the first time sees the skid marks. He looks back at the tires and is surprised to see no damage. "They must have hit an animal and then stopped. You know a lot about road kill, could you look for it while I talk to the troopers?"

Not even giving a thought to why Joe would know he knows a lot about road kill, Johnny simply nods, "Of course."

Johnny looks back at the road and sees the skid marks Joe must have seen. Judging from them, Johnny heads in the direction the animal would have been thrown. After a while Johnny gives up, unfortunately, finding nothing.

Still feeling important, Johnny heads over to a small cluster of people where Joe is talking. "That is as much as I know. This here is Johnny. He was kind enough to stop and see if he could help." A little embarrassed, Joe stutters as he continues, "Uh...

Johnny here, he... uh... knows quite a bit about road kill. I had him check the area for an animal kill that may have caused the accident. Did you find anything, Johnny?"

Johnny shakes his head, "No Sir, nothing. The only thing I can think of is that one of those critters that ate on those people may have dragged the road kill away!"

An elderly man approaches Johnny, "Johnny, my name is Dr. Thatcher. I have been doing some research in the area and would love to ask you some questions if you don't mind?"

Johnny shrugs his shoulders, "Sure."

Dr. Thatcher looks around at the officers and realizes he would rather talk to Johnny in his own environment. "Johnny, I know this may sound strange, but would you mind if we go for a ride and let these fine gentlemen finish their jobs?"

A little nervous, Johnny hesitantly replies, "I guess that would be ok."

One of the troopers speaks up, "Are you sure, Dr. Thatcher? I could have one of the boys run you back to town and then we could meet up later to do more of your research."

Dr. Thatcher shakes his head, "No, Johnny here is exactly the person I want to discuss my research with for now. I'm sure he won't mind taking me into town after our conversation, will you Johnny?"

Johnny looks a little disappointed as he thinks back to his fuel gauge. He mumbles, "I don't have much gas."

Dr. Thatcher is not about to take no for an answer. "No worries. I will fill up your tank when we get into town and pay you for your time."

Not one for charity, Johnny shakes his head, "No Sir, I'll be fine. I'll help you with whatever you need."

Dr. Thatcher is always surprised at the generosity of the hill people. They'd give you the last shirt off their back, but pride keeps them from allowing you to do the same for them. He decided to take a different approach, "I appreciate that Johnny and please realize this is for my research. It is no different than doing a job for me. The pay will be a tank of gas and money for your time."

Johnny can't believe his luck! Talk about being at the right place at the right time! His whole manner changes. Trying to sound sophisticated, Johnny smiles, "I would be honored!"

Dr. Thatcher returns the smile, "Lead the way."

Johnny and Dr. Thatcher get in the truck and get settled. Before Johnny takes off he asks, "Straight to town?"

Dr. Thatcher thinks about it, "Sure, we can start driving that way but let's let our conversation decide for us, ok?"

A little confused, Johnny shrugs his shoulders, "Ok. What is your research about?"

Dr. Thatcher looks out of the window sadly as they pass by the accident, "That is a very good question. It is a little complicated, but it has to do with road kill."

Johnny is surprised, "Road kill? As in animals or road kill as in humans, like back there?"

Now Dr. Thatcher is surprised, "Not too many people group them as the same."

Johnny offers his opinion, "As sad as it is, people getting killed on the road are exactly like animal road kill. We just clean them up quicker than the animals."

Dr. Thatcher is intrigued, "Please, explain a little more."

Johnny thinks about it, "No different than an animal, here we are going along our way and then BAM! Something happens, whether it is due to our own fault like looking at the phone or radio and not paying attention, or outside forces like the weather, or even an animal that isn't paying attention."

Dr. Thatcher is curious, "Why did the officer from town say you were well informed about road kill?"

Johnny gets quiet and then softly replies, "Sometimes I find clean road kill and take it home for Ma to cook."

Dr. Thatcher understands, "I hear things have been real tough since the mine closed."

Realizing Dr. Thatcher is not about to judge, Johnny adds, "And Pa getting killed didn't help."

Dr. Thatcher offers his sympathies, "I'm sorry to hear that. What happened to him?"

Johnny sighs, "Him and Uncle Rodney went hunting; only one of them came back."

Dr. Thatcher is curious, "A hunting accident? Did Uncle Rodney mention anything unusual about the animals?"

Johnny nods, "Yea, he said the animals were acting all strange that day. Tried to say there were these huge raccoons leading an attack on them! Uncle Rodney, though, was drunk as a skunk. We really couldn't understand or believe much of what he was saying that day!"

Dr. Thatcher, in contemplation, says, "You know raccoons are highly intelligent. They also have a manual dexterity that comes close to an ape."

Johnny wonders, "Are you a real doctor or a book doctor?"

Dr. Thatcher laughs, "A book doctor."

Johnny is not sure if Dr. Thatcher is laughing at him so he tries a little harder at asking a better question, "What's up with the road kill angle?"

Dr. Thatcher likes Johnny's forwardness, "Tell me, have you noticed anything different about your road kill?"

Johnny thinks back to his earlier revelation, "I think others may be getting in on my action! Animals have gotten scarce up in the hills and now road kill is becoming sparse too!"

Dr. Thatcher offers, "You think maybe the traffic commission might be doing a better job at their clean up?"

Johnny laughs, "Nah, they are some of my buddies. When I first started doing it, I ran into them from time to time. I guess they felt sorry for me and started leaving the better pieces for me."

Johnny thinks about it, "Eventually they began to spread the time farther and farther apart. They realized I was cleaning the messes up for them. As long as the road kill is either gone or far enough from the road that no one can see, they need not bother."

Dr. Thatcher is impressed, "It is sad that you are not getting paid to do their job."

Johnny does not feel that way, "What do you mean? The road kill is the pay. Ma and I have done alright because of it."

Dr. Thatcher thinks about all the spoiled college kids he teaches. Not one of them would ever think the way this kid does. No, they expect things to be handed to them on a silver platter. If Daddy and Mommy's money won't buy them what they need, they figure the government owes it to them even though they have never paid into the government!

Johnny interrupts Dr. Thatcher's thoughts and asks, "Why do you think the road kill is getting less?"

Dr. Thatcher becomes blunt, "Perhaps not less, but the tables are turning. Did you know that the accident back there was not the first one? In fact, the rise of auto accidents in that area has increased at an alarming rate."

Johnny is surprised, "Really? Never heard anything on the radio about it."

Dr. Thatcher shakes his head, "No, and you won't. The deaths have sort of been buried in paperwork to avoid a panic."

Johnny is still confused, "Then why haven't I seen more of them?"

Dr. Thatcher looks out at the passing scenery, "Let's say the cleanup crew for the government is much more effective than the transportation crew!"

Johnny is curious, "Then how did you learn about it?"

Dr. Thatcher sighs, "Quite by accident. My research is about how animals evolve to match their environment."

Dr. Thatcher proudly reveals, "In fact, I had just finished up a ten year long research out in Yellowstone Park. I'm sure you've probably even seen the video floating around out there on Facebook."

Johnny shakes his head, "What is Facebook?"

Dr. Thatcher laughs, "I keep forgetting, out here it's really not that important. Good for you!"

Dr. Thatcher continues, "Anyway, they released twelve wolves into Yellowstone Park. The idea was to see how the wolves impacted the environment."

Johnny is interested, "I bet they cleaned up the deer problem for them!"

Dr. Thatcher nods, "They did, but by doing so what else did that effect? Before long we started to see vegetation that the deer had been eating grow back."

Dr. Thatcher thinks back fondly, "Not only grow back but flourish, which in turn brought in more insects. The insects brought in different types of birds."

Dr. Thatcher explains more, "The vegetation also began to re-route waterways which brought back beavers that had almost gone extinct in that area."

Johnny is impressed, "Then the beavers changed the rivers with their dams?"

Dr. Thatcher smiles, "They did! It created small pools which brought in even more species of birds and before long the whole geographical area changed! All because of twelve wolves."

Johnny tries to connect the dots, "So, your thinking is that something here has been introduced to our environment and a chain reaction may be happening?"

Dr. Thatcher is impressed, "You are very smart Johnny, that is correct!"

Johnny is confused, "What changed?"

Dr. Thatcher has a theory but wants to see what Johnny's take is on it. "You tell me."

Johnny thinks about his life before living in the hills, "The mine closed?"

Dr. Thatcher nods, "Exactly! And what happened when the mine closed?"

Johnny thinks about what so many of them did, "People moved back to the hills."

Dr. Thatcher agrees, "Yes, and hunting became a way of life instead of entertainment."

Johnny realizes what must have happened, "The animals began to change because of us?"

Now it is Dr. Thatcher's time to shrug, "I think it has been slowly happening ever since the first road was built. Certain types of animals who live by a main road have slowly been changing to adapt to their environment, but it has been so slow none of us has noticed."

Suddenly it all clicks together for Johnny, "You think the animals have evolved because of us!"

Dr. Thatcher nods, "I do and it is my job to prove it."

At first Johnny thought Dr. Thatcher was smart, but now he isn't too sure, "Animals are dumb, there is no way they could have intentionally caused that accident back there!"

Dr. Thatcher argues, "Really? Have you ever seen a bird bait fish with a piece of bread? There is proof that some birds have actually learned how to fish!"

Instead of trying to figure it out Johnny decides to let Dr. Thatcher explain himself, "How do you think the accident back there happened?"

Dr. Thatcher sighs, "I've only got a couple of ideas. At night, perhaps a possum's eyes reflect more, causing their red eyes to look exactly like brake lights."

Johnny starts to laugh, "Seriously?"

Dr. Thatcher does not back down, "Think about it. A weary driver, driving at night or maybe even in the rain, sees red and is tricked into thinking it's another car. The driver swerves to miss it and wrecks alongside of the road."

Johnny has to ask, "And in the day time?"

Dr. Thatcher is not sure, "I don't know, maybe like the birds, something has learned how to bait us."

Just then something hits the side of the truck. Going sixty-five miles an hour the reaction is normal, Johnny turns the truck but overcompensates. The truck quickly goes out of control and before they know it, Dr. Thatcher and Johnny find themselves banged around inside the flipping truck.

Battered and bruised, Johnny finally comes to realize he is hanging upside down, held in place by his seat belt. He slowly turns and looks where Dr. Thatcher was sitting, but is surprised to see him gone!

Blood rolls down Johnny's face and into his eyes, causing his vision to be blurry. He feels hands unbuckling his seat belt and is thankful that someone is there to help; however, when he falls hard against the roof of the truck he blacks out completely.

Fading in and out of consciousness, Johnny realizes he is now completely out of the truck. He rolls his head on the blacktop and is shocked to see Dr. Thatcher motionless beside him. What is even more shocking is all the types of animals lined up as if they are at a smorgasbord. Johnny quickly realizes he and Dr. Thatcher are the main course!

Trying to get up, Johnny bats at the hands that are holding him. Hands? Whose hands are they anyway? Then he realizes that the largest raccoon he has ever seen is holding him down! In disbelief, Johnny watches as another raccoon is motioning for the next animal to come up and take a bite of Dr. Thatcher!

Dr. Thatcher may have been right! Raccoons may have evolved enough to not only look after themselves, but help other animals as well!

While Johnny fades back out of consciousness he can't help but think how ironic it is that after all those times he had collected road kill, he would now be road kill himself!

White Noise Stories Continued

As Lauren listens intently to the story on the radio, a loud noise startles her! It is as if she either hit something or something hit her, causing her to instinctively swerve the car. Feeling the car swerve, Roxy wakes up startled, "What the hell!"

Lauren quickly gets the car back under control, "I don't know!"

Roxy, frustrated, reaches over and turns the radio off. "Why is that crap on every time I wake up?" Sitting up and looking over her shoulder she asks, "Did you hit an animal or something?"

Lauren looks in the rear view mirror. "No, not that I know of! There was nothing on the road. It almost felt like something hit us!"

A slight chill comes over Lauren as she thinks about the story she just heard on the radio. What if animals did evolve to stop road kill? Maybe an animal hit her car with something trying to bait her? Realizing she missed out on what Roxy said, Lauren shakes her head a little to clear her thoughts and answers, "I'm sorry, what did you say?"

Roxy looks concerned, "Don't you think we should pull over and check the car out?"

Lauren looks at the desolate road and shakes her head, "No, the car is driving fine. Anyway, I don't think it is wise to stop on this stretch of road. There are no other cars around and who knows, someone or something could have hit us on purpose in hopes we would stop!"

Roxy looks out at the scenery and has to admit it doesn't give off a good vibe, "Maybe you are right! You know, I heard that somewhere they were leaving child car seats by the side of the road. People would stop to check on the child and then they would get robbed or worse!"

Lauren had heard that story too, "It can be scary out there. We need to be more aware of the signs!"

Roxy is confused, "What do you mean?"

Lauren blushes, "Never mind, you will think I am crazy!"

Roxy is wide awake now and ready to talk, "No, seriously, I want to know!"

Lauren sighs, "Believe it or not, my father is big on signs. When anything unusual happened he would say, 'See Sweet Pea, there's your sign.' It was his way of acknowledging a coincidence."

Roxy is curious, "Give me an example."

Lauren thinks of one, "Ok, I remember a couple years back I was driving him home from his surgery."

Roxy remembers, "That was such a scary time for you! Colon cancer is no fun!"

Lauren agrees, "Especially when we were told it was stage 4; it happened so quickly none of us were prepared!"

Roxy adds cheerfully, "True, but thankfully everything worked out ok!"

A slight pang of guilt comes over Lauren, "If it hadn't, I certainly would not be going with you now! I still worry that maybe I shouldn't have left. What he has, no one knows for sure if it'll come back or how quickly it could spread!"

Roxy shakes her head, "Nonsense! You can't live your life based on a 'what if' scenario; your dad doesn't and you know he doesn't want you to either!"

Roxy has to ask again, "So, what was the sign?"

Lauren can't help but smile at the thought of it, "On the way home from the hospital we had the radio on. Both of us lost in our own thoughts of what the future was going to hold for all of us."

Tears begin to form as Lauren remembers that difficult time; however, she clears her throat and continues, "The song 'I'm Alive' from the soundtrack Xanado randomly comes on the radio."

Lauren thinks fondly back, "That movie was very special to my dad and me. For my sixteenth birthday he made me watch the movie to see if I liked it. I loved it! He then surprised me with tickets to my first Broadway play... Xanado!"

Roxy smiles, "That is so sweet!"

Lauren agrees, "Yes, it was. Anyway, when the song came on, my dad gets the biggest smile I have ever seen on him! He patted me on the hand and said, 'There's you sign Sweet Pea, I'm alive and everything is going to be just fine!' and he was right!"

Roxy admits, "Definitely a cool coincidence!"

After a moment Roxy asks, "Do feelings count as signs too?"

Lauren nods, "Of course they do, but feelings can be harder to read. A lot of times we dismiss our feelings as illogical or not important. More often than not though, they are our internal signs!"

Roxy tries to understand, "A little ways back when I asked you why we weren't stopping, I looked out at the scenery and felt a bad vibe!"

Lauren had felt the same, "Me too! Let me ask, would you have listened to that feeling if you had been alone?"

Roxy thinks about it, "Probably not. I would have thought I was being silly and stopped anyway!"

Lauren sighs, "You need to start listening to yourself! Also, start noticing the little things out there that help us."

Roxy is curious, "If you don't mind me asking, why didn't you see the signs in your apartment? Or for that matter, listen to your own internal signs?"

Lauren has to smile, "Touché, my dear!"

Roxy looks seriously at her, "I'm not trying to be cute. Obviously you have very good intuition! I don't understand why it didn't work for you in the apartment."

Lauren thinks about it, "Honestly, I'm not sure. It was like I was in a fog. When I was outside the apartment complex I would completely forget everything that happened in the apartment!"

Roxy is surprised, "Really? That is why you never mentioned anything to me during that entire time?"

Lauren nods, "Yes, you know me, I tell you everything!" Although, Lauren admits to herself, she did not tell Roxy about the gas station incident. She's not sure why, other than not wanting Roxy to think she was going down the crazy road again!

Roxy interrupts her thoughts, "I never understood why I didn't know what was going on then. Mind you, that one night at the bar I have to say I knew there was something up with you, I just never dreamed it was so bad!"

Lauren remembers that night, "You can't beat yourself up over it! I told you before, I tried desperately to hide my appearance but you saw right through me that night!"

Roxy shakes her head, "But it wasn't enough! I should have insisted on staying with you! At least then, the next day I could have taken you to the doctor! Maybe some of what you had to deal with would have never happened!"

Lauren is surprised at her sincerity, "Roxy, it is done and over. You have more than redeemed yourself! Look what you are doing for me now!"

Roxy feels a little bit better, "I suppose. Hey, you never told me! Who did you think you saw that night at the bar?"

A slight chill comes over Lauren as she remembers the couple. Lauren tries desperately to remove the fog from her brain to understand the whole story. Surprisingly, the fog is no longer there! She is beginning to remember it clearly! "Oh my God, Roxy, it just came to me!"

Roxy begins to get a little excited, "Really? Tell me!"

Lauren looks over at her with wide eyes, "It's all so crazy! I don't think you are going to believe me!"

Roxy shrugs her shoulders, "Try me!"

Lauren plays the story over in her mind and tries to summarize it for Roxy, "There was this guy who had to have knee surgery. He tore up his knee so bad they had to use cadaver parts to fix it!"

Roxy is grossed out, "Can you imagine? Having a dead person's body parts in you! I mean, of course, it is amazing at what they can do. Still, the thought of it seems a little Frankensteinish!"

Lauren can't help but laugh, "You are right! Anyway, after the operation the guy finds his whole manner changing. His temper is out of control and he had never had an issue with it before the operation."

Roxy tries to be reasonable, "Couldn't it have been he was frustrated that he wasn't healing as quickly as he wanted?"

Lauren agrees, "Yes, of course! But he did heal and while trying to get stronger he found himself aimlessly walking farther and farther from his apartment."

Roxy is curious, "Where did he go?"

Lauren answers, "At first to nearby neighborhoods, but farther each day until one day he reached a neighborhood that seemed to be the place he wanted to go!"

Roxy wonders, "What was so special about that neighborhood?"

Lauren sighs, "A girl!"

Roxy jumps ahead of the story, "Are you trying to say that because of the cadaver parts in this guy he was taken to the neighborhood where obviously the dead guy's girlfriend lived?"

Lauren is impressed, "Exactly!"

Roxy tries to be optimistic, "Aw, that is such a sweet love story!"

Lauren is not so sure, "My only concern is, did the guy fall in love with the girl because of his own feelings or that of the dead guy? And what about the anger issue? What if one day the anger is stoked because the dead guy becomes jealous?"

Roxy thinks about it, "Yea, ok, maybe not such a good idea!"

A realization comes over Roxy, "Wait a minute! Are you saying that couple was at the bar that night?"

Lauren nods, "They were!"

Roxy is confused, "How in the world did you know who they were?"

A faraway look comes over Lauren, "I didn't at first. I just had this feeling I knew them from somewhere. Then when they left, the guy let the girl walk ahead of him. He stopped by me and whispered something along the lines of, 'They will never believe you but sometimes one of us does escape!' It was crazy!"

Roxy is curious, "It was very loud in the bar that night, are you sure that is what he said?"

Lauren thinks hard and has to admit, "I'm not sure, but I think so."

Roxy puts out a theory, "What if, being raised to look out for signs, you create your own signs? Maybe you had the dream because you saw this couple in real life, like on a bus or train. Then, when you saw them in the bar, you confused your dream with real events. With the bar being so crowded that night; you might have mistaken what he said and your mind filled in what you thought you heard."

Lauren thinks back to the girl at the gas station. Lauren thought she had heard the girl say it was time for her to leave the dime there. However, Lauren had already admitted to herself she was not sure what the girl said. Maybe her mind had simply put in what would have related to the story on the radio!

Lauren is beginning to get a headache thinking about it. "Believe it or not, I did think something similar! You know how you forget a dream? What if the dream, still being in your sub-conscious, creeps out during the day?"

Roxy whistles, "What a full circle! You subconsciously dream at night of events you had in a previous time, only to forget the dream and identify with it subconsciously during the present time! That's kind of a mind fuck, don't you think?"

Realizing how stressful all of this must be on Lauren, Roxy suggests, "Hey, I have an idea! I just saw a cool sign back there advertising a cute caboose that is a diner. Why don't we stop there for lunch?"

Lauren is happy to get a break from analyzing her stupid mind, "Sounds great!"

Roxy nods, "Awesome! We need to change our vibe back into vacation mode!"

Lauren laughs, "I was thinking the same thing!"

Lauren sees the turn off Roxy was talking about, "There it is, that was quick!"

Roxy's stomach rumbles, "Perfect, I'm starving!"

Lauren easily finds the Caboose. Hard to miss since it seems to be the only attraction in the small one street town.

Lauren parked the car and before going inside, she inspected it. Sure enough, on the back fender is a dent the size of a hefty rock!

Lauren shakes her head in disbelief, "Is it just me, or does this look like something that could have been thrown at us from the side of the road?"

Roxy looks at it and shrugs her shoulders, "I suppose, or it could have been a rock kicked up by the tire." She sighs and heads towards the Caboose, "Obviously, it's not a big deal! Let's not let it ruin our lunch!"

Still, Lauren can't shake the feeling as she thinks about the story on the radio. Is it unreasonable to think that animals have evolved enough to go hunting themselves? Look at the birds that learned how to fish, is that any different? Lauren thinks not; the only thing different is the prey!

Roxy holds the door for her and yells, "Come on, let's eat!"

Knowing Roxy doesn't want to be bothered with her dark thoughts; Lauren tries to shake the chills and focuses on the Caboose in front of her. It was a cute little thing, but unfortunately her chills are not going away! As she goes through the door she has to ask Roxy, "What is your feeling about this place?"

Roxy smiles, "A good one! Take in a deep breath, it smells so damn good!"

Suddenly the smell overcomes Lauren and she has to agree, "Oh yea, now I smell it!"

Ignoring her feeling, Lauren happily sits down at a small table for two with Roxy across from her. She looks around and sees only one other customer, a young man minding his own business. Something about him intrigues Lauren.

A bored waitress comes over with the menus, "Hi, I'm Stacey. The special today is barbecue pulled pork."

Roxy and Lauren smile up at her and in unison say, "Sounds good!"

Stacey can't help but laugh, "You two jinxed! Ok, two specials coming up. What kind of drinks?"

Again, both Roxy and Lauren say together, "Coke!"

All of them laugh as Stacey takes the menus back, "I'll be right out with those. Meanwhile, I want you two to work on talking separately!" Lauren and Roxy giggle.

Lauren is beginning to feel like she is on vacation! It felt good to laugh again. She looks around at the little diner and is impressed with all the old black and white photos on the walls. "I bet this thing has a lot of history to it!"

Roxy agrees, "I'm sure it does!"

Stacey comes back with their Cokes and Lauren has to ask, "What kind of stories do you have for this place?"

Stacey is surprised, "Funny you should ask! I have been trying to convince the owner to advertise the darker side of the history about this place!"

Lauren is intrigued, "And what would that be?"

Stacey makes sure the cook can't hear her, "This here Caboose was involved with one of the most gruesome serial killers of all times!"

Lauren is surprised, "Really? I thought I knew them all! In college, I read everything I could get my hands on about serial killers! I don't remember any Caboose killings though."

Stacey looks around before answering, "Oh no, you won't find it in any books! They never confirmed it, but my granddaddy used to tell my daddy all about the Hobo killings!"

Roxy is curious, "Why wouldn't the owner want to tap into something like that? People go nuts over sites that are haunted!"

Feeling uneasy, Lauren has to ask, "Is this place haunted?"

Stacey shrugs her shoulders, "I don't rightly know, I just started. But I can tell you, the place is sure dead! Tough making money! What better way than to promote it as haunted to bring people in?"

A bell rings and Stacey looks over, "Looks like your lunch is ready. I'll go get it for you!"

Stacey brings out two huge plates of food and places it in front of them, "Bon apatite!"

Before she walks away Lauren has to ask, "Why don't you have your father call into the radio station with his stories?"

Stacey looks confused, "Radio station?"

Lauren nods, "Yea, on our road trip I've been listening to unusual stories people call in the radio. Must be syndicated because every time I think I have lost the station, the next station has it on!"

Stacey thinks about it, "Actually, that is not a bad idea! Daddy loves to tell his stories and if he just randomly called in, not giving his true identity, then maybe it will get some publicity for this place!" She looks excited, "You two enjoy, I think I'll give him a call right now!"

Lauren and Roxy finish their lunch in record time. It was the best pulled pork either one of them had ever had! Stuffed, Lauren looks around and notices the young man must have left while they had been so involved in eating. Leaving Stacey with a big tip and a wish for good luck on her endeavors, the girls head out to the car.

Roxy suddenly stops, "Maybe, I better use the restroom. How about you?"

Lauren shakes her head, "Nah, I'm fine. I'll meet you in the car."

As Lauren walks to the car, she notices an old beat up pickup truck backing up beside her car. When she gets closer, she sees flies swarming all around whatever is in the back of the truck. A horrific stench suddenly comes over her, one she has never smelled before! Curious, as she walks by, she looks in. Her stomach suddenly lurches as she realizes it is piles of road kill with maggots and worms still crawling all over the carcasses! Trying desperately to keep her lunch down, she quickly turns her head.

Fumbling with her keys, Lauren does not notice it's the young man from inside sitting in the driver's seat. With the window down, the young man teases her, "Don't worry ma'am, at least you didn't see this at the back door where the kitchen is!"

Startled, Lauren agrees, "I guess I would be questioning that special right about now!"

The young man laughs, "Hey! Don't knock home cooked road kill! My ma was the best at camouflaging it! You would have never known if no one told you!"

Thinking about the bloody, maggot infested, smelly road kill piled in the truck makes Lauren fight even harder to keep her lunch down! Trying not to be rude, she quickly replies, "I bet! You have a nice day now!"

Before Lauren gets in the car, he answers her, "You too! Be safe out there, road kill ain't just for critters!"

Terrified, Lauren gets in the car and locks the door as she starts it up. Ignoring the truck beside her, she stares forward, willing Roxy to hurry up! The young man, now facing the way he wanted to go, pulls away.

Lauren had not felt threatened by what the young man said, it seemed nothing more than a sincere concern! What had frightened her was how quickly she identified that man with the young man in the story on the radio!

Roxy finally emerges from the diner. Once inside the car and heading down the road she senses something is troubling Lauren, "What's up?"

Trying to keep herself calm, Lauren simply asks, "Did you see an old pickup truck leaving when you came outside?"

Roxy looks around, "No, why?"

Thinking back to their earlier conversation, Lauren is a little reluctant to mention the truck incident to Roxy before she thinks more about it herself. Vaguely she answers, "This damn truck was parked beside us with road kill in the back. It was so gross!"

Roxy can't even imagine, "Glad I didn't see it! I'm afraid that special isn't agreeing with me as it is!"

Lauren sighs, "I have to admit, I had a hard time keeping mine down after seeing that God awful road kill!"

Roxy curls up, holding her stomach, "Mind if we don't talk any more about it? I think I'll try and go back to sleep before I throw up!"

Lauren sympathizes, "Of course! If we need to stop, just let me know!"

Roxy nods, "You'll be the first to know!"

A little ways down the road Lauren is happy to see Roxy has fallen back to sleep. With nothing else to do, Lauren thinks about the incident back at the diner.

We are up in the hills. It probably isn't uncommon for a truck with road kill to stop at a diner. Just because Roxy didn't see the truck doesn't mean it wasn't there!

It was no different than back at the gas station. By the time Lauren had turned off the gas nozzle, the girl she had been talking to could have easily walked away!

What bothers Lauren about both incidents is how easily she connected them with the stories she heard on the radio. Is this what she had done in the apartment?

Stands to reason, being alone day in and day out while having crazy dreams! Added to the fact that as the days went on it became worse! Although, why would being outside the apartment complex cause her to forget what was going on inside the apartment complex? Perhaps she had lumped her time awake and her time asleep together, causing the whole time to be nothing more than a foggy memory in her subconscious? Maybe, in the end, she simply was not able to tell her dreams and reality apart?

Lauren is frustrated with herself because it seems too easy for her to fall back into that situation! She had never done anything like this before the apartment. And yet, she did have a breakdown! Her psychiatrist warned her that it would take time for her to fully recover. Lauren knows she needs to give herself time, but then again, she was damned if she was going to let it happen again!

To divert her thoughts, Lauren turns her radio on and finds herself listening to a gruff old man talking about life on a train. Imagine that! This might be Stacey's father telling one of his stories! She can't believe her luck! Excited, she looks forward to hearing what he has to say.

Hobo

Hobo

In a gruff voice the old man starts his story, "I remember when Ronnie and I jumped on our first train. All of seven years old."

You can almost hear the smile in his voice as he remembers, "Yea, it was Ronnie's idea to jump on the train after the incident. He said it was destined to be since we had nicknamed ourselves R&R."

He explains, "Ronnie and Ray Ray is what they called us. Though honestly, more often than not, Ronnie and everyone else just called me Shadow. See, I was the Shadow because I stayed back and let Ronnie make the decisions. Ronnie, he took real good care of me."

"Anytime there would be incidents, he'd say, 'Shadow, don't you worry, I got this,' and usually he did. The incidents were real bad when we were young, but when we were old enough to fight back they got interesting."

The old man becomes quiet, reflecting back, "The incidents started at home with the beatings and what not from our drunken father. I suppose it was because of him that we became fighters." After a pause, "At least he planted the seed. When other incidents happened while we were in juvey and jail that seed continued to grow."

He can't help but chuckle, "Back then, they thought they were doing the right thing by throwing kids into juvey at such a young age. In fact, juvey was just as bad, if not worse, than home!"

A hardness comes over him, "One thing though, they never were able to separate ole Ronnie and I. For that, I was thankful."

"The first time we hopped that train we ran into a group of hobos. A decent lot of folk, they took us under their wing and taught us the hobo code. If we had been allowed to stay with them, more likely than not, our lives would have been much better!"

Disgusted, he shakes his head, "But no! They ripped us away from the only true family we had ever known!"

He explains, "Many people think hobos, tramps and bums are all the same, people who rode the rail to escape their troubles. However, each one was different in their own way. A tramp worked only when forced to. A bum did no work at all and counted on handouts. A hobo was a worker who wandered. The only thing they truly had in common was the rail."

He thinks back, "You know, I once heard they thought the word hobo came from the term hoe-boy which was a term for a farm hand. However, it was used more as a greeting such as 'Ho Boy'! In railroad terms it meant homeward bound."

He shrugs his shoulders, "Whatever the case, a hobo was what ole Ronnie and I aspired to be. Although honestly, at one time or another we were all three; hobo, tramp and bum."

"As I mentioned earlier, a hobo was a worker. He may take long holidays, but sooner or later he would return to work. A tramp never works if it can be avoided, he simply travels. A bum neither works nor travels unless forced to by the police."

He thinks back to the stories he would listen to around the campfires, "I guess it all started back when the Civil War ended and discharged veterans would hop freight trains to get back home. In the early 1900's people looking for work would jump on the freight trains. By 1930, it hit an all-time high with the Great Depression."

He sighs, "However, the life of a hobo was a dangerous one! Not only were they poor and far from home, the train crews were hostile towards them. The worst was the railroad security staff, nicknamed bulls, which had a rough reputation of being violent against them."

Sadness creeps into his voice, "Many hobos risked life and limb. It was easy to get trapped between cars, get feet caught under the wheels, or even freeze to death in bad weather. When freezer cars were loaded at an ice factory any hobo inside was likely to be killed."

He realizes he is rambling, "I'm sorry, but I wanted to give you an idea of what being a hobo was like before I told you my story."

"Yea, riding the rails almost made us lose our lives several times. Slow, painful, near death experiences. Whether it was from exposure to the cold, hunger or being beaten within an inch of our lives, it didn't matter. Each and every time we prayed for the sweet darkness of death." He sighs, "But death disappointed us and would not come even when we prayed the hardest."

Suddenly he gets tired as the painful memories flood down on him, "Let alone what it did to us mentally! The shame and abuse we dealt with changes you, makes you hard and bitter! Vengeful!"

His voice lowers, "That is where Ronnie shined the most, during his quest for vengeance. He grew stronger, excelled and lived life to the fullest! Funny thing was, our roles had reversed. He now lived in the shadows. I, on the other hand, lived in the daylight fulfilling my own part."

"We had a great set up. I landed a job manning the caboose. It was a perfect fit. Not having family or a home, already knowing the rails, it gave me a chance of coming close to having a normal life."

He chuckles a little, "They would have never hired Ronnie, the craziness in his eyes would have given him away. No, this time it was my turn to protect Ronnie. Only fair, after all he had done for me throughout the years."

"I didn't mind it so much. I was my own boss and was allowed to decorate the caboose like my own apartment. I lived that way for damn near ten years."

He sighs, "Ronnie, he still lived on the freight trains. He'd come visit me once in a while. Bring me new beer bottles from different states to add to my collection. I tried to get him to stay longer, knowing how dangerous his lifestyle was. But, he was happy and who was I to take that away from him? My job was to keep an eye on him, make sure he was safe, and more importantly make sure he didn't get caught!"

He has to admit, "Ronnie's mission was an important one. Not only was it to seek revenge for both of us, but also to protect any future victims."

Sadness creeps back in, "I have to admit though, through the years ole Ronnie became more vicious and crazy! No longer was it justice, he enjoyed it! He even began to prey on the innocent ones, breaking the code we had embraced in the beginning."

He proceeds to explain, "As I mentioned before, the true hobo has a code. The first hobos that cared for us as kids were true to that code and they tried to instill in us morals we had never be shown."

He cites the code in a trance-like way, "Decide your own life, don't let another person run or rule you. When in town, always respect the local law and try to be a gentleman at all times. Don't take advantage of someone who is in a vulnerable situation. Always try to find work, even if temporary, and always seek out jobs nobody wants. By doing so, you not only help a business along, but ensure employment should you return to that town again."

He takes a deep breath and continues, "When no employment is available, make your own work by using your talents at crafts. Don't become a stupid drunk. Respect handouts, don't wear them out. Always respect nature, don't leave garbage. Cause no problems with the crew on rails, act like an extra crew member. Don't cause problems in train yards. Don't allow other hobos to abuse children. Help all runaway children and help your fellow hobos whenever and wherever needed, you may need their help some day."

Disgustedly he adds, "Sounds like a perfect code doesn't it? As I said before, if they had allowed Ronnie and I to stay with the first group of hobos we met we would have turned out differently. Unfortunately, the authorities thought the rails were no place for children; however, the dark abusive place they threw us in was far worse!"

He sighs, "The next time, when Ronnie and I were finally able to escape, returning to the rails put us into a new hell. The hobos we met were nothing like the first hobos. They did the exact opposite of the code. As an abused child, trust is an issue. When that trust is finally earned, only for it to be taken away by the very group you trusted, words lose meaning."

He remembers, "That is when we learned the symbols. Hobos drew different symbols along the way to let the next hobos know what to expect."

He goes back to his monotone voice as he explains, "A cross signified food would be served to the hobos after a sermon. A triangle with hands meant a homeowner had a gun. A horizontal zigzag signified a barking dog. A square missing its top line meant it was safe to camp. A top hat and a triangle signified wealthy people willing to help. A spearhead was a warning to defend yourself. A circle with two parallel arrows meant get out fast, hobos are not welcome!"

He takes a deep breath to finish, "Two interlocked circles signified handcuffs. A medical staff signified a doctor who was willing to help. A cross with a smiley face in one of the corners meant the doctor would treat hobos for free. A cat signified a kind lady lived there. A wavy line above an X meant fresh water and a campsite. Three diagonal lines meant it's not a safe place. A square, representing a house, with an X, meant a hobo had been tricked by another hobo there. Two shovels signified work."

He remembers back to the time when he and Ronnie were kids. Neither one of them were able to read, but they had learned those symbols out of necessity! As time went by, they would not only put the customary symbols out for the next hobo, but also a few of their own. "Ronnie lived by the code as if it were burned into his soul. For the ones that didn't, he hunted them down."

"One symbol I didn't mention was Ronnie's personal calling card. It was a simple design, a scythe, the weapon death uses when he comes calling."

The old man can't help but be proud of the symbol as he brags, "It struck fear into anyone that saw it!"

He clears his throat, "By now, I am sure you have figured out Ronnie became a serial hobo killer. Ironically, a hobo that killed hobos. Many of you are probably anxious to know how many he killed, was he ever caught, and what happened to him."

He sighs, "I am not really sure how many Ronnie killed, though my beer bottle collection is what made him become known and also provided an idea of how many he did kill."

He chuckles a little sinisterly, "Have to say though, Ronnie had a good sense of humor. Those beer bottles were not only for me, but were a slap in the face of the railroad industry! They were displayed in their caboose for damn near ten years!"

He feels he has to explain. "In the early years, the crew in the caboose was there to make sure the train ran safely. However, their concern was for the safety of the cargo, not human life."

He shakes his head in disgust, "Many times they turned a blind eye to the violence that happened on their trains. Whether it was for their own safety, or to keep the railroad industry unblemished, either way it was dirty!"

"All I know is that when Ronnie and I needed their help the most, they would be the ones to give the final blow! Throwing us off their trains like they were nothing more than clean-up crews. One more dead hobo was one less problem!"

The old man sounds impressed, "Yea, ole Ronnie had his hands full hunting down all those hobos that molested us throughout the years, stopping new ones from continuing the abuse, and of course he didn't forget about the people who chose to look the other way! Since Ronnie couldn't go after the workers on the trains for fear of getting caught, having his handiwork prominently displayed was the next best thing!"

Continuing his story, the old man becomes serious. "It was in 1947. A train traveling from Pittsburg to New York entered a curve and jumped the tracks due to traveling too fast. Several passenger cars and the caboose went over the side of the mountain, killing twenty-four, hobos included, and injuring more than a 100. Ronnie and I happen to be on that train."

"It wasn't until the clean-up that they discovered Ronnie's dirty little secret. They found my beer collection spread out all over the mountain, most broken, with something unusual inside each and every one of them."

The man speaks matter-of-factly, "Even though Ronnie and I were still tight, Ronnie knew he had to keep me in the dark about some things. He knew I knew from the rumors and the symbols along the way; however, it was easier for me to keep him safe by looking the other way when I didn't know for sure. After all, I too, had become what we hated most."

The old man ponders, "I think, because of our situation, it was even more symbolic what Ronnie pulled off. Since a man has two balls, Ronnie would keep one from his victim and shove the other in a beer bottle for me. I guess it was a secret talisman to give me the balls I needed to do what had to be done. All were prominently displayed for the railroad industry that had caused it all. The irony was not lost on me when I found out."

You can hear the smile in the old man's voice, "After the train crash, they never found me. They never learned how much I knew or how much I participated."

He continues, "All I do know is that the railroad industry hushed it up real quick! They had enough on their hands with the accident, let alone the public finding out about a hobo serial killer on board. Finding a bag filled with the matching balls near a dead hobo cleared up a lot of unsolved murders. However, it was not something to brag about and was quietly swept under the rug."

The old man finishes up, "I hear they salvaged the caboose, cleaned it up real nice, and made it into a little restaurant. I'm sure if it could talk all those poor souls would have some mighty fine horror stories about their meeting with a hobo named Ronnie."

His voice lowers to almost a whisper, "I like to think ole Ronnie is still out there riding the rails, helping me whisper in the ears of some eager hobo willing to carry on his work. Speaking of which, I heard Angel Resendiz was executed. They said he was a serial killer on the rails back in the 90's. Killed fifteen that they know of. I remember him being one of the ones who liked to listen to an old man's story."

The man's voice becomes proud again, "None of them will be as good as Ronnie! If they were, they wouldn't have gotten caught!"

"I guess that old saying 'evil begets evil' was true in our case. Where we thought violence would destroy violence, it didn't. It only intensified the evil and gave it more power to live on."

White Noise Stories Continued

Lauren is shaken back to reality with Roxy's loud yawn. Roxy, annoyed, again turns off the radio. "God, how I hate that noise!"

Lauren smiles, "I am so glad you are awake! You will never believe who was on the radio!"

Roxy looks bored, "Knowing you, I bet it wasn't JayZ!"

Lauren is not going to let Roxy ruin her excitement, "No! But I do think it was our waitress' father..." Lauren stumbles, "or grandfather. He sounded old and his story was back before 1947."

Roxy is still not impressed, "I bet that was a real knee slapper!"

Lauren's feelings are a little hurt, but she persists, "Actually it was very interesting! He was talking about Ronnie, the hobo serial killer."

Roxy laughs a little, "Wait! Was he a hobo killer or a hobo that killed?"

Lauren smiles and answers, "Both!"

Roxy is confused, "Don't they have a code or something? A lot like honor among thieves?"

Lauren thinks about it, "Yea, but what was done to them as kids and later on, I can only imagine how messed up that made them!" She outlined the story for Roxy.

Roxy's mood changes, "Geez! They allowed that on the radio?"

Lauren shakes her head, "He was very careful about what he said, but you knew what he was implying!"

Roxy yawns, "Do you know what I want to hear more about? Your apartment! I can't get over someone died in it!"

Lauren sighs, "Not much to say. When my parents asked the apartment complex if someone had died in my apartment they instantly refunded my money and apologized that it had not been disclosed."

Roxy wonders, "Weren't they curious how you knew?"

Lauren thinks about it, "Not really. My parents told them I dreamed about it, but they didn't seem interested!"

Roxy persists, "What was the dream about? Can you remember any of it now?"

Lauren tries to open her mind; it is almost as if she is cleaning the fog out of her head. "He was a painter. His best friend's mom gave him a paintbrush from overseas for his birthday."

Lauren struggles with the memory, "The brush was cursed. It made you a better painter but it needed blood."

Roxy scrunches her face, "Ew!"

Lauren nods, "Worse than that, it needed more blood to keep the painting fresh! Unfortunately, before the painter knew that information he started making a self-portrait of himself."

Roxy is shocked, "Are you saying he painted a portrait of himself with his own blood?"

Lauren lowers her voice, "Worse, he was in the apartment when he did it!"

Not really wanting to know but having to, Roxy asks, "How did he die?"

Lauren squinted her eyes in determination to remember, "It was like he could never get enough blood for the painting from the cuts he inflicted on himself! In the end, he stuck the brush into his jugular!"

Roxy sits quietly for a moment thinking about it. Finally she asks, "Do you think it was a cursed paintbrush or did the painter just go crazy?"

Lauren sighs, "I don't know. They would not tell my parents how the previous owner died. The only thing that ties it to my dream is that when I had my breakdown in the lobby one of the guys remembered the former tenant being a painter! I think that strengthened my belief that the dead were dreaming. Now that I have taken a step back, I'm wondering if you weren't right. It may have been my mind trying to fit my dreams into reality!"

Roxy is impressed, "Look at you, self-analyzing over there! The long ride must be doing you some good!"

Lauren blushes, "I have had plenty of time to think, I'll give you that!"

Lauren looks out the window at the passing scenery, "Interesting concept though, the dead dreaming! So often we use the words, 'put them to sleep' like with a dog. If that is the case, would they not dream?"

Roxy tries to laugh it off, "Please, aren't you being a bit literal? Just because we say things, it doesn't mean there is a belief in them."

Lauren disagrees, "Not true! Many things we say today are based on what was a belief in the past!"

Roxy argues, "Ok then, if the dead are sleeping what would wake them up?"

Lauren thinks for a moment before answering, "I don't know, maybe reincarnation? Perhaps they are in limbo until their souls are either collected or re-used?"

Roxy is surprised, "You are serious, aren't you?"

Lauren, embarrassed, shrugs it off, "I never said I had all the answers to the reason for our existence!"

Roxy begins to yawn again, "Damn these pills! I hate how tired they make me! Are you ok if I fall back asleep?"

Lauren smiles, "Do I have a choice?"

Roxy looks a little concerned, "I'm sorry. I'll try to skip the pill next time!"

Lauren shakes her head, "Honestly, I would rather you be sleeping than throwing up!"

Roxy agrees as she grabs for her headset, "Me too!"

Lauren waits until Roxy is all settled in before she turns her radio on. At first all she can find is music on the radio. She is a little disappointed, but then admits to herself it is a nice change.

Several miles down the road her radio station begins to fade out. Lauren is about to change the station when she hears a man telling a story. She peeks over at Roxy and is relieved to see her sleeping soundly. Excited to hear the story, she turns up the radio.

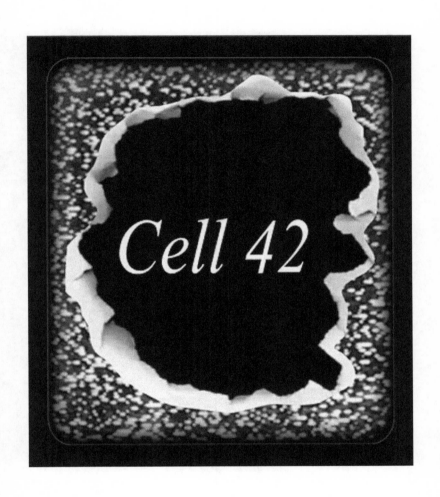

Cell 42

Cell 42

Mike checks the duty roster, "Damn!"

Rosey looks up from her desk, "Problem Mike?"

He looks disgustedly at her, "Yea! They put me on duty with that sniveling, snot-nosed, new kid Jiminy!"

Rosey corrects him, "It's Jimmy, not Jiminy!"

Mike disagrees, "Nah, its Jiminy the Cricket! He's like your little conscious sitting there always warning you to do the right thing!"

Rosey never liked Mike. Letting her disgust shine through she mumbles, "Maybe that's not such a bad thing for you, Mike!"

Mike looks suspiciously at her, "You didn't arrange the schedule to teach me a lesson, did you Rosey?"

Rosey shakes her head, "You know I don't do the scheduling! Just give the kid a break! I remember when you first started, not everyone liked your ways either!"

Mike sneers, "Yea, but I got the nickname Mechanic because I know how to fix things around here! Being nicknamed Jiminy is nothing to be proud of!"

Rosey shakes her head and would love to say 'giving yourself a nickname doesn't count!' Plus, Mike is the only one that calls him Jiminy! Having a conscious is not a bad thing, but obviously Mike does not have one and can't understand that. She was sure of that ever since the incident with Mike and that poor inmate Roger! Rosey knows, deep in her heart, Mike killed that kid intentionally! But of course, this damn facility always protects one of their own.

Roger, the inmate, was just a hardened criminal in their eyes. And yet, Rosey saw him for what he was, a poor sick kid that everyone picked on, including the guards! Roger's crime was falling in with a bad crowd to try to fit in, who in return got him into trouble and left him to serve out his time still trying to fit in! Mike, the Mechanic? Yea, he fixed Roger alright! Put him right out of his misery!

Rosey knows it is better to choose your fights and this one was not worth it. She focuses back on the work in front of her, hoping this arrogant ass will get the hint and leave!

The door opens and in walks Jimmy with a big smile, "Hi Rosey, how are you this fine evening?"

Rosey rarely smiles in this God forsaken place, but looking at Jimmy's smiling face she can't resist, "Very good Jimmy, thank you for asking!"

Mike is sickened by the pleasantries, "Come on Jiminy, time to make our rounds!"

As Mike walks out the door Jimmy looks back over at Rosey and winks, "Oh goody, I'm sure you will make it an interesting night for us Mechanic!"

Rosey winks back and whispers, "That a boy! Don't take no shit from him!"

Jimmy nods and catches up with Mike, "Where to first?"

Mike sighs, "Ole Leroy is back at it again!"

Jimmy's whole mood changes instantly, "He's still in the Hangman's Gallows?"

Mike smiles, "Yup, good ole cell 42."

Jimmy is curious, "How many have hung themselves in that cell, do you think?"

Mike shrugs his shoulders, "Don't rightly know, some of them we moved to other cells after the fact so the administration wouldn't stop us from using that cell all together."

From day one, Jimmy had been told the stories about cell 42. How the very first cell mate to be in that cell hung himself. Ironically, he hung himself while waiting to be hung. Story goes that the guy knew he sinned and didn't want to be judged by God. Since committing suicide automatically takes you to Hell, he figured he would by-pass God all the way. No one was going to judge him but himself!

After the first hanging, the next prisoner in cell 42 complained of hearing a whisper at night telling him to hang himself. It got so bad that he finally did. From then on, anyone put in cell 42 complained of hearing voices tempting them to commit suicide, thus giving cell 42 the nickname Hangman's Gallows.

When the suicides began to add up, the warden decided to use it to their advantage by putting any new prisoners who came to the prison after doing a horrendous crime into cell 42. Between their own guilt and the whispers at night it wouldn't take long to find them hanging in the cell.

However, the warden knew they had to start being careful. The damn prisoners would start complaining to their lawyers. The warden realized if a prisoner died in that cell after talking to the lawyers there could be problems.

Mike came up with the idea to move the prisoners, after they hung themselves, to another cell and fix the records to prove they had already moved the prisoners at the lawyer's request. Nobody would be the wiser. That was the incident where Mike decided he became the Mechanic because he "fixed" the problem.

Even though the prison had the highest suicide rate in the country, no one really cared, after all, they were hard core criminals. When they committing suicide it saved the taxpayers' money.

Anyway, any logical person would dismiss that cell 42 was genuinely haunted as nothing more than the other inmates putting fear into whoever moved into cell 42. It was simply a vicious game the inmates played with the new guy. At least that was what Jimmy had figured out, "I told Leroy to ignore the other inmates, they are just messing with him!"

Mike stops and looks dead serious at Jimmy, "He has a right to be afraid of that cell; however, what Leroy did to those kids takes away that right! He needs to listen to those voices and follow through!"

Jimmy disagrees, "I don't think Leroy hurt those kids like they said he did. Things just don't add up!"

Mike turns away and starts walking, "He was tried and sentenced. Nothing you can do about it now!"

They walk the rest of the way in silence. Jimmy doesn't bother to ask Mike if he thinks cell 42 is haunted. What would be the point? Either Mike would bust his balls for being a scaredy cat, or he would try to convince him it is haunted and later make fun of him. There was no winning with Mike.

They get to the cell and Leroy is anxiously waiting for them, unashamed tears of fear running down his face. "Man, I'm glad to see you! You gotta get me out of here! The whispers... I can't take it anymore!"

Mike sneers at Leroy, "Why don't you go back to reading the Good Book over there, it'll protect you!"

Jimmy speaks up, "Leroy, we've talked about this. Just ignore them! You can't let them get inside your head! You know what happens if they do!"

Leroy shakes his head, "Nah, you don't understand. They want to make a deal with me! Said they would leave me alone if I get my friend, Father Thomas, to come in here and exorcise the place!"

Mike laughs meanly, "Why in the world would they want that? If the voices are ghosts, would not having your priest friend come in and exorcise them be signing their own death warrant?"

Leroy looks confused, "I don't know, maybe they just want peace?"

Mike glares at him, "No! They want you to pay for what you did to those kids! Sitting here alive in this cell ain't payment enough!"

Leroy shakes his head, "I didn't do nothing to those kids that I can remember!"

Mike spits on him with pure hatred, "That's what all of you perverts say!"

Leroy wipes the spit from his face, goes to his cot and sits down, and begins to silently sob. Jimmy can barely stand it. Poor ole Leroy didn't have much more mentality than a kid himself, for Christ sake! "Leroy, you tell those voices to leave you alone tonight! I promise to ask the warden about all this in the morning."

Leroy looks up at Jimmy hopefully, "God bless you Jimmy!"

Mike walks away disgusted, "Oh good grief! C'mon Jiminy, we have work to do!"

As they walk Jimmy lowers his voice, "What would be the harm in asking the warden? If we make a big deal, like an exorcism or something, maybe the inmates will leave Leroy alone."

Mike shakes his head, "Still believing it is the other inmates?"

Frustrated, Jimmy answers, "Alright! What if the cell is haunt-ed? Wouldn't it be good to get rid of whatever is causing all these problems?"

Mike can't argue with Jimmy, it would be good to get that damn cell exorcised! He had his own encounter with cell 42 after going too far with the inmate Roger.

The prison was able to cover up the murder Mike committed. They believed his story over that of the inmates who were, more than likely, covering up for one of their own. With no substantial proof, there was no reason for the warden to sacrifice one of his own.

However, Mike knows the truth. What he did to that inmate was vicious and uncalled for, and yet, he felt invincible after-wards! He was looking forward to a new encounter where he could feel that power and control again!

All was good and fine until Mike had to clean out cell 42 one day. That was when he heard the whispers for himself. They told him he had sinned and it was time for him to judge himself! Funny thing was, he had been tempted to carry the judgment out right then and there! However, before Mike could carry out the deed, the coward fainted! When he fainted, he fell half out of the cell which allowed Mike to come to his senses and get the hell away from that cell!

He was so shaken by the incident that he approached the warden and said perhaps Roger's death affected him more than he thought. The warden took pity on him and let Mike take a short paid leave of absence to clear his mind.

You would think during the time away from the prison Mike would realize his wrong doing and be thankful he was not caught. On the contrary, he couldn't wait to get back to work! He reveled in the idea working where there were no consequences!

And yet, there was the problem of cell 42! So far, Mike had been able to avoid it at all cost. Having an exorcism might solve his problem; however, deep down, he can't for the life of him understand why the spirits would be asking to be exorcised. What would it benefit them?

To shut Jimmy up Mike finally agrees, "Ok, we will talk to the warden in the morning, but let me meet with him first to grease the wheels!"

That morning Jimmy waits patiently outside the warden's office while Mike and the warden have their meeting. Not convinced Mike is on board with the exorcism, Jimmy can't help but worry that he was going to make him out as the bad guy to the warden. Since Mike had the seniority, what chance did Jimmy have to convince the warden otherwise?

Rosey finally motions him in, "You can go in now Jimmy." She whispers in his ear as he passes by, "Make it seem like it is his idea or will be good for the prison, not anyone else's!"

Jimmy nervously walks in and takes a seat beside Mike. The warden clears his voice, "I hear you have some crazy thing you want to ask me, for an inmate no less!"

Jimmy realizes Rosey was right and decides to heed her advice, "Actually, I thought it might help us out more than the inmate."

The warden is intrigued, "Go on."

Jimmy quickly tries to form the right words, "I know we've been having some trouble from Leroy's lawyer about moving Leroy out of cell 42."

The warden answers angrily, "This ain't no God damn Holiday Inn! What does he expect?"

Jimmy agrees, "Of course! We can't have these lawyers undermining your authority! That is why I think it would be good to let Leroy have his priest friend come in and do an exorcism."

Jimmy quickly explains, "It would look like we were accommodating the current inmate and, whether it works or not, in the future we can say the cell was exorcised. That would take the only other reason for the suicides, beside inmates doing it completely on their own, away."

The warden thinks about it and then finally begins to smile, "I like it! It just may work! Ok, make it so!"

Relieved, Jimmy gets up and reaches over to shake the warden's hand, "Thank you, Sir!"

The warden shakes his hand as he looks over at Mike, "Mike, I think you may be wrong about this kid! He may go about things differently than you, but it looks like his first interests are the prison and the administration! That is what I like to see!"

The warden pulls his hand from Jimmy's, smiling, "In fact, I like you two as a team. We have a bad cop/good cop going on here, exactly what we need!"

As the warden dismisses them he finishes up, "Keep up the good work!"

Mike and Jimmy leave the office. Mike continues ahead while Jimmy falls back enough to whisper to Rosey as he passes by her, "You are the smartest lady I know! Thank you!"

Rosey blushes, "And don't you forget it!"

Jimmy chuckles as he leaves. Quickly he catches up with Mike, "That went pretty well. Will you go with me to tell Leroy before you leave?"

Although Mike likes the idea of the exorcism, for his own reasons, he is not too happy about how much the warden liked how Jimmy presented it. Mike shakes his head, "No, you love him so much, you go tell him! I am ready to go home!"

Jimmy, feeling a little empowered by the warden's comments, uses it to his advantage, "I think we should go together, the warden says we are a team! If it looks like we are all on board with this it may convince the other inmates it's for real!"

Mike sneers, "Ok, fine! But let's make it quick!"

As they walk to cell 42 in silence, Jimmy thinks about what the warden said and what it will mean. Mike and he were going to be a team and that in itself was going to be hell on earth!

Mike is not only nasty to Jimmy, when it comes to the inmates he is far worse! There had already been many times Jimmy had to step in when Mike was taking discipline too far.

Jimmy's main concern now is, what if one of these times he tries to stop Mike and he turns on him? How easy would it be for him to blame anything that happened to Jimmy on an inmate? Although Jimmy had not started working here until after Mike's incident with the inmate Roger, he knew the rumors. If he got away with it before, what was stopping him from doing it again? Certainly not his conscious!

Jimmy doesn't want to think about it and seeing Leroy anxiously waiting for him at the cell puts him in a good mood, "Hi Leroy! Looks like you got some sleep last night!"

Leroy nods happily, "I did what you told me! I told the whispers you were going to talk to the warden and if I got the request I needed my rest to make the arrangements."

Jimmy smiles, "Ok then! You call your priest friend up at lunch and get it all set up."

Leroy's eyes glisten with tears, "Thank you, Jimmy! You have no idea how much this means to me! I can't wait for you to meet Father Thomas!"

Leroy reaches over for his bible and shows Jimmy, "Father Thomas gave this to me! During the trial he stood with me the whole time! In fact, sometimes Father Thomas would tell them where I was when I couldn't remember!"

Jimmy is curious, "How did he know where you were?"

Leroy explains, "Oh, I worked for Father Thomas for several years doing yard work around the church. Father Thomas rescued me off the street when I was very young. He even let me live in the storage closet while I worked for him!"

Mike looks at his watch impatiently, "C'mon Jiminy, we need to wrap this up so we can get home and get some sleep!"

Leroy looks over at Mike a little fearfully, "Thank you too, Mike! I know you would like to see these whispers go away as well!"

Mike is about to ask him how he knows but thinks better of it. Keeping his tough guy image, he answers gruffly, "Whatever, Leroy. Get this shit set up soon so we can put all this nonsense behind us!"

Leroy nods happily, "Don't you worry! Father Thomas will come tonight! I just know it!"

Somehow, someway, Leroy convinced Father Thomas to come that night. In fact, Jimmy and Mike were the ones to escort Father Thomas to cell 42.

Jimmy is a little surprised at what Father Thomas looks like. He thought he would be a much older man, but on the contrary, he is quite young.

Mike is not concerned with his age. After all, no matter the age, a priest is a priest, "Father Thomas, did you bring all the stuff you need for an exorcism?"

Father Thomas chuckles a little, "I made it look like I did, what with all the robes and stuff. However, between you and me, I don't really believe in the whole exorcism scene."

Mike looks disappointed, "So, you will not be performing an exorcism?"

Father Thomas looks over at Jimmy and winks, "Oh, I'll be performing, just not an exorcism! Honestly, I don't have the authority to perform one."

Jimmy lowers his voice as they get closer to the cell, "I wondered about that. On all the movies you see today they always portray getting an exorcism approved is a hard task."

Father Thomas agrees, "More like impossible! The church does not like getting involved anymore. Too much of a risk!"

Mike wonders, "Then won't you get into trouble 'portraying' you are doing an exorcism?"

Father Thomas shakes his head, "There is nothing wrong in doing a blessing or a cleansing. Ole Leroy is too stupid to know the difference, so it'll be fine."

Jimmy can't help but mumble aloud, "Leroy thinks of you as his friend."

Father Thomas is a little embarrassed and clears his throat, "C'mon, you guys know what I mean. He has the mentality of a twelve-year-old."

Mike blurts out disgustedly, "Even a twelve-year-old can be lethal! What Leroy did to those kids was unthinkable! There is no excuse! He may have the mentality of a twelve-year-old, but even twelve-year-olds know right from wrong and that was plain wrong!" Realizing his own hypocrisy on knowing right from wrong, Mike quickly adds, "Kids should never be harmed!"

Jimmy rolls his eyes at Mike's feigned innocence, "Father Thomas, do you really think Leroy did what they said he did?"

Father Thomas bristles, "Of course he did! The kids identified him, it was done in his own room, and kiddie porn was hidden under his bed! It was clearly an open and shut case!"

Jimmy is confused, "If you truly believe that then why did you help him during the trial? Or for that matter, why are you helping him now?"

Father Thomas sighs, "We all have our own cross to bear. I brought Leroy into the church and he was my responsibility. I will never forgive myself for what he did to those kids!"

Determined, Father Thomas continues, "However, I do believe in forgiveness. In the end, God will have the final judgment."

Jimmy wants to ask more questions but they are approaching cell 42. He does not want to ruin the appearance of a real exorcism in front of the rest of the inmates.

Leroy is anxiously waiting for them, "Father Thomas! I knew you would come! Thank you so much!"

Mike unlocks the cell and Father Thomas steps in. He is surprised when Father Thomas asks, "Mike, do you mind coming in here with me? You seem to have a strong faith and you can help me prepare."

Not wanting to go into the cell, but being too arrogant and full of self-importance to turn him down, Mike agrees.

Father Thomas looks at Jimmy, "Leroy seems comfortable with you Jimmy. Can you take him to another cell temporarily? This may take a while."

Surprised, Jimmy nods, "Yea, I'll take him to cell 28 and then come back."

Mike looks nervously around the cell and back at Jimmy, "Ok, but hurry back! We may need you."

Leroy obediently follows Jimmy, "Do you think this will work, Jimmy?"

Jimmy answers him reassuringly, "I don't see why not, Leroy."

As they walk to cell 28 Jimmy is still curious and asks, "Leroy, do you not remember what you did to those kids?"

Leroy thinks real hard, "Ever since Father Thomas took me in I have had blackouts."

Jimmy does not understand, "Blackouts? What kind of blackouts?"

Leroy shrugs his shoulders, "The doctors say I might have had them due to bad things that were done to me while I lived on the street."

Jimmy begins to understand, "I suppose because of what was done to you, you did it to those kids?"

Leroy looks at him sadly, "I guess so."

Jimmy opens up cell 28, "I will be back for you when they are finished."

Leroy is relieved to be in a cell with no whispers, "Ok, I'm going to get some more sleep!"

As Jimmy is about to leave, he gets a call on his radio. "Jimmy, we're having trouble with Mike's radio. Can you come to the office and get him a new one?"

Jimmy replies, "On my way."

Meanwhile, back in cell 42 Father Thomas starts performing. He hands Mike his bible. "Mike, would you read the passage that is highlighted while I start the cleansing?"

Mike should feel safe with Father Thomas, but instead he feels vulnerable. Almost as if God himself knows they are pretending and He is not impressed. Instantly, the voices start to whisper, almost as if they had read his mind! They whisper, "Yes Mike, your God is not here! He has forsaken you for what you did!"

The whispers cut through to Mike's soul, "You claim at any age you should know right from wrong. Obviously then, when you killed that inmate you knew what you were doing was wrong!"

Trying to ignore the whispers Mike whispers over to Father Thomas, "Are you hearing anything?"

Father Thomas is dealing with demons of his own! They are whispering in his ear and he is deathly afraid Mike will hear! He abruptly answers, "I think that does it! We can leave now!"

Father Thomas had barely sprayed the room with holy water. The verse he said aloud didn't even sound finished but Mike was not about to argue with him!

They both turn to leave but the cell door violently slams shut! Mike instantly gets on his radio, "Command, can you hear me? Father Thomas and I are locked in cell 42! We need to have someone let us out immediately!"

Command didn't hear Mike's frantic call. They could only hear patchy white noise from Mike's radio, the reason they called Jimmy to come and get a new one.

Mike tries to reassure Father Thomas, "Don't worry, someone will be here in minutes. Even Jimmy should be back by now!"

Father Thomas screams in agony as he puts his hands over his ears, "Stop it! No! I won't admit it! You can't make me!"

Mike looks confused by what Father Thomas is saying and the whispers in his own ears are loud and persistent. He finds himself yanking the sheet off the cot.

The other inmates sit in silence and awe as they watch the events unfold. No one says a peep for fear that what is happening in that cell will overflow to their own!

In record time, Mike has tied the sheet to the ceiling and placed his neck into a noose that magically appears. Hanging is the only relief from the damn whispers! However, once he starts to hang it is a slow process to die, giving his mind time to understand what is happening. As he gasps for his last breath, Mike desperately claws at his noose until his hands are bloody, but to no avail.

Father Thomas watches helplessly as Mike hangs himself. Fearing for his own life, he screams out, "Ok! I confess! I was the one who did those horrible things to those kids!"

The whispers are not content and force Father Thomas to say more, "It was easy! Leroy had blackouts due to all the shit I had done to him for years!"

Tears stream down his face as he continues, "Leroy always wore a floppy hat and sunglasses outside to work in the church yard. I knew I could easily pass for him. I would make him do a stupid mindless chore while I dressed up like him. Then I took the kids back to his room. I planted some of the kiddie porn I already had. It was the perfect set up!"

Suddenly, his long scarf starts to slide up to the ceiling on its own. Father Thomas screams out, "No! I already confessed! You have to forgive me! God forgives me! I have been a servant of Him all my life! My work for Him more than compensates for what I have done!"

The whispers laugh out loudly enough that even the other inmates can hear them, "Taking the innocence of a child can never be undone! What right do you have to hide your perverted ways behind God's work?"

Another voice harshly continues, "We want to make sure true justice is served! Doesn't suicide take you to your hell?"

As Father Thomas struggles against being hung, he cries out, "This is murder, not suicide! God will know!"

A voice stronger than all the others answers sinisterly right before Father Thomas loses consciousness, "I am the judge here! You will be sentenced to an eternity of hell, whether you believe in it or not! For this is my hell!"

Jimmy comes back to cell 42 to an eerie silence. At first, he can't believe his eyes! Both Mike and Father Thomas are hanging quietly in the cell. He shakes his head in disbelief and screams out, "Oh my God! What happened?"

An inmate nearby whispers in disbelief, "What happened in there had nothing to do with God!"

Jimmy quickly radios for help as he tries to unlock the cell. A different inmate speaks up, "Dude! Don't go in there alone, wait for backup!"

Realizing Father Thomas and Mike are already dead, Jimmy stops short of going into the cell. Instead, he decides to wait for backup. While waiting, he observes the two men hanging in front of him. Jimmy can't help but ask again, "What happened?"

An inmate simply says, "They hung themselves."

Jimmy finds that hard to believe. If that were the case, why did both of them die so violently? He could see where they clawed at their nooses until they were bloody. In fact, Father Thomas fought so hard he had thrown off one of his shoes!

Jimmy walks over to the closest inmate, "Why did they hang themselves?"

The inmate looks fearfully at cell 42, "Because of their sins. I guess Mike did it over the guilt of killing Roger."

The inmate continues in disgust, "I mean, it was one thing for all of us to bully that dumbass Roger, but Mike went too far! Sticking the guy's inhaler up his ass and then watching Roger gasp for air as he died was even too sick for any of us to do! And yet, when we all told the warden what he did, they cleared him! Mike got what he deserved!"

Jimmy sort of understands that one. "What about Father Thomas?"

The inmate sighs, "Better let ole Leroy out. Come to find out the poor kid is innocent."

Eventually they did let poor Leroy out. What the inmates heard that tragic night was enough for the police to re-open the case. Upon further investigation, they found a second floppy hat, sunglasses and kiddie porn in Father Thomas' room. Now it truly was an open and shut case.

As for the two hangings, they were never fully explained; although it was evident the two did in fact hang themselves. The reason why, together in that cell, is still unknown except to the inmates in the surrounding area. Never did you see a group of inmates so quickly become model prisoners.

Cell 42 was officially retired after that incident. However, some inmates walking by the cell swear they can still hear whispers tempting them to provide true justice in their own cells. To this day, that facility still holds the record for having the most suicides.

White Noise Stories Continued

The story fades out as they are entering the final state in their drive for the day. This time it is Lauren, in deep thought, who turns off the radio. Miles get eaten up as she thinks about the story she just heard. Could something like that really happen? Maybe what she experienced in that damn apartment was something unnatural!

Lauren looks over at Roxy when she becomes a little restless in her sleep. What about Roxy? Had something really happened to her when she looked in that mirror as a kid, but then she convinced herself otherwise? Damn if it wasn't easy to go back and forth on this subject!

Feeling Lauren staring at her, Roxy wakes up a little self-conscious, "What? Was I drooling, snoring or talking in my sleep?"

Lauren smiles, "No, you are fine!"

Roxy pulls off her headphones and looks around. She is surprised to see they are so close to their hotel. "Wow! I really slept hard! I am sorry! Are you doing ok?"

Lauren stretches a little, "I am. Although, I am not going to lie, getting out of this car for the day will feel nice!"

Roxy watches the cornfields go by, "This is your ole stomping ground, huh? Way different than Jersey!"

Lauren nods, "Actually, it has changed a lot in just the last couple of years!"

Roxy pulls her phone out, "I'm going to call Teresa and tell her we will be at the hotel by 6:30."

Lauren agrees, "Good idea! It will give her plenty of time to get ready to meet with us at the restaurant."

Roxy calls Teresa and talks briefly to her. Afterwards, Lauren can't help but comment, "It is nice that you are trying with my old friends."

Roxy admits, "I get a little jealous sometimes because I know all of you go way back. You and I have only known each other since the last year in high school!"

Lauren becomes serious, "It was a dark time for me when I had to leave all my old friends before my senior year! I was very fortunate you were so friendly towards me!"

Roxy shrugs it off, "It was easy, you looked lost and I picked up on it. I have to admit, when I met Teresa during Christmas last year she was very sweet to me! She never made me feel like an outsider. I'm sure Jodi will be the same."

Lauren smiles, "They are good people, always there for you no matter what! I am a lucky girl to have such good friends!"

Before long, Lauren pulls into their hotel parking lot. Roxy is surprised, "I thought this was going to be some hole in the wall! This is very nice!"

Lauren parks the car, "Wait until you have dinner at Grays! Best home cooked meals around! I can't wait to get me some of their chicken livers and gravy!"

Roxy looks over at her and wrinkles her nose, "Please tell me they have more than chicken livers!"

Lauren laughs as she gets out of the car, "Where's that sense of adventure you kept telling me about before we left?"

Roxy pulls her bag out of the car, "Oh, it's there. I was just wondering if I should be wearing my bibbed overalls tonight."

Lauren shakes her head, "Careful girlfriend, you are in my territory now! Don't be making fun of my folk here!"

Roxy is not backing down, "Oh no! How many times have you busted my chops about my friends in the city with their stretch pants and stilettos? What's fair is fair!"

Smiling, Lauren holds the door open for Roxy. "You are right! I deserve that, but the difference is that here you are going to meet real and genuine people, not fake wannabes!"

Roxy sighs, "Alright, some of 'my folk' might be like that, but not all of them!"

Lauren reaches over and gives her an affectionate hug, "I'm teasing you!"

Roxy sighs, "One of the hardest things I have yet to figure out about you!"

Lauren heads to the counter laughing, "I guess it's just a 'thang' we do here."

Lauren and Roxy take their bags to their room, freshen up, and head back out to meet up with Teresa at Grays. Roxy is happy to see Lauren so excited to see her friend Teresa. Lauren seems to be returning to her happy self!

Lauren maneuvers through the little town she grew up in easily, happily showing Roxy different places where some of her happiest memories were from. Once at Grays, they find Teresa sitting in her truck waiting for them. Lauren and Teresa hug for what seems like an eternity but then Teresa gives Roxy a big hug too.

The dinner at Grays was everything Lauren had said it would be! A huge cafeteria with lots of home cooked items. Roxy was so overwhelmed she was not sure what to get! Fortunately, they each got something different and Roxy was able to sample a number of things. And yes, she even tried the chicken livers and was pleasantly surprised!

After dinner and gossip, Teresa didn't want the time with her best friend to end. "Mind if I follow you two back to the hotel and maybe we can talk there for a while?"

Lauren is excited, "That is an awesome idea! Are you sure? I know you have to work tomorrow. I don't want to make it too late for you!"

Teresa shakes her head, "Oh please! How often do I get to see you? Anyway, I'm the one that feels guilty for not letting you get your sleep! You've driven all day and you have a lot of driving to do tomorrow!"

Lauren is too excited to sleep, "Not a problem, tomorrow is going to be fun too! Sure, we'll drive the whole day, but by dinner I'll get to see Jodi! I will be too excited to be tired!"

They drive back to the hotel, Teresa closely following Lauren. Teresa, always one for being observant, notices a passenger van following them from the restaurant. Could be just a coincidence, but the roads Lauren is taking back to the hotel is not a direct path. Yet, the van follows them right into the parking lot of the hotel! Anxious to pick up their gossip, Teresa quickly forgets about the van as she and the other two head towards the lobby.

Wanting to give Teresa and Lauren some quality time alone, Roxy speaks up, "I'm going to call it an early night! Even though

I was a bum and slept most of the day, I want to go up to the room, relax and brag on Facebook about our road trip!"

Teresa gives her a big hug goodnight, "As always Roxy, it was a pleasure!"

Roxy returns the hug, "Right back at ya! You two don't have too much fun down here!"

Lauren can't stop smiling, "Oh, we will!"

Lauren gives Roxy a brief hug goodnight and whispers, "Thank you!"

Lauren and Teresa find a cozy spot in a corner and begin their gossiping. After finally getting caught up, Teresa looks concerned. "How are you really doing, Lauren?"

Lauren is relaxed from their intimate conversation and answers honestly, "Not bad. I think this trip was exactly what I needed! In fact, I think this whole idea of moving is a good idea!"

Teresa looks a little sad, "I have to admit, I have wanted you to move from the East Coast for a long time, just not all the way over to the West Coast!"

Lauren understands, "I know, but if anything, me living on the East Coast proved to us that no matter where we live we will always be friends!"

Teresa nods, "You are right! Look at Jodi, I miss her too! Though I have to admit I am a little bit jealous of her having Jady, her new husband!"

Lauren can't help but laugh, "I know, right? Lucky girl found her soul mate early! It's so cute that their names match, Jodi and Jady! Can't get more perfect than that!"

Teresa wonders, "You sure you are going to be alright with Roxy?"

Lauren is a little surprised, "I thought you liked Roxy?"

Teresa sighs, "I do, I was just a little surprised. After your incident you felt you could tell Jodi and I everything; however, you hardly told Roxy a thing!"

Lauren hesitates, "It's not that I didn't want too. Roxy had a lot going on in her life at that time. Her sister got married, she got back with her ex briefly, only to remember why he was an ex. It was all about timing."

Lauren can see Teresa's skepticism and quickly adds, "Actually, Roxy has been very interested during our trip. In fact, talking to her seems to be lifting the fog."

Teresa can't help but wonder, "Maybe the farther away you get from that apartment complex the more you will remember!"

Lauren is impressed at how much Teresa believes her, "I can't thank you and Jodi enough for believing my crazy story! From the minute I told you two, neither one of you questioned my sanity. You truly believed me! I don't know why or how but you did!"

Teresa reaches over and pats her on the hand, "Because, my dear, for as long as we have known you, you have never lied to us nor made up stories! Of course we are going to believe you!"

Lauren thinks about it, "I guess we've been naïve all our lives to think strange things don't happen when, in fact, it is all around us!"

Teresa does not follow her, "What do you mean?"

Lauren explains, "On the way here I have been listening to this syndicated show on the radio. People call in with the strangest stories you have ever heard!"

Lauren finds herself not wanting to get into the strange incidents that happened after hearing the stories on the radio. Even though Teresa would have understood, Lauren is simply too tired to get into it!

Teresa is not surprised, "Look at all the shows on TV, or all the stories we see on Facebook. There definitely is strange crap happening all over!"

Lauren can't help but wonder, "Do you think instead of making us aware of things, it simply is making us numb?"

Teresa thinks about it, "I am sure to some degree it is! But then again, since we have heard and seen these stories, perhaps it makes it easier for us to understand when something happens like it did to you. Not so quick to jump to the conclusion that someone is crazy for what they say they experienced."

Lauren yawns and then blushes, "Sorry. You are right though, it is a good way of looking at it!"

Teresa stands up, "As much as I hate to say goodbye, I want you to get your rest!"

Lauren stands up and walks her to the door, "It was so good seeing you! Promise me you will visit me in California!"

Teresa sighs, "Only for you. You know me, that city life ain't my cup of tea!"

Lauren hugs her hard, a little tearful. "And I love you for that!"

Teresa hugs her back, "I love you. Now you take care of yourself and if you need anything call me day or night! The phone is always on!"

After saying their goodbyes, Teresa walks to her truck. Out of the corner of her eye she sees an older man standing by the van that followed them from the restaurant. A slight chill comes over Teresa. At first she thought the man had red glowing eyes, but then realized it must have been the butt of his cigarette glowing.

As she gets in the car, Teresa can't help but think she recognizes the old man; however, for the life of her she can't think of who he is! Teresa is a little surprised as what seems like a slight fog comes over her mind. She shakes her head a little as if to clear her thoughts. Now what was she just thinking about? Frustrated with herself, she shrugs her shoulders. Maybe she will think of it later.

Lauren and Roxy wake up the next morning completely refreshed. After having another home cooked dinner for breakfast they find themselves back on the road.

Even though Roxy wanted to stay up, Lauren assures her she will be fine. With a lot of convincing, she finally gets Roxy to take her pill.

Miles down the road, after talking endlessly about the night before with Teresa, Roxy finds herself getting sleepy.

Once Roxy is asleep, Lauren turns her radio on in hopes of finding her show. She is in luck! A young girl has already started her story. Lauren hopes she has not missed too much of it!

Hitch Her

Hitch Her

Jackie and Don drive in silence. Both are on a vacation that will hopefully put their marriage back on track, although so far it was not working. Earlier, Don had made the mistake of correcting Jackie on the way she had used a certain word in a sentence. She, of course, had gotten pissed off that he had corrected her instead of letting it slide. Ever since then, they rode in silence.

Realizing the sun is about to set, Jackie breaks the silence by asking, "Maybe we should start looking for a hotel for the night?"

Bored, Don agrees, "Fine with me."

Jackie tries to ignore Don's attitude, "Look at that sunset, isn't it beautiful?"

Don shrugs his shoulders, "I suppose."

Frustrated, Jackie hotly replies, "You can never get excited about anything, can you?"

Don tries to defend himself, "What? It's a freaking sunset! What is there to get excited over?"

Jackie sighs, she will never be able to make him understand.

Realizing he needs to make an effort, Don apologizes, "I am sorry. You are right, it is pretty."

Jackie sits in silence. Sometimes it is better to be quiet than harp on something. Anyway, at least Don apologized this time.

Looking out the window Jackie sees a shadow. She squints her eyes and sees a little girl ahead of them. "Slow down, Don. It looks like a little girl is walking down the road ahead of us!"

At first Don does not see what Jackie is talking about, but when he squints his eyes against the last of the sun's rays he sees her too. "I see her! Wonder what she's doing out her alone? Do you see any other cars?"

Jackie looks over at the embankment alongside of them, "No, but it's hard to see anything for sure. Try not to scare her when we pull up beside her."

Don slows the car down to a crawl before they approach the girl. She looks no older than six or seven, carrying a dirty old teddy bear.

On closer inspection, Don is not sure he wants to stop. Something seems off with the kid, almost as if she was waiting for them. Like she is used to hitching for rides.

However, Jackie's maternal instincts kick in to high gear, "Oh, that poor thing! She must be terrified!" Before Don can caution her to be careful, Jackie rolls down the window, "My sweet, are you ok?"

The little girl stops walking and slowly turns towards the car, "May I come inside?"

Don finds it odd that she is asking permission. Then again, he is not used to kids having manners these days! He puts the car in park and reaches to the back, opening the door for her. However, the little girl just stands there waiting for a reply to her question.

Jackie assures the little girl, "Of course you can come inside!"

As the little girl gets in, Don has to say, "You need to be careful out there, being a hitcher is not very safe!"

The little girl is curious, "What is a hitch her?"

Jackie cringes when she hears the little girl repeat the word back incorrectly. She waits, knowing for sure her husband will quickly correct the child.

Surprisingly, Don doesn't catch it! Instead, he quickly gives her a text book definition of the word, "It is a person that asks for rides along the road, although there are several other definitions for it. It could mean fasten or tie, like hitch a horse up to a post."

Obviously liking to hear himself talk, Don continues, "The other meanings are sayings. One is 'back in my day we used to hitch up our pants' which means pull them up. Another is when two people got married, they 'got hitched.' However, in this case slang would be more appropriate. A person alongside of the road who needs to get a ride is called a hitchhiker or some might call them a hitcher."

Jackie looks over at Don, annoyed, "Seriously Don? This is not your classroom! I'm sure the poor girl does not want to hear your nonsense!"

The little girl speaks up, "No, I like being called Hitch Her. It sounds cool."

Jackie is a little confused by the little girl's calm manner, "Honey, why are you out here?"

Don jumps in, "You aren't hurt, are you?"

The little girl shakes her head, "No Sir, but I am afraid the rest of them are dead!"

Don is shocked at what the little girl says and instantly grabs for his phone to call the police. As Don is busy looking at his phone, Jackie turns completely in her seat to see the little girl better. She gasps as the final light from the sun shines down on the little girl. She is stark white and her eyes are as black as night itself!

Jackie's hands tremble as she reaches over to Don to get his attention. Fumbling with the phone he asks curtly, "What?"

Not wanting to bring attention to what she is trying to do, Jackie asks, "Don Honey, can you check to see if her door is shut?"

Don sighs and looks up from his phone. Just as he is about to reply to Jackie that he was sure it was, he catches a glimpse of the creature, the little girl, in their back seat. He shivers uncontrollably and looks down at his phone, only to see that he has no service! Worried, he looks over at Jackie, "There is no service!"

Trying to convince herself that it is just a little girl who needs their help, Jackie clears her throat, "Let's start over. My name is Jackie and this is my husband Don. What is your name?"

The little girl answered quietly, "Anna."

Jackie sighs with relief, surely there are not too many creatures named Anna! "Anna, can you tell me what happened?"

Anna nods, "Daddy was driving when all at once a deer jumped in front of us. He swerved and the next thing I know we are flipping over and over. I thought we would never stop!"

Now Don is beginning to feel foolish, this poor girl has just been in a major accident and may have lost her whole family. The sunlight must have been playing tricks on their eyes for the girl to come across looking so evil. "Do you remember where the car is?"

Anna hesitates, "A ways back, I think. I found myself walking before I even realized I was walking."

Jackie's motherly instincts kick in again and she quickly takes her sweater off and places it around Anna's shoulders. "You poor thing, you must be in shock!"

Anna agrees, "I am! I can't believe the transfer didn't happen!"

Don is confused, "Transfer? What are you talking about?"

Anna replies matter-of-factly, "When my twin sister Diana died I was supposed to get her soul!"

Suddenly the air in the car turns frigid and both Don and Jackie are frozen with fear. Jackie trembles as she asks, "Why would your sister's soul go to you?"

Anna rolls her eyes, "Because silly, that is how it works! I was Diana's doppelgänger so I have no soul. That is, not until Diana died, then I would get her soul!"

Jackie and Don are at a total loss and don't know what to do. Hoping the poor child is simply in shock, Don tries to think of an excuse to get out of the car, "Maybe I should get out and check on your family? Perhaps you are mistaken and they just need help?"

Anna smiles sinisterly, "Oh no, they are all dead! The steering wheel went through Daddy's chest. Mommy was thrown into the windshield. She is half in and out of the glass, nearly cut in half!"

Anna continues, "And dear Diana is smashed into a puddle of goo. To think I fought with her to sit on that side! For once, I am glad I let the bitch have her way!"

Jackie and Don sit there motionless, not sure what to do next. Anna is enjoying the uncomfortable atmosphere, "The problem is, I am caught between this universe and the next."

Jackie suddenly jumps into action and tries to open her door but it is fruitless, the doors are locked! She screams out, "Don! Unlock the damn doors!"

Don has already been trying, but to no avail. "Damn it! I can't get them to unlock!"

Anna laughs, "Trying to leave before my story is over is a bit rude, don't you think? Remember, you invited me in!"

Suddenly a distant memory pops into Jackie's mind and she whispers, "The dark eyed children!"

Don looks at her questioningly, but it is Anna who answers, "Ah yes, you have heard of us!"

Like Don did with her earlier, Anna takes on a lecturing voice as she explains, "You see Don, we are an internet urban legend. It started sometime in the early nineties, but we've been around for a lot longer than that!"

Jackie whispers, "What are you, an alien? A creature? Vampire or demon?"

Anna smiles, "Take your pick. We can be any of them or all of them. Depends on the culture and what your own beliefs are."

Anna sighs as she contemplates the different terms Jackie had used, "An alien? I suppose we are alien to this universe and yet we are growing in numbers."

Anna looks a little sad, "Creatures? I suppose in my form, yes. Although, if I had gotten my true form you would have never been able to see under the disguise!"

Anna continues, "Do we like blood like a vampire?" Teasingly she licks her lips loudly, "Of course we do!"

Anna speculates on the last term, "Demon? Do we want your souls? Absolutely! Unfortunately, since I am an in-between, I can't collect your soul. The upside is, I am human enough to be able to kill!"

Anna thinks about it, "However Don, I like your new term. Hitch Her. You can add a new meaning to that word. I will be a 'hitch her' to the two of you. I will be tying myself to you and your souls until I can move out of the in-between!"

Now Don realizes Anna is not saying the word hitcher correctly. Looking over at Jackie who is staring helplessly back, he realizes he doesn't want to piss his wife off one last time. For once, he will let it go.

Don and Jackie were never found, but at the end their marriage finally seemed to be on the right track!

White Noise Stories Continued

Trembling, Lauren turns the radio off abruptly. For some reason that story had bothered her! Reluctantly, she nudges Roxy to wake her up.

Roxy wakes up groggily and takes her headphones off, "What's up?"

Lauren looks a little embarrassed, "I'm a little un-nerved, that's all."

Roxy sits up and gives Lauren her full attention, "Why? Something wrong with the car? Did we almost wreck?"

Lauren shakes her head, "No, it was something I heard on the radio."

Roxy instantly becomes concerned, "Oh my God! Did we get bombed?"

Feeling foolish, Lauren shakes her head, "No, nothing like that. It was a story I heard on the radio."

Roxy is shocked as she looks around at the bright sunshine, "Honey, it is broad daylight! What possibly could have scared you so much?"

Lauren is not sure how to start, "Remember when I told you about the mirrors and the doppelgängers?"

Roxy rubs her eyes trying to wake up, "Yes?"

Lauren tells her the story she just heard. "It is so similar to what I dealt with in that apartment, except without the mirrors!"

Before Roxy can answer Lauren rushes on, "What if we were wrong about my apartment? What if I really did tap into the dead dreaming? Why else would my dream be so close to the story on the radio?"

Roxy can't help but laugh, "You just answered your own question! Probably because you had heard a similar story before and simply dreamed it!"

Lauren hates Roxy's condescending tone but defiantly goes on, "I'm telling you, I think it's all real!"

Roxy shakes her head, "Listen to yourself, you are getting all caught up in stupid scary stories and your mind is trying to force it all into a reality it is not!"

Lauren is beginning to realize it is much easier for Roxy to not believe in the unknown than to actually entertain the idea it could be a possibility. "Whatever!"

Lauren drives in silence. Frustrated, Roxy tries to apologize, "I am sorry, maybe I handled that wrong!"

Lauren is not moved and continues to drive in silence. Suddenly, Roxy and Lauren see a billboard in front of them and can't help but read it together. After reading it, they both burst out laughing! In between giggles Roxy reads it aloud, "Uranus Fudge Company – proudly packing fudge in Uranus since 2015."

Lauren is shocked, "Oh my God! How funny is that?"

Roxy agrees, "It's hilarious! Let's stop!"

Lauren nods, "Yes, I definitely think we should stop at the Uranus fudge making company!"

Not sure if it is all the stress Lauren has been under, or all of the driving, but she can't help hysterically laughing at that stupid billboard! Tears are literally running down her face! Roxy is laughing along with her and she is so relieved! That stupid billboard was the perfect distraction they needed to relieve the tension between them!

Lauren follows the signs and before they know it they are sitting in front of a tourist trap advertising Uranus, Missouri. Lauren didn't even know there was a Uranus, Missouri!

Excited, they both go in the store. Tons of memorabilia is packed inside. Buying their first souvenirs of the trip, Lauren buys her father a T-shirt with the famous fudge packing Uranus logo on it. Her father will love it!

Roxy decides they have to buy a vanity license plate for Lauren's car to show it has traveled Route 66. Since California requires a plate only on the back, it is perfect to put on the front!

At the register a woman gives them a big smile and asks loudly, "Did you find everything you wanted in Uranus?"

Lauren and Roxy giggle like school girls and blush, "Why yes, we did!"

The friendly woman nods, "Good to hear it! You girls heading out West for the solar eclipse?"

Lauren looks a little confused, "Solar eclipse?"

Roxy nods, "Yes silly! How could you not know? It's been plastered on Facebook, the news, everywhere, for days! It only comes once every 40 years!"

Lauren is shocked, "Gosh, I had no idea! I haven't been paying attention to social media lately. Where is it going to be?"

The cashier lady answers, "Across the whole United States, though they did say out West you will be able to see it best! It's going to be a total eclipse. Make sure you pick yourself up some Uranus Solar Eclipse glasses free with a purchase!"

Lauren and Roxy get their glasses. Lauren smiles at the cashier, "Thank you! You have such a cute little store here! I love it!"

Roxy agrees, "Yes, it is! I checked us in on Facebook when we first got here. You would not believe how many people are getting a kick out of this store!"

The cashier smiles, "That's what we want to hear! You two be safe out there and enjoy the solar eclipse!"

Lauren and Roxy get back in the car. Lauren has to ask, "You really knew about the solar eclipse?"

Roxy nods, "I did! In fact, I sort of planned our trip around it. I have us staying at a small secluded town where the internet said it would be the perfect place to see it! A once in a lifetime type of thing! I couldn't resist!"

Lauren is surprised, "I don't recall you saying anything about it."

Roxy looks disappointed, "I was going to surprise you! I knew you really hadn't been paying attention to what is going on in the world. It looked like I was going to get away with it, until now! I thought it would be something cool we could share together. Forty years from now we can tell our grandchildren where we were when we saw it!"

Lauren is impressed, "I had no idea, so it still was a surprise! I can't wait, I've never seen an eclipse! And you're right, definitely a cool story to tell one day!"

Roxy perks up, "I'm glad! I wasn't sure if you would think it was dumb or not."

Lauren feels bad about getting upset with Roxy earlier. Obviously, Roxy had put more thought in this trip than she realized, "Look, I am sorry about earlier. I know you mean well. Maybe I overreacted?"

Roxy shakes her head, "No, I get it! I certainly wouldn't like it if someone didn't believe in what I said!"

Lauren understands, "You handle it differently than Teresa and Jodi. Where they believed me instantly, you try to be logical and look for a sane reason. Nothing wrong with that, in fact, it gives me a different perspective!"

Roxy watches the scenery go by, "I'm not saying that I don't believe you. You may have encountered something in that apartment complex I can't explain! I just don't want you to dwell on it. Honestly, I want my fun loving Lauren back!"

Lauren nods, "I do too!"

Hours go by while they talk about Roxy's ex, her sister and then their plans for California. Roxy points at an exit sign, "Looks like there are some fast food places here. Can we stop? I am starving!"

Lauren gets over and takes the exit, "I am too!"

After a quick late lunch, Roxy gets settled in for her nap. Lauren tries not to be jealous. The driving is beginning to get to her, especially after eating! Lauren finds herself fighting to stay awake.

Turning on the radio, she becomes frustrated at not being able to find anything she likes. Just as she is about to turn it off, Lauren hears a woman telling a story. She smiles, realizing she has found her show! Hopefully the story won't be like the last one! If it is, no way is she telling Roxy. This trip is long enough without adding tension over differences of opinion. Best if Lauren keeps certain things to herself.

Mermac Caverns

Mermac Caverns

A haunting voice begins to speak, almost as if she is whispering in your ear, "I am sure many locals know of the stories surrounding the Mermac Caverns."

"It is a cavern system that runs 4.6 miles in the Ozarks, near Stanton, Missouri. The caverns were formed by the erosion of large limestone deposits over millions of years."

She speaks monotone like a tour director, "The Mermac Caverns is a huge tourist attraction with more than fifty billboards along Interstate 44 and is considered one of the primary attractions on Highway 66."

"In 1935 the cave system was opened to the public as a tourist attraction by Lester Dill, who in 1960 also invented the bumper sticker as a means of promoting the caverns. In fact, Mermac Caverns rented out billboard space in the caverns, claiming it was the only underground billboard in the world."

A little more upbeat, the woman continues, whispering mischievously, "Mermac Caverns was recently closed down with the official reason that high levels of toxins had been discovered and they had to install vents. However, in a little while, I will tell you the real reason!"

"For now, let me explain some of the formations found in the cavern. On the fifth level is the Wine Room. It has the world's rarest cave formation, the Wine Table. It is an onyx table that stands six feet high and is supported on three natural legs. The table was composed almost entirely underwater. The table and room are adorned with grape-like clusters."

The woman can't help but add, "Sounds to me like the perfect place for a sacrifice!"

"The cavern also contains a massive sheet wall of formations formed during the past several thousand years; here they display a light and sound show."

Sighing, she continues, "There is also a room called Hollywood where some movie scenes were shot. One was where Tom

Sawyer and Huckleberry Finn found the gold. There was also a TV episode of Lassie shot in the room."

"Another room in the cavern is called the Ballroom. It was first used in 1890 for large community events and square dances."

Her voice begins to reflect a bit more enthusiasm, "I saved my favorite for last, the Mirror Room. This part of the cavern contains a stream of water that is only about two feet deep. However, when a group of lights are turned on the depth of the water looks like fifty feet due to the reflection of the cavern's roof."

"Here are a couple of interesting facts about the cavern. During the 18th century it was used for extracting saltpeter for the manufacture of gunpowder. During the Civil War the plant was discovered and destroyed by the Confederates."

The woman has to chuckle, "Even Jesse James and his gang were thought to have used the caverns as their hideout."

"All of what I have told you is pretty mundane and what you will hear if you go to see the Mermac Caverns yourself or do any online research. Strangely, these are the only interesting facts you will find about the caverns!"

The woman pauses a moment and then asks, "Doesn't that make you stop and wonder? Surely a dark dank cavern would have dark deep secrets too, would it not?"

"The Mermac Caverns have existed for 400 million years. In centuries past, Native Americans used the cavern system for shelter, to be precise, the Osage Tribe."

The woman settles in for her true story, "It begins with the beginning of the Osage Tribe here on Earth. The Osage Tribe once lived in the sky, way beyond the Earth. They wanted to know where they came from so they went to the Sun."

Her voice soft but strong continues, "The Sun told them that they were his children. This only prompted the tribe to find out more, so they traveled farther until they came upon the Moon."

"The Moon told them that she gave birth to them and that the Sun was their father."

Sadness creeps into the woman's voice, "The Moon told them they must leave the sky and go down and live on Earth."

"A nearby jealous universe named Mo Sa Ne overhears and suggests that she should be the protector for the tribe. The Sun, being impressed, agrees and gives the universe a task to fulfill once she is on Earth. Since Mo Sa Ne means Arrow of Life, her task on Earth would be to keep a balance between life and death."

"Her red arrows were for life and the black ones for death, both fired to the west so life and death can ever pursue night and day."

The woman sighs, "The tribe obeyed, but the Earth was covered with water. Not knowing how to return home in the sky, they wept and called out. However, there was no answer."

"You see, Mo Sa Ne wanted the tribe to fail. She wanted to have her own tribe with the Sun. She already had children, but they were not from the light and had no souls. A soul allows you to be reincarnated so you can live throughout the ages."

The woman returns to the perils of the Osage Tribe, "Fortunately, the animals had sympathy for the tribe. The Elk instilled confidence in all creatures because of its beauty and grace. The tribe asked the Elk for help."

"Eager to help, some of the Elk jumped into the water and began to sink while others called out to the winds. Soon, rock appeared and the tribe came down to live on them."

Irritated, the woman continues, "Unfortunately, the tribe was impatient. They didn't like living on the rocks with no food! Again they cried out and this time Mo Sa Ne answered with a bargain. She would raise the water to mist, but only if the tribe would give away their awareness after death."

The woman realizes she needs to explain, "Mo Sa Ne could not take away their ability to be reincarnated, she could only take away their awareness of each life they lived before. The Osage Tribe thought it was a small price to pay."

"With the bargain in place, the water on Earth rose up as a mist revealing the soft earth below. The Elk, in their joy, rolled over and over leaving loose hairs clinging to the soil. The hairs grew and from them sprang all the vegetation on Earth."

"As time went by, the Osage Tribe thrived. Even though Mo Sa Ne had their awareness, it did her no good since none of the tribe would remember she had it in their future lives."

The woman sighs, "Mo Sa Ne's jealousy grew as she watched the Sun and Moon embrace morning and evening. How could the Sun love the Moon when it was obvious Mo Sa Ne was a much better mother!"

"Her jealously became bitter. Why should the Moon's children be blessed with the light of a soul when Mo Sa Ne's were not?"

The woman pauses, "Mo Sa Ne had to figure out a way to take the souls from the Moon's children and give them to her own. But how? Although the tribe had easily given away their awareness, they were not so likely to give away their souls for there was no more need to bargain."

The woman continues, "This is where the Mermac Caverns come into the story. Mo Sa Ne had taken up residence in the caverns. It was a place where she could travel between universes to be able to see her children and keep an eye on the Sun and Moon's children on Earth."

"The caverns became a bad place where members of the tribe would mysteriously disappear while visiting it. Legends began about dark things happening to one's soul if they entered the caverns."

The woman explains, "In reality, it was a bad place where Mo Sa Ne had figured out how to steal the Osage's souls and place them into her own children."

"Without having awareness to warn their future selves, the Osage Tribe tried to keep in place stories of warnings in hopes of keeping their souls intact."

Sadness enters the woman's voice, "As the tribe grew, so did restlessness and the younger generation didn't like listening to the old ways. Because of their ignorance and naivety Mo Sa Ne's children were able to grow in numbers and soon were able to go to different parts of the world to feed."

The woman states the obvious, "Mo Sa Ne had invented temptation. Her children were good at tempting or chipping away at the soul, yet it was a slow process. They had to target the souls they had tempted through each lifetime for the soul to be weakened and eventually taken."

"Once taken, the soul had to be baptized into another vessel. The only time Mo Sa Ne found she could do this without the

Moon and Sun noticing was when they were too involved in a random embrace such as a solar eclipse."

The woman chuckles a little, "That is how 'solar eclipse' got its name, although now it is spelled differently. Originally, it was called souler eclipse, as in the eclipse of souls."

"For Mo Sa Ne to baptize the souls she needed to find water that had been on Earth from the beginning of time. The Mermac Caverns were perfect! When the water rose up to become mist it was trapped in the caverns. Pure pools of water that was here on Earth before the Osage Tribe was left behind. It was exactly what Mo Sa Ne needed for the baptisms."

The woman's voice trembles, "As for today, the Mermac Caverns continue to be an eternal source for soul domination."

Playing to her audience the woman asks, "So, what does this story have to do with you? Where is the fear factor here? Think about it, a mundane little tourist trap hiding one of the darkest secrets in the world!"

The woman whispers menacingly, "Why is it still a secret? Why were those toxins that recently closed the caverns down not contributed to all the decomposing soulless bodies, accumulating throughout the centuries, floating in the cavern's waters?"

"Maybe, just maybe, all of our awareness has been taken?"

White Noise Stories Continued

Lauren looks over at Roxy as she turns the radio off, "Roxy, are you awake?"

Roxy yawns, sits up and takes her headphones off, "I am now."

Lauren stretches, "I am sorry! I am really tired and I thought maybe talking would wake me up!"

Roxy gets a couple of waters out of the cooler and hands one to Lauren, "Here, maybe this will help too."

Lauren takes the drink appreciatively, "Thanks, I'm sure it will!"

Roxy is surprised the radio is turned off, "Couldn't find the show you like so much?"

After taking a drink Lauren shakes her head, "No, I found it. At the end of the story I turned it off to give myself a break."

Roxy shakes her head, "I don't know how you don't fall asleep listening to people talk! I need music!"

Lauren teases her, "And yet, you seem to fall asleep so easily with your music!"

Roxy smiles, "Ok, you've got me there. But at least it's not boring!"

Lauren chuckles and points as she sees the next billboard advertising the Mermac Caverns, "Check that out! That was what the last story was about on the radio!"

Roxy reads the billboard, "Mermac Caverns, what is it?"

Lauren chooses the words from the woman on the radio and whispers it in an eerie voice, "An eternal source for soul domination!"

Roxy looks at her shocked, "No kidding? Oh, we have to stop! Do we have time?"

Lauren is curious too so she nods, "We'll make the time!"

Lauren pulls off at the next exit. Excited, she follows the signs but her excitement turns to disappointment when they turn into an empty parking lot. She suddenly remembers, "Damn, that's right! The woman on the radio show said it was closed due to high levels of toxins!"

Roxy is curious, "What sort of toxins?"

Lauren teases her with the whisper of the evil voice again, "Millions of years of decomposing soulless bodies in the water!"

Roxy smiles, "Nice! Wonder if they sell it bottled?"

Lauren laughs, "Leave it to you! I don't know, why don't you can ask that cute guy over there?"

Roxy looks over to where Lauren is looking and suddenly gets out of the car, "I think I will!"

Not sure what to do, Lauren stays in the car while she watches Roxy talking to the cute guy. After a couple of minutes the guy looks around cautiously and then nods his head.

Roxy runs back to the car and grabs her empty water bottle, "C'mon! He says he can sneak us into the Mirror Room and we can get a sample of the water there!"

Lauren is shocked, "Are you kidding? What about the toxins?"

Roxy replies, "No big deal, it's all cleaned up. Think about what a cool story it will be displayed in our new apartment! Anyway, they are allowed to open up next week!"

Lauren is still a little unsure about being out in the middle of nowhere and following some random guy into a dark cavern, but her curiosity overcomes her fear. Why not? She catches up with Roxy, "Who is this guy?"

Roxy shrugs her shoulders, "Some guy that works here. The other workers haven't been called back yet. He thinks he can sneak us in with no problem!"

The guy walks up to them and puts his hand out to Lauren, "Hi, I am Marty and you must be Lauren?"

Lauren blushes slightly, "I am. Thank you for doing this for us! I hope we don't get you into any trouble!"

Marty looks around as he takes them to a private opening to the caverns, "We should be alright. The foreman left for supplies and won't be back for hours!"

Roxy assures Marty, "It should only take a few minutes to retrieve some water."

Marty looks at Roxy's water bottle doubtfully and stops, "Why is it you need the water again? You won't be testing it to give Mermac Caverns a bad name will you? A lot of us here count on this job!"

Lauren shakes her head, "We are on a road trip from the East Coast to the West Coast. I heard a stupid story about this place on the radio."

Roxy agrees, "She's right! I wanted the water as a souvenir to sit in our new apartment. You know, a conversation piece from our road trip!"

Marty smiles, "Cool, I am more inclined to help out thrill seekers than professionals! Professionals tend to screw everything up for people."

Marty, not bashful, adds, "Plus, you're so damn cute! How could I resist?" He starts walking again, "Follow me. If we do run into anyone, Roxy, you are my cousin on my mom's side. That will explain a lot! I guarantee you, no one will ask any more questions."

Roxy is not sure if she should be insulted, "That bad, huh?"

Marty realizes now how it sounds, "I'm sorry. Yea, my ma was from the East Coast and hooked up with my pa. She soon realized living in the Midwest knocked up with a kid was not the type of life she wanted so she left me and Pa when I was two."

Roxy understands, "It's ok, I am sorry. It must have been very hard on you!"

Now it is Marty's turn to be a little embarrassed, "Nah, it's all good."

Changing the subject, Marty asks Lauren, "What is this story you all heard?"

Lauren hesitantly replies, "It was a story about the caverns being... haunted, I guess you could say."

Marty shakes his head, "I am a little surprised something like that was on the radio! We have to sign waivers around here not to speak of what we've seen."

Lauren is curious, "Have you seen anything?"

Marty shakes his head, "Not that I can recollect. The strange thing is that after you leave this place you think you may have seen something, but your mind becomes all foggy so you aren't sure."

Chills come over Lauren when she realizes it is no different than what happened to her at the apartment complex! Lauren has to ask, "What about the other workers? Don't any of you talk about strange things you may have heard or seen?"

Marty leads them down a path into the caverns, "Not really, the foreman keeps a close eye on us. For instance, if we are doing a tour and one of the guests asks if we've seen a ghost..." he hesitates as he points down, "watch your step here." Marty continues, "Before we can answer, the foreman will say something like 'the only ghost around here is the founder, Mr. Dill, and he don't take kindly to people talking about him!' We are never allowed to talk about personal experiences!"

Lauren asks, "Do you think ole Mr. Dill haunts the place?"

Marty thinks about it, "Not sure. There are rumors that people have seen a tall dark shadow with a hat on and automatically they assume it is Mr. Dill!"

Roxy is curious, "You don't think it is him?"

Marty continues to lead the way while the girls are in awe of the formations surrounding them. He turns his big flashlight on since the main lights are off. "Not sure, I just know there are a lot of shadows down here. There are things you can only see out of your peripheral vision, and yet, you're comfortable like you've always known they were there, just..." Marty stumbles for the right words.

Lauren helps him, "You feel it but are not aware?"

Marty is surprised, "Exactly! How weird is that?"

Lauren sighs, "Very! But it was along the lines of what the woman said on the radio!"

Marty ushers them in, "Here's the Mirror Room, where Roxy said you wanted to come."

Lauren wonders, "Roxy, how did you know about the Mirror Room?"

Roxy shrugs her shoulders, "I didn't. I just asked Marty where there was a stream in the cavern where we could get water."

Marty looks a little confused, "I could have sworn you asked for it by name. My bad, I guess I assumed everyone knows the name!"

Marty wants to know more about the story Lauren heard, "What was on the radio?"

Lauren feels foolish, "It was folklore about the Osage Tribe. They were the Sun and Moon's children. When they came to live on Earth a jealous nearby universe offered to watch over the tribe."

Lauren can't help but feel like they are being watched by the shadows jumping around Marty's light, "She wanted her children to have souls like the Osage Tribe. The first time the tribe needed help she responded by bargaining with them. She stole their awareness, meaning they would not remember the lives they previously lived when they are reincarnated."

Lauren rubs her arms, a little chilled, "The tribe felt that was a small price to pay since she agreed to have all the water that covered the Earth rise up in a mist. The tribe thrived and filled the Earth; however, the jealous universe had her own children prey on the tribe. They chipped away at their souls through each life-time until their soul could finally be taken."

Roxy is confused, "What does the cavern's water have to do with anything?"

Lauren looks down at the crystal water, "The caverns kept Earth's original water which the universe needed to not only keep the souls, but baptize her children in to transfer the souls."

Marty lets out a long whistle, "That there is some story!"

Roxy squats down and sticks her empty water bottle into the cool cavern water, "I know right? A very cool story to tell when people come over!"

After filling the bottle Roxy gets up and takes a pen out of her pocket, "Would you mind writing Mermac Caverns on the bottle and signing it?"

Marty takes the bottle and pen, "Sure, why not? Probably be the only fifteen minutes of fame I'll ever know!"

Teasing Roxy he asks, "Can I put my phone number on there too?"

Roxy blushes but quickly takes her phone out, "No, but I'll put it in my phone!"

As Marty leans over to give Roxy the number, Lauren quickly takes her phone out and takes a picture. Roxy looks up angrily when the flash goes off, "Seriously? You know how much I hate pictures taken when I am not ready!"

A little hurt, Lauren tries to defend herself as she puts her phone away, "Sorry, thought it was cute. Marty holding the bottle and leaning into you with the cavern in the background. It's a perfect picture to add to our little story!"

Marty is now not so sure he should have given Roxy his number! Maybe, she is a bit more like his mom than he would like!

Roxy quickly realizes her mistake, "I'm sorry Lauren, you're right! However, we all need to be in the picture! C'mon guys, let's get a group selfie!" She uses her phone to take the selfie.

Still feeling a little awkward after Roxy's big blow up, Marty decides it is time to go, "I better get you two out of here before we get caught!"

As they walk out, Lauren takes one last look at the cool water. Small ripples emerge. A little frightened, Lauren asks, "Are there any fish or other things living in the water?"

Marty shines his light over the water but the ripples are no longer there. "Surprisingly, no. It is almost like the Dead Sea, there is no wild life that lives in the water!"

Roxy looks at her water bottle with concern, "Maybe there are more toxins in here than you know!"

Marty laughs, "No, actually the toxins were in the walls and air. The water tested completely pure!"

As they walk back up the path Lauren is curious, "Do any of you go swimming in the water here? It is so cool and the water looks tempting!"

Marty is a little surprised, "Really? For the most part people stay away from the water, almost as if they are afraid of it! No, I have never heard of anyone going swimming intentionally." He then lowers his voice, "Although, there have been several drownings around here."

Lauren is surprised, "I thought the water only looked deep?"

Marty nods, "That's the crazy part! The people died in only two feet of water! Basically, all they had to do was either stand up or for God's sake just roll over!"

Lauren looks around and matches his voice, "I thought you said nothing strange ever happens here?"

Marty shakes his head, "Oh no! Plenty of strange things happen here all the time, but they are stupid things that stupid tourists do! Like drunk college kids, or couples trying to rekindle their flame, or even little kids walking in their sleep! Nothing really paranormal, just stupidity!"

As they walk back to the car Lauren looks out over the parking lot, "As much of an entrepreneur as Mr. Dill was, I am surprised he didn't try to market this place as having some sort of special healing water."

Roxy nods and raises up her bottle proudly, "And he could have bottled it!"

Marty laughs, "You're right, maybe I will bring that up at the next meeting. If they take me seriously I may have that fifteen minutes of fame after all!"

Lauren shakes his hand, "Good luck with that Marty, and if you are ever in California look us up! I'm sure once our story gets out people will want to meet the man that made it happen!"

Marty shakes her hand warmly, "Thank you Lauren, I will keep that in mind."

Roxy wiggles in, "Hey, don't forget I have your number! Don't be surprised if I start pestering you to come out soon!"

Marty reaches down and kisses her on the cheek, "I look forward to it. You girls have a safe trip now!"

Minutes later they find themselves back out on the highway. Roxy looks a little miserable. "Why do I do that?"

Lauren knows what she is talking about but asks innocently, "Do what?"

Roxy sighs, "Scare men off with my attitude."

Lauren offers comfort, "I think maybe he would have been a little skittish anyway with his whole mom situation!"

Roxy nods, "I suppose you are right and it seems that long distance relationships never last!"

Lauren agrees, "That's what I've heard. Anyway, he was cute, I'll give you that, but not really your type! I'm sure you will find someone really cool in California."

Roxy is curious, "What about you?"

Lauren thinks about it, "Guess I'm just looking for my soul mate. I'll know him when I see him!"

Roxy chuckles, "Soul mate? Seems like all we've talked about this trip are damn souls!"

Lauren has to laugh, "I know! I suppose it has a lot to do with the radio show I have been listening to, but I can't help it, I'm addicted!"

Roxy yawns, "Hey, if it keeps you moving on down the road I'm not complaining!"

Lauren wonders, "Did you take another pill already?"

Roxy nods her head, "Yea, I took one while we were walking back."

Lauren looks over at her with alarm, "You didn't take it with that water, did you?"

Roxy bursts out laughing, "Oh, God no! The pills are small, I can dry swallow them!"

Lauren looks relieved, "Oh ok, I guess I really didn't like the idea of you drinking water that may have left over soul residue!"

Roxy smiles, "Left over soul residue. I have to say the way you say it makes me tempted!"

Lauren rolls her eyes, "Didn't you find it weird that there is no wildlife in the water?"

Roxy nods, "Maybe the water is too pure for animals, or people for that matter? We've all been exposed to pollution and what not for so long; perhaps our bodies can't handle something so pure?"

Lauren thinks, "It was pretty amazing when you think about it! I am always bummed that America is so "new" compared to other countries when it comes to history. We stood somewhere that has been around for 400 million years! That was pretty impressive!"

Roxy looks out the window, "I think we will be impressed with the Grand Canyon too! I am sure there are little niches all over it that hide some dark secrets of their own as well!"

Hearing Roxy say that makes Lauren want to listen to another story. "Mind if I turn on my radio? Maybe you would like to listen with me?"

Roxy grabs for her earphones, "No offense, but I have gotten used to falling to sleep with my music on!"

Lauren waits for Roxy to get settled. Finally she is able to turn the radio on. Not realizing it, Lauren is beginning to be like she was at the apartment.

Towards the end of her stay in the apartment Lauren found herself hooked on dreaming! She couldn't wait to go to sleep to see what the next dream held for her!

Anything can become an addiction, but surely a syndicated radio show could not hurt her, could it?

Witchin' Time

Witchin' Time

Mandy passes the bottle over to Nick. "C'mon guys! Can't we think of something to do in this one horse town?"

Steff looks over at Jeff, "I suppose we could take her over to Cry Baby Bridge?"

Mandy perks up, "Oh cool! What's that all about?"

Steff sighs, "The tale goes that this poor woman was repeatedly raped by her father. She would then throw the babies off the bridge. At night, you can hear the babies cry."

Jeff nods, "Yea, it's pretty cool! Nick and I went with some guys last year. I swear, you really do hear babies crying while on that bridge!"

Mandy gets excited and looks at Nick, "That sounds awesome! Can we go?"

Nick hands her back the bottle, "Sure, why not? Gotta give this little city girl the full effect of the local décor!"

Steff looks disgustedly at her cousin, "Yea, God forbid the little princess becomes bored with our way of life!"

Mandy sneers over at her, "Look cuz, I don't like being here anymore than you do!"

Jeff tries to keep the peace, "Now girls, let's try to have fun tonight!"

Nick takes the bottle from Mandy and gives it to Steff, "Drink up and get in the mood! After seeing the bridge we could go on over and see the witch's house!"

Mandy is excited, "Oh, my God! There is a witch's house too? This should be a bitchin' time!"

Finishing a big swallow, Steff hands the bottle over to Jeff. Trying to get into the spirit of things, Steff laughs, "Nah, tonight it's gonna be a witchin' time!"

The four teenagers have to drive only to the outside of town. Within minutes they reach the Cry Baby Bridge. Before they go over the bridge, Jeff stops, "If we are going to truly experience the effect of Cry Baby Bridge, maybe we should enhance our senses!"

Jeff pulls out a bag of weed. Hoots and hollers erupt inside the car. After taking several hits, Jeff tries to remember the story that was told to him before he went over the bridge, "As Steff said, rumor has it a local girl was raped repeatedly by her father."

Nick nods, "Yea, and the babies she kept having were deformed!"

Jeff agrees, "Deformed so much that they looked like monsters!"

Nick jokes, "I suppose that would be why the poor girl would be able to throw her own babies off the bridge. Those things were not something even a mother could love!"

Steff interrupts seriously, "No, from what I heard the poor girl desperately loved the babies. Each one she would hide and try to keep; however, her father would find them and make her get rid of them!"

Mandy wonders, "Why did she throw them off the bridge? Why not just suffocate and bury them?"

It sickens Steff to hear Mandy talk so casually about killing a child; especially since the whole reason for her being here was the trouble she had gotten caught up in back home. Having an abortion had thrown Mandy's parents into a realization that perhaps they should have been a little stricter with their princess. That was the reason why, out of the blue, Steff's parents were good enough to volunteer to watch Mandy for the summer.

Steff looks at the lit joint in her hand and the bottle at her feet. She wasn't a great influence, but at least her parents knew she was smart enough to not get knocked up! The things she did, didn't hurt anyone but herself. Coming here to Cry Baby Bridge was a way for her to try and wake Mandy up to what she had done. Looking at the back seat and seeing Nick pawing all over Mandy she realized something needed to work or Mandy was going to find herself knocked up again!

Steff finally answers, "The poor girl said she wanted to baptize them before they died so at least they would have a chance to go to heaven."

Mandy is not dumb, she knows all too well what Steff is trying to do. She throws it right back at her, "Really? I thought no matter what, bastards weren't allowed in heaven?"

Nick has to laugh, "She has you there, Steff!"

Jeff clears his throat, "Whatever the case, it's sad what happened to that girl and her children. Moreover, it is scary as shit! Are you guys ready to go? Looks like a perfect night with the fog coming off the river and a full moon!"

Mandy is surprised as they all start to get out of the car, "Wait! We are walking, not driving over?"

Jeff hesitates, "She's right you know. Let's drive over the bridge and park the car on the other side since we have to head that way to the witch's house."

Everyone agrees and gets back in the car. Jeff drives the car slowly to get the full effect of the bridge. Mandy is not impressed, "This is lame!"

Nick sighs and gives her another joint. "Shut up Mandy and take another hit! Let yourself get caught up in the story! It is only fun if you allow yourself to be afraid!"

Mandy does not like being told what to do, but maybe Nick has a point, "Alright, fine!"

They all take one last hit before they get out. As they begin to walk away Jeff stops and goes back to the car, "I think maybe it is a good idea if I hide the key under the seat. That way, if something does happen, anyone will be able to go for help!"

Mandy giggles, "Oh Jeff, that was a nice touch!"

Jeff shrugs his shoulders after placing the key under the seat, "What? How many times have you seen a horror story where the guy with the key is the first one to get killed and the rest are stranded?"

Steff places her arm around Jeff and teases, "Don't let him fool you, he's just trying to increase his odds by not having the key!"

Mandy laughs as she cuddles up to Nick while they walk to the bridge, "This is fun! Thanks for putting me in the mood!"

Nick squeezes her ass, "Baby, just know that I am always in the mood! Anytime you want it!"

The four of them stumble up onto the bridge a little drunk and high. They peer over the railing. None of them had realized before how long of a drop it was.

Steff is the first one to speak, "Is it just me, or do we seem a lot higher up than we are supposed to be?"

Jeff laughs loudly, "I don't know about you, but I am pretty high right now myself!"

Steff punches him playfully, "No, seriously! It didn't seem like we went that high up on the road to cross the bridge!"

Nick agrees, "Must be a gradual incline. I am a little surprised how far down the river is too!"

Mandy shivers, "Did it just suddenly get colder?"

Steff nods, "Oh my God, yes! It's freezing up here!"

Nick whispers in an eerie voice, "An unnatural cold!"

Jeff shushes him, "Listen! Do you hear them?"

Mandy rolls her eyes, "Please! You guys are not scaring me!"

Nick hears what Jeff hears, "Yo man, I hear it! That's our cue isn't it?"

Mandy hesitantly asks, "Cue for what?"

Jeff sighs, "To leave! You are supposed to leave the minute you hear the babies crying!"

Mandy's eyes suddenly get real big, "I hear them! Don't you hear them, Steff?"

Steff listens and is shocked to hear babies crying! Real babies crying! She stutters, "Ok, ok Jeff, we all heard them, now let's go!"

Jeff shakes his head, "No, damn it! The last time we all left like scared little kids! This time I want to see what the hell is making that noise!"

Nick agrees, "I'm with you, dude! Last time, I was not nearly high enough to have the balls but tonight I am ready!"

Steff looks a little concerned as she sees Jeff leaning way over the railing to get a better look. He yells out at Nick, "Nick, come over here and hang onto me! I think there's a trestle I can reach. From there I may be able to get a better look!"

Steff is not happy with that idea, "Why don't you two find a pathway down to the river from the road?"

Jeff shakes his head, "I think it's something under this bridge that is making that noise! Maybe frogs or crickets? Coming down by the road may not give me the answer!"

Nick nods, "What's the worst that could happen? If he falls he will go in the river and get wet. It won't kill him!"

Steff slaps Nick upside the head, "Uh, hello? It is called Cry Baby Bridge because babies were killed after being thrown off it!"

Nick laughs as he rubs his head, "Ouch! Relax! Jeff is a grown man, not a helpless baby!"

Steff mumbles, "Man my ass, he's acting like a foolish kid if you ask me!"

Jeff kisses her on the forehead, "Remember this was all your idea! I am just prolonging the moment!"

Mandy giggles, "About time, right Steff?"

Steff can't help but laugh, "Yea, right. Ok you idiot, get it over with!"

Nick positions himself against the railing holding onto Jeff as he lowers down onto the trestle. Jeff makes sure of his footing before he looks around. He was right! The baby noises were louder here under the bridge! Cursing himself for not bringing a flashlight, he pulls out his lighter. As soon as the lighter was lit so he could see more clearly, Jeff started screaming, "Oh shit! Oh my freaking God! Are you guys seeing this?"

Above, Steff thinks she hears Jeff screaming but it is hard to tell due to the babies screaming louder, "Nick! What's going on?"

Nick leans way over the railing to see, "Oh my God! Jeff, give me your hand dude! You've gotta get out of there!"

Mandy begins to think about it, "Oh, ha ha you guys! What did you do, stick a recorder down there and then Jeff turned it up once he got under the bridge? Great joke on the city girl! I get it, now let's go home! This is stupid!"

Steff looks at her with wide eyes, "Seriously Mandy, this is no joke! I think Jeff is in trouble!"

Mandy is becoming frustrated because Nick is ignoring her so she yells out, "C'mon Nick, tell him to turn the damn thing off!"

Mandy leans over the railing to see what Nick is seeing. When she sees it, she nearly falls off the bridge in fear! "What the hell?"

Mandy can't believe her eyes! The light from Jeff's lighter sways back and forth giving her a glimpse of all of the deformed babies crawling up and under the bridge towards Jeff! In fact, some of them are actually surrounding Jeff, stopping him from grabbing at Nick's hand! She watches in horror as he tries to punt the babies away from him like footballs!

Nick, not seeing any other choice, screams out, "Jump dude! It's your only chance! I will come down by the river from the road to help you!"

Mandy can see the fear in Jeff's eyes. He takes a deep breath in and pushes himself off the trestle. Mandy and Nick watch as Jeff plunges to the water below. It was the most horrific sight they had ever seen! You would have thought Jeff's body had been devoured by piranhas! Although it is pitch black, they could still see the river turn red!

Steff screams out as she too watches Jeff jump, "Oh my God! Why did he jump?"

Just then Nick screams as he brings his hand out from under the railing, "The little bastard bit my finger off! Run! They are coming up onto the bridge!"

Mandy starts running without looking back. Steff just stands there crying, "What about Jeff? What bit you, Nick?"

Nick grabs her arm and forces her to run, "The damn babies, that's who! Now run!"

Suddenly, tiny hands and fat fingers claw at the edge of the bridge, bringing up their bloated baby bodies to where the three of them are!

Since Mandy had a head start on them, she had a good chance of getting away. She ran like never before! All she kept thinking about as she ran was, thank God Jeff left the keys under the seat! All she had to do was make it to the car, get it started, and get the hell out of here!

Nick and Steff were not so lucky. The babies may be bloated, deformed, even dead for Christ sake, but man were they fast!

Nick got into a good rhythm of kicking them like Jeff; however, poor Steff was not that talented! The one time she did kick one of the babies her foot smashed into the bloated baby's belly, causing her foot to actually get stuck in the damn thing!

Nick had contemplated going back for Steff but he was already off the bridge and realized he was safe. Apparently the babies could go no further than the bridge or the water below.

Seeing that Nick had made it to safety, the babies turned and swarmed over Steff, consuming her in minutes.

Not able to watch, Nick runs toward the car holding his bloody hand. He is thankful that Mandy has the car started and has not left him!

Mandy screams as she watches in the rear view mirror, "Hurry, Nick!"

Out of breath, Nick reaches the car and jumps in, "Go!"

Without hesitation Mandy floors it. "What about Steff?"

Nick lowers his voice, "I'm sorry, she didn't make it!"

Mandy shakes her head, "Great! This will be all my fault somehow! My parents are never going to forgive me!"

Nick looks at her in disbelief, "What? This isn't about you! I just lost two of my best friends since grade school and Steff was your blood!"

Through gritted teeth Mandy answers, "No, she wasn't! I was adopted!"

Nick is still shocked, "Whatever! The poor girl is dead! She was right about you, you are a self-centered bitch!"

Mandy screams back at him, "Shut up! Just tell me where I should go to get out of this freaking hick town!"

Nick looks around to get his bearings, "We're on the wrong side of the bridge! This road only takes us to the witch's house!"

Mandy slows the car down, "Are you kidding me? What the hell is up with you people? Deformed eating babies, witches? Why couldn't we have robbed a liquor store like back home?"

Nick sighs, "Honey, right about now I'd gladly sit in a jail cell! At least it would be safe!"

Mandy stops the car and pulls out her phone, "Perfect! No reception! Why does that not surprise me?"

Nick shrugs his shoulders, "Why do you think none of us own one? It's not worth it out here!"

Mandy looks helplessly at Nick, "What are we going to do?"

Nick thinks about it, "Let's just stay in the car until morning. By then, maybe we will be able to cross back over the bridge."

Terrified, Mandy whispers, "Won't the babies come out here to find us?"

Nick shakes his head, "I don't think so. It looked like they couldn't leave the bridge or the water underneath it."

Mandy thinks about how Jeff was devoured in the water. Shaking her head to get rid of the memory, she asks, "Tell me about this witch. What do we have to worry about from her?"

Nick simply answers, "Fire."

Mandy does not understand, "What do you mean fire?"

Nick thinks about what he can remember of the old folklore, "The locals burned her house down. They thought she was in it but she was not. While leaving the burning house they ran into the witch. Supposedly, she turned their torches onto them and they all burned to death."

Mandy shudders at the thought, "Who was this broad?"

Nick shrugs her shoulders, "I don't really know. All I know is that sometimes you can see smoke coming out of the fireplace that was left behind when her house burned down."

Mandy stares in front of her and points, "Let me guess, when you see the smoke you are supposed to run?"

Nick slowly nods as he looks to where she is pointing to, "Yup."

Mandy screams at him, "Run to where?"

Before Nick can answer he sees a light in the distance coming towards them. He grabs his door handle, "Mandy, get out of the car now!"

Mandy yanks at her door and quickly hops out. A second later the car erupted into a ball of fire! If Nick hadn't of told her to get out she would have been consumed by the fire!

Nick comes over to Mandy, holding his bloody hand tenderly, "Are you ok?"

Mandy looks at his hand sympathetically, "I forgot all about your finger! Here, let me wrap it!" She quickly yanks off her second shirt and carefully wraps his hand. "Thank you! You saved my life!"

Nick can't believe what he sees walking towards them. "Don't thank me yet, it's not over!"

Mandy looks down the road and sees an old hag stumbling towards them. Instead of fear, she is overcome with anger and yells, "Who are you, you stupid witch? We did nothing to you, leave us alone!"

The witch gets closer and loudly cackles, "You are right my dear! You and your ancestors have done no wrong to me!"

She raises a crooked finger towards Nick, "But he has!"

Terrified, Nick pleads with her, "Whatever they did to you, I did not! I am so sorry!"

The witch shakes her head and hisses out, "No! That is not good enough! Your people turned a blind eye to me when I needed them the most!"

Getting closer she explains, "My pa, the good preacher, couldn't possibly sin in their eyes, but they all knew what he was doing to me!"

Suddenly Mandy realizes who the witch is, "You're the poor girl that was raped over and over by her father! Those bastards on the bridge are yours!"

A little offended, she glares over at Mandy, "Funny, coming from an offspring born out of wedlock who doesn't realize she is a bastard herself!"

The old lady looks at Mandy in deep thought, "Let me tell you a little something about your own past before you judge my offspring!"

"Your momma didn't even love your daddy! Before she got knocked up with you, she told him she was going to try and find someone better!"

The witch has to admit, "However, he tried to do right by you. Even asked the bitch to marry him, but she said no."

"The self-centered bitch didn't even try to hide having a bastard by getting married immediately! Nah, your momma was more worried about what time of the year to have her perfect wedding!"

"So self-centered was she, she gave it no thought at all to what it might do to a child later on to know her parents didn't care enough to make themselves a family."

"She eventually met another man. One who didn't want to be bothered by another's offspring. Since she had never had to sacrifice for her child, you, it was easy enough for her to get rid of you."

The witch smiles, "So you see my dear, my bastards are no different than you or, for that matter, what you would have had! Your monstrousness is just on the inside!"

"As bad as your mother was, at least she didn't kill you! Unlike you! Who truly is the monster here? I was forced to kill mine, you had a choice!"

She rambles on bitterly, "I prayed feverishly to God for help but my prayers were unanswered! Instead, I became pregnant because of my father's sick twisted abuse."

"Being brainwashed by my father and his religion, I believed a bastard, even though a victim themselves, would never be allowed into heaven!"

Disgusted she continues, "Father treated the child no different than an unwanted deformed farm animal! He told me if I didn't get rid of it, he'd take a shovel to it himself!"

"Beaten down and knowing no other way, I prayed to another. The Other told me to baptize the child by throwing it over the bridge. The Other would graciously accept it into His Kingdom!"

Nick tries to reason with her, "Don't you see? I too am a victim! I am innocent! I have never done anything to you!"

The witch ignores his pleas and forces Nick back towards the bridge with a line of fire from her fingertips. "Funny thing about religious folk, they never heed their own teaching!"

Nick gets closer to the bridge, trying to figure out which way he would rather die, by fire or by babies? As the fire dances closer to Nick, he sees no other choice than to throw himself into the river like Jeff. At least that will be quick!

After Nick's screams fade out the witch looks calmly over to Mandy, "Yes, they easily forget another saying in the Bible – The sins of the fathers shall be visited upon the sons."

Mandy stands perfectly quiet. Not sure what to do, Mandy has to ask, "Why did they come after you and your house?"

The witch looks sadly at her, "I was a constant reminder of what they had allowed. Everyone was afraid of Pa and his righteous ways. It wasn't till after he passed they turned on me. They couldn't understand why I wasn't a God fearing woman."

The witch chuckles, "God was not what I was afraid of! I had not seen anything from God, but I knew all too well what man could do! They figured since I refused religion I was nothing more than a heathen or perhaps even a witch!"

The witch starts walking wearily back from where she came from, "Wasn't until they tried killing me that I felt a fire deep inside me rise up."

"All the years of hurt and pain had burned my soul. Finally consumed, the soul turned outwards and sought its revenge."

The witch's words fade in the wind as does she, "The only happiness I get now is seeing my babies get fed!"

White Noise Stories Continued

"Lauren? Are you ok?" Roxy becomes concerned when Lauren doesn't answer her, "Lauren, can you hear me?"

Lauren can hear Roxy but she seems so far away. She shakes her head a little as she answers quietly, "Yea, I'm ok."

Roxy turns the annoying radio off, "Are you sure? Maybe we should pull over?"

Lauren focuses on the road in front of her and is surprised at how far down the road they had gotten, "No, I'm fine, really!"

Roxy is curious, "My God girl, where were you?"

Lauren sighs, "I guess I was daydreaming, lost in thought."

Lauren realizes that is not much of an explanation so she continues, "It's weird, when I hear these stories on the radio I find myself in the story! Like I am actually there living the story!"

Chills come over Lauren as she thinks about the last story. Cry Baby Bridge is not something she is going to forget easily!

Roxy shakes her head, "You have way too much imagination! I swear you were born in the wrong generation! Our generation needs visualization! You, on the other hand, would have been fine sitting beside an old radio listening to something like The Lone Ranger!"

Lauren is not so sure, "Not too good of an imagination. Even though I feel like I am re-living the story it all is in black and white! These stories are a lot like the dreams I had in the apartment complex. Those were in black and white too."

Roxy questions her, "Even the painter's dream?"

Lauren nods, "Yea! I mean, during the dream it was like I knew what the colors were supposed to be, but..."

Lauren stumbles for the right words, "You know how when you watch an old black and white movie you know the sky is blue, even though it is not? It's the same thing when I listen to these stories!"

Roxy is beginning to be really concerned about her friend, "Maybe you should lay off the radio for a while?"

Lauren understands Roxy's concern and has to agree, "Maybe you are right! Hey, can you do me a favor and call Jodi for me? We're almost to the hotel and we can meet up with them at the restaurant by 8:00."

Roxy grabs her phone, "Not a problem!" She talks to Jodi briefly making their arrangements.

They find the hotel with no problem and freshen up. The restaurant is not far and before they know it, the four of them are sitting down to dinner.

Like the visit with Teresa, Lauren catches up with Jodi on all the gossip. Roxy and Jady, Jody's husband, carry on their own conversation.

With it being such a long day, Lauren calls it an early night but promises to have breakfast with Jodi and stop by to see her horses. A little disappointed, Jodi understands. Her disappointment quickly turns into concern after talking to Jady on the way home.

Jodi asks, "So, what did you think of my better half?"

Jady pretends to be shocked, "I thought I was your better half!"

Jodi blows him a kiss, "I stand corrected! You are now, but my girl Lauren was before you came along! Did you like her?"

Jady nods, "Yea, she's a real sweetheart! I can see why you two are so close!"

Jodi is curious, "What did you think of that Roxy girl?"

Jady shrugs his shoulders, "She was nice enough."

Jodi can't help but tease him, "Not bad on the eyes either! I was a little worried she may be after my man!"

Jady sighs, "You always think that! No, actually she is concerned about Lauren!"

Jodi becomes quiet, "Why? What did she say?"

Jady becomes serious, "She's afraid Lauren may be slipping back into the state of mind she had at the apartment that led to her breakdown!"

Jodi's heart drops, "What makes her think that?"

Jady looks over at the radio, "Roxy says that every time she wakes up Lauren is listening to the radio."

A little miffed, Jodi blurts out, "What's wrong with listening to the radio?"

Jady answers, "Nothing, unless it's white noise!"

A shiver comes over Jodi, "White noise like the white noise that was coming from her sound machine in the apartment?"

Jady nods, "Exactly! And get this! Lauren keeps talking about this syndicated talk show that has weird stories on it, yet Roxy has not heard one word of them!"

Jodi states the obvious, "She thinks Lauren is receiving more dead people's dreams through the white noise on the radio."

Jady clears his throat, "Uh, not exactly! Roxy doesn't really believe that stuff, she just thinks Lauren had a breakdown."

Jodi grabs her phone furiously, "That's because she doesn't know Lauren like we do!"

Jady looks over at her, "Who are you calling?"

Jodi listens to the phone ring, "Teresa! I want to know what she thinks!"

Jodi has a brief conversation with Teresa and afterwards tells Jady, "Teresa said Lauren acted fine when she saw her although she was not impressed with Roxy!"

Jady has to laugh, "When are you girls ever impressed with another girl?"

Jodi smiles, "You're right! We may be a little protective of our Lauren!"

Jady corrects her, "Jealous you mean?"

Jodi rolls her eyes, "Please! That girl Roxy ain't got nothing on our friendship with Lauren!"

Jady pulls into the driveway, "Then I guess there is nothing to worry about!"

Jodi becomes serious, "Actually, there is! Teresa said she had been trying to think of something she forgot that night. It seemed like there was a fog in her mind! That sounds a lot like what Lauren used to say happened to her when she was away from the apartment complex!"

Jady turns the car off, "Did she finally remember?"

Jodi nods, "Teresa said there was a guy that followed them from the restaurant to the hotel. Later that night when she went out to her truck she saw him again."

Jady tries to reassure her, "Maybe Teresa is being overly cautious?"

Jodi looks at him with wide eyes, "No, I don't think so! While I was talking to her, she remembered who he looked like."

Jady is caught up in the story, "Who?"

Jodi lowers her voice, "He looked just like Lauren's description of Mr. Akeru!"

Jady is not sure if he believes Lauren's story, but he does believe his wife and if she thinks it is real then he would support her, "Maybe you should tell Lauren tomorrow?"

Jodi agrees, "I want to do it when the two of us are alone. Even though I don't like the idea, do you think you can keep Roxy busy while I do?"

Jady can't help but tease her, "I'm sure I can think of a couple of things to do to... I mean... with her."

Jodi reaches in for a kiss, "The risks I take for my girls! They better appreciate it!"

The next day after breakfast, Lauren and Roxy follow Jodi and Jady back to their house. Lauren is amazed how perfect it is! Jodi gets to have her horses, Jady has a nice barn for tinkering on his cars, and the house Jodi has is a beautiful home!

Lauren hops out of the car and rushes over to Jodi, "Oh Jodi! It's all so beautiful! Everything you always wanted! I am so happy for you!"

Jodi gives her a quick hug, "You're right, I am happy! C'mon, let me show you the house!"

Jodi looks over at Roxy and Jady, "Jady, honey, why don't you show Roxy your car and then bring her in to see the house."

Jady looks happily over at Roxy, "Do you like cars?"

Roxy looks a little confused, "Yea, I guess." Seeing Jady's smile begin to fade and not wanting to be rude, she changes her manner, "Of course! Show me what you got!"

Jodi walks arm in arm with Lauren. Lowering her voice, "We may not have much time alone! Roxy doesn't look like much of a car girl!"

Lauren giggles, "What gave you the clue? Maybe because she doesn't drive?"

Jodi laughs along with her, "Quit teasing me! It's the only thing I could think of to get you alone!"

Jodi takes Lauren through the house to her bedroom to give them as much privacy as possible. Lauren looks at the bed and blushes, "So, this is where the magic happens? Lucky girl! I really like Jady! You two make the perfect couple!"

Jodi smiles proudly, "I'm so glad you like him! He likes you too!" She sits on the bed and pats the space next to her, "Time for a heart to heart!"

Lauren smiles as she remembers how many times the two of them said that to each other. Lauren has a seat, "What's up?"

Jodi is not sure how to start, "How are you feeling?"

Lauren suddenly knows where this is going, "What did Roxy say?"

Jodi sighs, "She told Jady she was concerned about you listening to the radio!"

Lauren tries to brush it off, "It's nothing! You know what kind of imagination I have! So what if I get caught up in the stories?" Before Jodi can interrupt she quickly goes on, "And you know how sometimes when you are tired you zone out a little? Everyone does it on a long road trip, it's no big deal!"

Jodi changes the subject, "I talked to Teresa last night. She said she really enjoyed your visit!"

Lauren looks at her curiously, "And?"

Jodi chooses her words carefully, "She thought she saw a man following you from the restaurant!"

Lauren is surprised, "Really? She didn't mention it to me."

Jodi agrees, "I know. She said she was too excited to visit with you to bring it up. Then she saw the guy again when she walked to her truck."

Worried, Lauren quickly asks, "Is she ok? I knew I should have walked her to her truck that night!"

Jodi assures her, "She's fine! In fact, it wasn't until I called her that she remembered who the man looked like!"

Lauren is not sure she wants to know, "Who?"

Jodi sighs, "Your Mr. Akeru!"

Lauren is confused, "Mr. Akeru? Are you kidding? How would Teresa even know what he looks like?"

Jodi is the one surprised now, "Because of the way you described him to us! Even I would know him!"

They both hear the front door open. Lauren has to know, "What does this have to do with me listening to the radio?"

Jodi looks sadly at her, "Because what you have been listening to on the radio," she hesitates, "is white noise!"

Before Lauren can reply they hear Roxy and Jady enter the house. Jody whispers, "We better go. We can talk about this later!"

Although in a complete state of shock, Lauren agrees. Jody proceeds to show them the house but Lauren has a hard time focusing on what she is saying! All she can think about is the radio! White noise? That can't be possible! All those stories she listened to were from different people in different states! In fact, Roxy heard those people telling stories too!

Lauren stops herself. Wait a minute! Did Roxy really hear them? She remembers Roxy always complaining about the noise on the radio when she turned it off. Could it have been white noise Roxy was talking about instead of making fun of what Lauren was listening to? And what did Mr. Akeru have to do with all of this?

Lauren finds herself outside saying goodbye. Jodi hugs her hard and whispers in her ear, "Watch for the signs, listen and take heed. Please be careful!"

With tears in her eyes Lauren hugs her back, "I will! Thank you for believing in me! It's where I will get my strength!"

Back in the car Roxy and Lauren drive in silence. Roxy finally breaks it, "What did Jodi have to tell you that was so important I couldn't hear?"

Lauren is not surprised at Roxy being jealous. Lauren quickly thinks of something, "Teresa's mother is pretty sick. She wanted me to sign a card she was sending her."

Trying to be convincing, Lauren sighs heavily, "I wish Teresa had told me when I saw her!"

Roxy lightens up, "I'm sorry to hear that. I'm sure Teresa figured you had enough going on already and didn't want to bother you!"

Lauren agrees, "You're probably right!"

Roxy can still feel a distance between her and Lauren, "I figured Jady told her how worried I am about you!"

Lauren decides to be honest, "He did and of course Jodi was concerned! However, she knows how hard driving long distances can be. She understood I was just in the zone."

Roxy doesn't buy it, "She didn't ask you about the radio show?"

Lauren shakes her head innocently, "No. Although I wish I had told her, she would have liked some of those stories! Strange that I didn't tell her, I tell her everything!"

Roxy smiles, "Things will start changing between you girls! You will all be getting your own lives and it will get harder for you to maintain the friendship you had growing up!"

Deep down Lauren knows Roxy is wrong! No matter how old they are or where they are in their life, Teresa and Jodi will always be there for her! Roxy on the other hand, she is not so sure she can trust her! What was the real reason Roxy told Jady about the radio show?

Lauren wonders, is Roxy trying to plant a seed of doubt in people's minds about her? Is she trying to make it look like Lauren is losing it again? If Roxy was so concerned about her, why didn't she mention the white noise on the radio to her? Sure, there was white noise at times, but that was just when they were in between stations!

Was Roxy so jealous of Teresa and Jodi that she was fabricating this to put doubt in their minds about Lauren's sanity? Unfortunately, Lauren wouldn't put it past Roxy! It is how Roxy becomes when she feels threatened! Lauren thinks about it. It must have been hard for Roxy to see her bond with her old friends. Maybe she was being too hard on Roxy!

Roxy interrupts her thoughts, "I'm sorry, I sort of pushed us to leave but we do have a lot of driving ahead of us."

Lauren agrees, "I know! I appreciate you letting us stop by to see Jodi's house! I am happy for her now that I know who she is with and where she lives!"

Roxy is a little surprised, "Aren't you a little jealous? I mean, the girl has everything! A guy she loves, a beautiful house and property for her horses. Even I am jealous!"

Lauren smiles, "No, not at all! When you love someone their happiness makes you happy!"

Roxy has to admit, "Girl, I think you are going to be a good influence on me!"

Roxy settles in for her routine of taking her pill, "Are you going to listen to the radio?"

Lauren looks a little afraid of it, "Not right now, but maybe in a little while."

Meanwhile, Jodi and Jady are busy trying to settle their horses down after Lauren and Roxy left. They were too busy comforting the terrified horses to notice the van pass that had Mr. Akeru at the wheel.

Bored while Roxy sleeps, Lauren finds herself tempted to listen to the radio. This time though, if she can find the station with the stories she will record it on her phone! If Roxy tries to tell anyone else it is nothing but white noise she will be able to prove her wrong!

Elevator Game

Elevator Game

Ryan and Nicole sit on the swings quietly looking up at the dark sky. Ryan finally breaks the silence, "Ok Nicole, are you going to tell me what's bothering you tonight?"

Nicole sighs, "Something I read."

Ryan shakes his head, "You've been reading Emma's journal again, haven't you?"

Nicole nods guilty, "Yes."

Frustrated, Ryan replies, "You do know she writes things in her journal hoping you will read it? You are playing right into her hands!"

Nicole answers miserably, "I know."

Ryan is curious, "What did she say this time?"

Nicole shrugs her shoulders, "The same things. How she hates living under my shadow, she can't stand me being popular at school, and of course, she thinks my parents favor me!"

Ryan has to know, "Anything about me?"

Nicole answers curtly, "Yes, you already know she has a crush on you!"

Ryan secretly likes hearing what Emma writes about him but realizes now is not the time to push it, "Ok, so everything is the same. What's the big deal?"

Nicole thinks about it, "Emma is going to see my cousin in the city this weekend. She wrote that she plans on playing an elevator game."

Ryan is encouraged, "Good for her! It sounds like fun! What is wrong with Emma finally getting to do something on her own?"

Deep down, Ryan really doesn't blame Emma for her feelings. Emma has been under Nicole's shadow and her parents do show favoritism. For Nicole to be jealous of a little weekend getaway for Emma is a little uncalled for.

Nicole shakes her head, "It's not like you think! I know you automatically think I am jealous, but do you even know what the elevator game is?"

Ryan feels bad, "No."

Nicole sighs, "Honestly, I didn't either. Emma wrote about how it will take her to another dimension where she will finally be the only girl that matters. Ryan, what if the 'elevator game' is nothing more than a metaphor for Emma committing suicide?"

Shocked, Ryan can see Nicole is genuinely concerned, "Emma and suicide? No way! Emma is too vibrant and full of life to do such a thing!"

Nicole looks at him a little surprised, "You say that like you admire her or something!"

Even though Ryan does find Emma attractive in a bad girl sort of way and has thought about how it would be to be with her, he stumbles, "Oh c'mon! Now who's being paranoid? You know how much I love you!"

Nicole is not so sure but decides to let it drop. "So, you don't think I should say something to my parents?"

Ryan shakes his head adamantly, "No way! You know how your parents are about privacy! They've already warned you about reading her journal! Emma knows we're going away this weekend. Perhaps she set you up? What better way to get you grounded and ruin our weekend?"

Nicole agrees, "Maybe you are right."

Ryan gets off his swing and pulls Nicole up towards him as he whispers, "You know I am. Now enough about Emma, let's concentrate on us!"

****

Nicole and Ryan went away for the weekend like they had planned, but when they got back they found that all hell had broken loose. Nicole's parents were furious that she was not at the place she told them and even worse, Emma was missing!

Nicole whispers on the house phone, "Ryan? I don't have much time, my parents took my phone and I am grounded from everything!"

Ryan answers miserably, "I am too! The only reason they let me keep my phone is because of work. Did they find Emma?"

Nicole shakes her head, "No, not yet. Actually, for once I have to thank Emma! She's really taking the spotlight off our weekend with her little stunt."

Ryan is curious, "Why, do they know any more?"

Nicole thinks she hears her mother coming. She quickly answers, "They have a video of her on the elevator acting strange. It's in the middle of the night and she keeps hitting buttons. She looks really scared!"

A little relieved, Ryan answers, "She'll show up. You know Emma, she'll want to come back for the drama! Bitch probably did this on purpose so your parents would try to find you during our weekend!"

Nicole blushes as she thinks about the incredible weekend they had, "It was worth it! Look, someone's coming, I gotta go. Love you!" She doesn't even wait for Ryan's reply as she quietly hangs up the phone and makes her way to her dad's computer.

Her mother comes into the room expecting to catch her daughter on the phone, but is surprised to see her on the computer, "You, young lady, are grounded! What do you think you are doing on your father's computer? I took yours away for a reason!"

Nicole looks innocently up from the screen, "I was doing some research on Emma."

Not believing her, her mother comes over and looks at the screen. She is surprised to see the Elevator Game listed on the search engine, "What's this all about?"

Nicole figures they can't ground her any more than she already is so she confesses, "I read in Emma's journal that she planned on playing the Elevator Game while she was in the city."

Her mother is curious, "The police have Emma's journal. When did you get a chance to read it?"

Nicole looks down miserably, "Last week."

Her mother shakes her head, "How many times have I told you about privacy?"

Nicole's eyes begin to tear up, "I know, but I was worried about her!"

Frustrated, her mother raises her voice, "Then why didn't you tell your father and me about your concern?"

Tears now fall freely while Nicole answers, "Which am I supposed to do, respect someone's privacy or tell someone?"

Her mother now has tears too. She grabs Nicole and hugs her, "Oh honey, I don't know! Now you know how hard it is being a parent! Please, tell me everything you know about your sister so we can get her back home safely!"

Nicole wipes her tears, "She hates being in my shadow and she thinks you play favorites, but you know what I really think?"

Breaking the hug, her mother is a little afraid to know but needs to, "What?"

Nicole sighs, "Emma has a crush on Ryan. She knew Ryan and I were going away for the weekend. I think she planned all of this to get Ryan and me in trouble!"

Her mother is instantly relieved, "Oh, I hope so! I mean, yea it was a crappy thing to do! There will be consequences for her too but I pray that is all it is!"

Seeing her mom desperately hanging onto the idea that it is nothing more than Emma being vindictive, Nicole can't help but agree. She clicks the computer off, "You're right Mom, I am sure that is all it is."

The next day Nicole is increasingly worried. Emma had been missing for two days. Finally, not knowing what else to do, Nicole goes back to her father's computer and researches the Elevator Game more thoroughly. Apparently, it is a real thing!

It is an urban legend ritual game that comes from Korea. A player needs to locate a building that has ten floors or more. Nicole thinks about it and remembers their cousin lives in such a building!

You are supposed to ride the elevator alone, visiting different floors in a specific order. One of the main rules is to not trust any other passengers if they get on the elevator, especially if it is an old woman or a young girl. These are thought to be ghosts or other beings from another universe. If you make any contact with them, they will kill you!

Nicole chuckles at the absurdity of it all. What could possibly be the appeal to Emma to actually play this game? She reads on.

Once in this other universe, you will be the center of it. You will become all important. Everything will revolve around you. Nicole thinks back to all the times Emma had screamed at her, "You are not the center of the universe! Not everything revolves around you!"

Was the allure of becoming the center of the universe worth it to Emma to play the game? Had Emma thought by going to this universe she would find the attention she craved? Become center of the universe like she accused Nicole of being?

The more Nicole thinks about it the more it seems like something Emma would do. Seeing her poor parents so distraught, Nicole decides she needs to find out herself.

After briefly talking to Ryan, Nicole sneaks out of the house to go meet up with him. She quickly makes it to his car down the street and, out of breath, gets in. Nervously, she leans over and gives him a quick kiss, "Thank you for doing this for me! I know it sounds crazy!"

Ryan shakes his head as he drives, "I can't believe I agreed! If my parents find out, I'm done for!"

Nicole is curious, "How did you pull it off?"

Ryan smiles mischievously, "They think I had to work tonight. I told them we are doing inventory which will make for a very late night."

Nicole is a little worried, "Do you think they will check on you?"

Ryan shrugs his shoulders, "I don't know. They did the first couple of nights but then stopped. To be on the safe side, I have Rob covering for me. I gave them his cell phone number." He winks at her, "You know, that special phone number we use when we're in the back doing inventory."

As Ryan drives towards the city he has to ask, "Why are we doing this? You don't honestly think Emma disappeared on an elevator to another dimension, do you?"

Nicole sighs, "I don't know. I researched it and people really believe in it! Also, there is that unexplained YouTube video of one girl who played the Elevator Game."

A chill comes over Ryan when he thinks about it, "Yea, I saw that! Didn't they find her in a water tower up on the roof?"

Nicole lowers her voice, "Yea, naked! And yet, all of her clothes were in with her in the water tower. Did you see how strange the girl acted in the elevator? That is exactly how Emma acted in the video they have of her."

Ryan is suspicious, "Exactly? Then who is to say that Emma may not have seen the same video and is using it as a prop to run away?"

Nicole stares out the window, "I thought that at first, but then I became unsure. What would she have to gain? Where would she run away to? Emma has never had to work a day in her life! She may complain about life at home but everything is still handed to her! I would think that if Emma was on the street she would wise up real quick and realize what she had!"

Ryan is confused, "Then I have to ask again, why are we doing this?"

Nicole answers miserably, "I don't know! I feel like I have to do something! Plus, what if Emma did stage this and is waiting to see if I care enough for her to play the game myself?"

Ryan can see Nicole's point. Whether it is for sisterly love or peace of mind, he can understand why she is doing it. "Ok, so what do you need me to do?"

Nicole sighs, "Nothing really, I have to do this alone. It's one of the rules."

Ryan is curious, "What are the other rules?"

Nicole pulls out a piece of paper. "I wrote them down so I wouldn't forget. All you have to do is hit a sequence of floors and not talk to anyone on the elevator!"

Ryan takes the exit to the city, "That sounds easy enough."

She agrees, "It does, doesn't it? At least no looking into any mirrors having to say bloody something or other!"

Ryan has to laugh, "I'm with you babe! Mirrors can be creepy!"

Nicole points to the building her cousin lives in, "That's the building, you can park here."

Ryan parks the car. As they get out he looks around nervously, "Do you think the police are watching this place?"

Nicole shakes her head, "Nah, they've pretty much written Emma off as a runaway, especially since they have her journal."

Ryan whispers, "What about your cousin? Aren't you afraid he will see you?"

Nicole opens the lobby door, "No, we should be ok. It's a pretty big building."

Ryan is still glad he's never met that part of Nicole's family, less chance of him getting discovered! However, he had to hand it to Nicole, she seemed very determined to see this thing through.

Nicole gives Ryan a quick kiss, "Ok, the quicker I get this done, the quicker we can go home! I will meet you right here, all you have to do is wait."

Nicole pushes the elevator button and it instantly opens. Taking a deep breath, she steps inside. As the door closes she tells Ryan she loves him.

Nicole looks around the empty elevator and chuckles, "Go figure, there are mirrors. Good thing Ryan didn't come!" She looks down at her notes and mumbles aloud, "Ok, first button I hit is the 4th floor." She presses the button.

As the elevator rises she glances back down at her notes and reads aloud, "Next is the 2nd, 6th, 10th and then the 5th floor where supposedly an old woman will appear."

Nicole carefully follows the sequence and to her shock and surprise, the doors open up on the 5th floor and an elderly woman enters the elevator! Nervous, she continues to look forward, avoiding eye contact. Nicole hits the last number in her notes. The old lady smiles, "I see we are going to the same place."

Not normally rude, Nicole decides this is too much of a coincidence not to be cautious! She decides not to acknowledge the old woman. Strangely, the elevator does not go down but starts moving upward!

The old lady is surprised too, "Oh my goodness, that's strange! I saw you hit the 1st floor button. I wonder why we are going up?"

Nicole wills herself to not answer. She keeps thinking to herself, if this damn elevator stops on the 10th floor this game may actually be real!

Sure enough, the elevator stops on the tenth floor! The doors open slowly. The old lady whispers, "Are you sure you want to get off here, dearie?"

Nicole is not sure. Then again, she is sure she does not want to stay in the elevator with the creepy old lady! If anything, she will catch the next elevator to meet up with Ryan. She's had enough of this nonsense and is ready to go home! She steps out into the hallway.

As soon as the elevator doors close, all the lights go out! Nicole takes a deep breath to calm herself. She tries to remind herself of what the urban legend says. It says once she is in the alternate universe all the lights will be out. What with the old woman, the elevator stopping on the tenth floor, and now the lights being out, it stands to reason this is actually happening!

Nicole stands there in the dark paralyzed with fear. She listens intently but there is no sound. Her eyes try to adjust to the darkness but have a hard time focusing in the blackness around her. She slowly turns around, trying desperately to find some sort of light. In the distance there seems to be a faint red glow. She instantly knows what it means, the last thing that tells her if she is in the alternate universe or not.

Having a sick feeling in her stomach, Nicole wills herself to walk towards the light. The game said you would see a red cross outside the window suspended in the air. Nothing else.

Sure enough, as Nicole looks out the window she sees a red cross. Incredibly, there is nothing else! No stars, no moon, and no buildings! Simply a red cross suspended in midair! Terrified, Nicole realizes she did it! She is in an alternate universe! Now what?

Nicole looks around in the darkness and decides to look for Emma as she walks back to the elevator! Fortunately, the first door she comes to is unlocked. She opens the door cautiously, "Hello? Is anyone in here? Emma, are you here?" The total silence is deafening, let alone the blackness! For fear of losing her way, Nicole hangs onto the door and calls out again. No answer.

Nicole, stumbling in the darkness, continues down the hallway as she keeps calling out for Emma. Even her own words seem to have a darkness to them. Getting more terrified with each passing moment, Nicole quickly opens each door she comes to. Frustrated, she begins to concentrate more on getting to the elevator than searching for Emma.

A nagging thought keeps trying to surface just beyond Nicole's reach. What the hell is it? Something to do with the game! Suddenly it comes to her! What a fool she has been! What was she thinking? The game clearly states that the alternate universe would make you the center of it!

What an idiot she was! Nicole would never be able to find Emma because she's not here! She can't be here! The game is all about you becoming the center of the universe! The only way you could truly be the center of the universe is if you were by your-self! You would become all important because you are the only one in this universe! This was all for nothing! Nicole has to get out of here!

Trembling, Nicole tries harder to get back to the elevator; however, the closer she gets the farther away it seems to be. Tears stream down her face as she reminds herself the game had said this would happen; however, you can make it back to the elevator and back to our universe! Not giving up, she finally makes it back to the elevator.

Clumsily, Nicole slides her hand over the wall to hit the button for the elevator. Silently the doors open up. The elevator is enveloped in darkness. Knowing this is her only way out, she steps inside.

Nicole instantly goes to the control panel and lightly runs her fingers over the buttons as she counts. The way home is to do the exact sequence she used to get here. The problem is, it is too dark for her to see the buttons! She has to be careful and count first, you only get one shot. If she hits the wrong button it will break the sequence and she will be trapped here forever!

Feeling confident in her selection after counting it several times, Nicole holds her breath as she hits the button. As soon as she hits the button the lights come on. Relieved, she starts feeling better! Agonizingly slow, she proceeds to put in each floor, checking her paper to make sure of the sequence.

On the 5th floor as the elevator doors open, Nicole turns her head to the side, making sure not to make contact if someone should step inside. Someone does step inside. In the mirror she can see who came in. Her tears flow freely as she realizes who it is.

****

Down in the lobby, Ryan patiently waits for Nicole. It has been over twenty minutes. He is expecting her to arrive at any time now. While he watches the elevator closely, he is surprised to hear a voice call out, "Ryan? Is that you?"

Ryan quickly turns around and is surprised to see Emma walking towards him, "My God, Emma! Where have you been? Everyone is sick with worry!"

Emma comes close and gives him a quick hug, "Oh please, not you too? I just got an ass reaming from my cousin and my parents are frantically on their way over here!"

Ryan's eyes get big, "Damn it, you did it to us again! Now your parents will know Nicole is with me, which in turn means my parents know! We're going to be in such deep shit over this!"

Emma looks innocently, "I don't know what you are talking about, but as for me it was all a big misunderstanding! I told my cousin I was going camping with Gigi from the 4th floor, which is where I have been the whole time! I didn't think it was a big deal. My cousin was always working and I was bored!"

Ryan looks at her in disbelief, "Seriously? You had to know people were looking for you! What about your phone?"

Emma looks a little hurt, "I forgot my charger at my cousin's, you can ask him! I went back tonight to get it and he bombarded me with all kinds of accusations. I showed him the note I left stating I was at Gigi's. I even had Gigi come up and explain that I was with her the entire time!"

Ryan shakes his head, "Why would you not bother telling your parents where you were?"

Emma sighs, "I figured Dave would have done it! If there was a problem, he'd come and tell me!"

Ryan is beginning to come around except for the note. "Why didn't Dave see the note?"

Emma explains, "It was buried under some papers. Apparently he threw his mail on top of it. He never saw it."

Changing the subject, Emma looks around, "You said you were with Nicole. Where is she?"

Ryan sighs, "Looking for you!"

Confused, Emma asks, "Why did you two split up?"

Ryan begins to feel foolish, "Because it was one of the rules."

Emma is not following him, "Rules? What are you talking about?"

Ryan lowers his voice, "Rules for the Elevator Game."

Emma's eyes get big, "Don't tell me Nicole is playing? Even I know not to mess with that shit!"

Worried, Ryan nods, "She is playing because she thought you were!"

Emma's eyes narrow, "That bitch read my journal again, didn't she?"

Ryan looks away, "Yes, but why would you write it if you weren't going to play?"

Emma looks uncomfortable, "I was going to but then I told Gigi. We did more research on it and it seems legit! We both figured it wasn't worth taking the risk if it is true!"

Ryan walks over to the elevator and pushes the button, "It's just a game, it can't be real!"

Emma shakes her head, "No, I'm telling you it is! There are all kinds of stories on the internet about it!"

Ryan tries to keep calm, "Yea, I know! Nicole did her research too!"

Beginning to worry the game may be real, Ryan tries to reassure himself, "If it is real, if anyone can make it back it will be her!"

Emma is not so sure, "If you can make it to the alternate universe that in itself is impressive; however, making it back is almost impossible!"

Ryan looks at her concerned, "Why is that?"

Emma nervously plays with her hair, "Because you're not supposed to talk to anyone during the game!"

Ryan nods, "Yea, Nicole knows. It's an old woman or a young girl, right?"

Emma sighs, "The old woman is at the beginning of the game, but it can be anyone at the end of the game!"

****

Nicole turns around in the elevator and grabs the girl who has entered the elevator, "Emma! I'm so glad to see you!"

The girl who looks like Emma embraces Nicole. Smiling, she whispers sinisterly, "Got'cha!"

****

Nicole was never seen again. Emma, on the other hand, had fulfilled her wish. Her parents doted on her since she now is their only child. Her popularity grew at school due to everyone's shock and curiosity over poor Nicole. And yes, feeling a bond with her as they comforted each other over Nicole's mysterious disappearance, Ryan eventually became her boyfriend!

As to what Emma had to think about the whole Nicole business, the entire set up went much easier than she had ever hoped!

Emma had hidden the note under Dave's stack of mail, knowing he would never see it. Gigi and she had gone camping, but only for one night. The rest of the time they stayed at her apartment, giving Emma the chance to be on the lookout for Nicole. She had no regrets. The bitch shouldn't have read her journal!

White Noise Stories Continued

Seeing Roxy beginning to stir, Lauren quickly stops her phone recording and puts it away. She reaches over and turns the radio off.

Roxy looks sleepily around, "Are you doing ok?"

Lauren nods, "No complaints. You have perfect timing! The gambling casino Jody and Jady told us about last night is the next exit!"

Excited, Roxy pulls out her bag and starts putting makeup on, "Now I feel like we're on a road trip! It'll be great getting out of the car and not having to share you with anyone!"

Lauren tries to ignore Roxy's jealousy as she makes the turn off. As they pull into the parking lot she can't help but admire the beautiful casino, "Wow! Jodi was right! This place is really nice!"

Roxy agrees, "A Hard Rock Café and all! It's a shame we had such a big breakfast and it's too early for lunch!"

Lauren gets out of the car, "I'm sure we'll still get something to snack on while we're here. I know us!"

Once inside though, the two of them couldn't make up their minds where they wanted to go first. Roxy wanted to try gambling, but Lauren was more interested in seeing the shops.

Instead of doing things together, Roxy promptly tells her, "You go do what you want! I am going to gamble!"

Normally she would cave in and do what Roxy wants but Lauren really wanted to explore the big hotel! Gambling was not a top priority for her, "If you don't mind, I do think I will go wander around while you gamble."

Annoyed, Roxy replies flippantly, "Fine, whatever! You'll know where to find me when you're done!"

Surprised at Roxy's attitude, Lauren tries to brush it off. They both have their phones on them. If they need to contact one another they can.

A little lonely, Lauren thinks about Jodi and Teresa. There would have been no separating any of them if they were here! Of course, if one of them wanted to gamble they would have asked the others to do it with them a little while and then they would do other stuff. Roxy was different. It always had to be her way or no way! Lauren realizes that is something she is going to have to learn to live with now!

Lauren comes to a huge lobby. She looks up and realizes there are more shops on the floors above them. Happily she finds the elevator. The elevator is beautifully decorated with mirrors all around. She is quickly reminded of the story on the radio. A slight chill comes over her as she presses a button, realizing the hotel has over ten floors!

Lauren finds herself tempted to play the elevator game herself. There was no one else on the elevator so what was the big deal? And yet, she couldn't bring herself to do it! Nervously, she laughs out loud and mumbles, "Chicken!"

Her mind answers her back, "Damn straight, some things are better left alone!"

Concerned, Lauren stops herself. She refuses to get back in the mode of talking to herself like in the apartment! She quietly waits for the doors to open.

After browsing around the shops for over an hour, Lauren realizes she better go find Roxy. Lord knows, Roxy would never come to find her!

Lauren gets in the elevator and just as she is about to turn away from the mirrors, goose bumps envelope her! The hair on her arms and neck literally stands up in fear! Quickly she turns around, afraid of facing what she saw reflected in the mirror! But the doors had already started closing, she is no longer able to see past them.

Lauren's goose bumps turn into a fine sweat over her body as she thinks about what she saw. Could it be possible? Was that really Mr. Akeru she had seen? If so, what are the odds that he would be here in this casino at this particular time unless he was following her! Maybe Teresa had been right and she did see Mr. Akeru at the hotel!

The elevators open up to the large, loud casino. Lauren begins to doubt what she saw; however, she knew she would never forgive herself if she did not make sure! Hiding behind a pillar, she watches the elevator for the next person to get off. Only a woman with a stroller comes out. Not satisfied, she waits until the elevator opens up again. This time a young couple is its only occupants. As she waits for the next time, Roxy comes up behind her, "Hey stranger, find anything good at the shops?"

Lauren jumps with her heart racing, "Damn it Roxy, you scared me!"

Roxy rolls her eyes, "Excuse me!"

Lauren sighs, "Sorry, I wasn't expecting you to come up behind me!"

Roxy is curious, "Why are you here behind this pillar?"

Lauren shrugs her shoulders, "I thought someone was following me. I guess I was wrong."

Roxy looks around, "Was he at least cute? Right about now, I would hook up with even a stalker!"

Lauren laughs, "Nah, it was nothing like that! How did you do at the tables?"

Roxy smiles, "Not bad! Almost lost it all at the beginning, then I won it back. I finally got up ten whole dollars and decided it was time to stop! How about you? Anything worth seeing up there?"

Lauren is not sure she wants to go back up there and risk the chance of bumping into Mr. Akeru, if he is here. "Not really. Typical high priced casino type stores!"

Roxy sighs, "Ok, now what?"

Lauren suddenly becomes very tired, "If you don't mind, I think the trip is catching up to me! I wouldn't mind going back to driving."

Roxy yawns and agrees, "I could go for another nap myself!"

Lauren is becoming resentful of how easy Roxy has it on this trip but decides to let it simmer some more before she says anything. They return to the car in silence.

Within minutes Roxy is fast asleep. Lauren admires the scenery around her. It's a shame Roxy isn't up to see it. She had been right, not much of a road trip for her!

Even surrounded by beautiful scenery, Lauren finds herself becoming bored. The lure of the radio calls her!

No longer able to resist, Lauren turns the radio on. Before she knows it, she finds a station with a new story already in progress! She quietly retrieves her phone out of her pocket and decides to record this story too. Although she had recorded the last story, it couldn't hurt to record another one!

Lauren wishes she could have caught these stories at the beginning. It always seems like she tunes in while the story is already being told!

Down By The River

Down by the River

Mark looks nervously at the navigation, "Wendy, it's like this town does not exist! How are we ever going to find it?"

Wendy assures him, "It's going to be alright! I printed out the directions just in case. I know how squirrelly navigation can get when you get deep in the woods!"

Mark begins to relax, "Thanks honey. Sometimes I don't know what I'd do without you!"

Wendy pats his leg, "It's ok. You need to calm down more. It's like you have all this energy pent up inside. I can only imagine how wild you were as a child!"

Mark chuckles, "Mom said I was a handful!" He becomes serious, "Maybe that is why my real mother gave me up?"

Wendy sighs, "Now Mark, you know that can't be the case! Sharon says she adopted you when you were a newborn. She has pictures of her taking you home from the hospital. Your birth mother would have never been able to know if you were going to be a handful! You can't blame yourself!"

Mark knows she is right, "I wonder what the real reason was for giving me up?"

Wendy looks out towards the beautiful scenery, "A town this far from civilization? My bet is they are very religious and your mom was made to get rid of you!"

That doesn't make Mark feel any better, "Great! Either my mom was the town whore or she got knocked up by family and I'm an inbred!"

Wendy can't help but laugh, "Would you stop! You're going to make yourself crazy!"

Wendy looks at the navigation. A circle is still spinning as it says over and over "searching". Frustrated, she turns it off and looks down at the directions she printed out. "We should be getting close."

Mark lowers his speed, "Sort of creepy out here, don't you think?"

Wendy nods, "Yes, and don't forget this is all your idea!"

Mark argues, "The ancestry site contacted me!"

Wendy sighs, "Honey, I tried to warn you when you signed up there may be answers you would not like!"

Mark agrees, "I know, Mom was pretty devastated that I found out. She really thinks of me as her own."

Wendy says, "Because you are! She raised you and loved you as her own! I'm still not sure meeting your birth family is the right thing to do. I hate to see Sharon hurt, she's been so good to us!"

Mark feels guilty, "I know and the last thing I wanted to do was hurt her. After what Dad did to her, I had no right. However, I had a heart to heart with her and explained that we might want to start having a family of our own and I wanted to make sure there were no surprises."

Wendy is shocked, "Do you really mean it?"

Mark looks over at her, "Of course I do! Why do you think I joined that dumb ancestry site to begin with?"

Wendy's eyes tear up, "I don't know. I just thought it was a new hobby. You never seemed interested in kids and we never talk about it. I was finally coming to terms with not having a family."

Mark has to admit, "There are some times when I feel like a kid myself and I wonder how I could ever be a father. More importantly, I worry I may turn out like my own father!" He hesitates, "Well, at least like the one who raised me. Who knows what my real father is like?"

Wendy is beginning to understand Mark's motive, "Ok, I get it. Geez, why don't we communicate like this more often?"

Mark sighs, "Our jobs consume us! If it's not mine, it's yours. I swear, sometimes I get tired just thinking about all we do!"

Wendy is a little hesitant, "Perhaps if we are thinking about having kids we should actually get married too?"

Mark agrees, "Yea, I've been feeling really guilty about lying to Mom, I mean Sharon, this whole time."

Wendy sighs, "She really gave us no choice. With that religion of hers, you know she would have disowned you for living with me out of wedlock!"

Mark nods, "I know. My father would have made sure of it! Meanwhile, it's ok for their friends in the same religion to still have contact with their children who have done far worse things!"

Mark has to admit, "Using our cruise was a perfect cover-up but I never thought it would take on a life of its own! Now, everyone truly believes we're married!"

Wendy chuckles, "I know, right? You have to admit we covered ourselves pretty good, down to putting it on Facebook. Now how are we going to handle getting married if we are already married?"

Mark sighs, "Well, it was going to be a surprise. I wanted to wait until this whole thing is over, but I was thinking we could tell Sharon we felt bad she was not at the wedding on the cruise. Then we could have a small wedding for all to attend."

Wendy is shocked, excited and a little nervous. She has to tease Mark, "What if I had said no?"

Laughing, Mark pats her on the leg, "Then I would have had to divorce your ass!"

Wendy notices a river, "It is so beautiful here! I bet people here have all the time in the world!"

Mark turns off the air conditioning and rolls down the window, "And no traffic! We haven't passed another car in miles!"

Wendy sees a sign, "There's Main, we're almost there!"

Mark's heart skips a beat as he drives through the sleepy town, "It's just like I imagined!"

Wendy notices only one church, "A one church town, this should be interesting!"

As they drive through the town they realize how quiet it is. An unnatural quiet. Mark wonders, "Maybe this is a bad idea. This place looks like a ghost town! Where is everyone?"

Wendy tries to be positive, "Let's get it over with. If we don't, we will always wonder. It should be after the next bend."

Wendy checks the addresses as Mark slowly drives, "There's the house! It looks like we're expected!"

Mark suddenly lets his foot off the gas, "What the hell?"

Cars are lined up in front of the house. Scores of people in the front yard and on the big wraparound porch. Streamers line the trees and balloons seem to be everywhere. Right above the garage is a huge sign, "Welcome Home Mark!"

Mark looks at Wendy wide eyed, "Oh honey, I had no idea! How awkward is this?"

Wendy chuckles nervously, "Very! Looks like the whole town is here. You, my dear, are famous!"

Mark moans as he realizes the people in the yard have noticed them and started pointing. "Oh geez, we've been discovered!"

Wendy smiles out at the people, "Put your best smile on and keep it on! Is it me or is it strange to have so many people gathered around and it still be so quiet?"

Through a strained smile Mark answers softly, "No, this is all too bizarre!"

A woman who resembles Mark walks towards the car with several women around her. She waits for Mark to get out of the car, takes a long look at him, and asks, "Are you my baby Mark?"

Blushing Mark answers, "I guess so."

Wendy looks around at the strange setting. The streamers and balloons seem out of place. Even though they are trying to portray it as a celebration, the party itself seems somber and subdued.

The woman steps forward and awkwardly hugs him, "Welcome home, Mark!"

The woman looks over at Wendy, "You must be his wife Wendy. Please come with us so you can meet everyone." Both Mark and Wendy cringe. Apparently, the lie lives on, even here!

Wendy keeps her smile plastered on. She should feel honored to be included and yet she instantly feels like it is more of an obligation then a friendly gesture.

Mark reaches out and takes Wendy's hand. He jokes, "Of course honey, come meet the family since you are part of it too!"

Mark and Wendy proceed with meeting the people there. It was Brother so and so and Sister so and so. At first, Wendy thought it was Mark's real brothers and sisters, but she quickly realized it was a religious thing.

Finally they come to a table in the middle of the yard. Mark and Wendy have a seat along with his mother and a few chosen ones. The remaining people stand in a circle around them, watching intently. Wendy and Mark feel like they are on display.

Mark notices several children and is surprised at how well behaved they are. "The children here are so quiet! There's no need for them to stay, is there? Why not let them go and play?"

His mother answers him sternly, "There will be time for that later!"

Mark jokes to Wendy, "I would have never been able to stand that quiet when I was a kid!"

Mark's mother looks at him curiously, "Were you not a well behaved child?"

He stumbles a little, "Not really. My mother, I mean Sharon, always teases about how much of a handful I was!"

Mark's birth mother cringes a little when he speaks of his adopted mother, "Well, you need not concern yourself with her anymore!"

Wendy has to speak up, "Excuse me, uh..."

Mark's mom answers for her, "You can call me Mary."

Wendy takes a breath in, "Ok, Mary. Sharon has been very good to both Mark and I. She loves Mark as her own!"

Mark takes over, "Wendy is right. Sharon raised me. She was the only mother I knew and she will continue to be part of my life."

Mary sighs, "Of course. Perhaps we should discuss what happened when you were born."

Nervous, Mark agrees, "I won't lie, I am anxious to hear your reason for giving me up."

Mary looks at him with wide eyes, "Oh no, child! I did not give you up! You were taken from me!"

Mary explains, "Your father and I had to travel outside of town for supplies we needed for the Passover." She looks around at the brothers and sisters for support, "I was pregnant with you and went into early labor. We had no choice but to go to the hospital there."

Mary motions for the crowd to separate, "That is where your twin brother Luke was born too."

Mark gasps as he sees a man that looks identical to him, "Oh, my God!"

Mary whispers harshly, "Please do not use His name in vain!"

Mark, still in shock over seeing his brother Luke, mumbles, "Of course, sorry."

Luke quietly reaches the table and has a seat. Although Wendy can clearly see how much Luke resembles Mark she can also sense they are nothing like one another.

Mark is at a complete loss for words. Already knowing the answer, Wendy wants to hear it from her, "Why did Luke come home with you and not Mark too?"

Mary sighs, "During the labor I passed out. John, my husband and your father, was not in the delivery room. We never knew there was a Mark."

Mark does not understand, "You didn't know you were having twins?"

Mary shakes her head, "Not a clue."

This is not the story Wendy had heard from Sharon. Both she and Sharon thought it was best to not tell Mark until after they heard what story the birth mother was going to come up with.

Wendy asks innocently, "You seem comfortable with Mark's name. How is that?"

Mary looks annoyed, "Because Wendy, at the time of their births I was having a hard time deciding between Mark and Luke for a name. I believe the nurse who took you simply named you the name I decided against!"

Mark sits there reeling from what he has just learned. On one hand, it is obvious his mother is not the town whore or that he is inbred and that in itself is a relief! On the other hand, she is trying to say he was stolen! He doesn't see how that could be possible. And for that matter, why would he have been stolen? It couldn't have been for money. As stingy as his father was, he would have never allowed Sharon to "buy" him no matter how desperately she wanted a child!

Mark glances around and he can't help but be thankful he had been taken. Although his childhood was far from perfect, with his own parents' religion, this whole town seemed even more cult-like!

Mark has to ask, "And what of John?"

Mary looks down sadly, "John passed a few years back. He was a good man."

Mark knows he should feel something but it is hard since he never knew the man. Instead, he feels the loss of not ever being given the chance to know him.

Wendy is a little confused and asks Mary, "How were you able to find Mark?"

Mary clears her throat, "The ancestor site contacted me after Mark submitted his DNA when he signed up. They gave me Mark's information if I wanted to contact him. I discussed it with Luke and we decided we needed to finally get you home where you belong!"

Luke mumbles quietly, "I always had this feeling I had a brother. I was the one that contacted the site on a whim. I convinced my mother it would be fun to see what it came up with. Did you have the same feeling?"

Mark looks like a deer caught in the headlights, "Honestly, no! I had no clue!"

A man makes his way through the crowd and looks at them, "The sun will be setting soon. Best we all make our way down to the river. She's waiting!"

Everyone starts to walk away while all at the table rise. Mark looks at Luke questioningly, "Who is she?"

Luke motions for Wendy and Mark to follow them. As they walk, Luke explains, "This town was born during a very violent time of the West. Folks came here to escape the crime and violence that plagued other towns." He sighs, "However, like anywhere the crime and violence began to rear its ugly head here too. It's in our genes. It doesn't matter how strict your religion is, mankind's imperfections will always shine through. Lust, greed, disobedience and eventually murder!"

Mark and Wendy find themselves getting closer to the sound of a river. Luke continues, "A woman living here long before the town was here, came to the elders with a solution."

Luke looks proudly out at the river, "She told them instead of baptizing people like they normally do in the river, bring them to her. On her land there was a special inlet the river flowed through.

She guaranteed anyone baptized there would be washed free from sin."

Luke smiles, "She was right! Our little town is over 120 years old. To this day, there is no lust, greed, disobedience and not one single murder!"

Wendy looks down at a little inlet where an old woman holds a screaming baby high in the air. Suddenly, she plunges the baby into the water and holds it there. Wendy becomes concerned, "Oh, my God! She's drowning that baby!"

Luke shakes his head, "No, she is not. Wait and see."

It takes everything for Wendy not to run down there. Just as she is about to go save that poor baby, the old woman lifts the baby out of the water. Not a sound comes from the child.

Wendy looks horrified, "She killed that baby, Mark!"

Mark takes Wendy in his arms. He sees everyone is watching him. He whispers, "Shhh… it'll be ok. I think we need to be careful."

Wendy becomes stiff in his arms as she realizes everyone is watching her.

A young woman goes and retrieves the baby from the old woman. Smiling, she brings the baby up close to Wendy, "He's ok, see? Now he will be easier to take care of and with no sin!"

Wendy is shocked to see the baby breathing normally. The child is quiet and seems to be content. She suddenly looks around at all of the children and sees how unnaturally quiet they are. None of them are even fidgeting! They all simply stand by their parents complacently.

Suddenly Wendy asks, "At what cost? Is that the same woman from over 120 years ago?"

Wendy frantically looks at Luke, "What did this town barter with this old woman? What did she have to gain from the bargain?"

Luke smiles, "It's true, she is able to receive our essence which in turn gives her youth."

Wendy looks at the ancient woman, "What youth?"

Luke sighs, "I am told she was a beautiful vibrant woman before my time. The deal she made with the town was everyone in town had to give up their essence. For some time she has been losing her youth. No one knows why."

Two large farm men come up to Mark and begin to force him down to the inlet. Luke continues, "We think Mark is the solution."

Mary stands at the edge of the inlet. Before they force Mark into the water she whispers, "It'll be alright my son, you are home among your brothers and sisters."

Wendy can't believe what is happening! They plan on taking the very essence from her husband that she loves! His free spirit is the difference between Luke and Mark!

Wendy is terrified. She looks at Luke, "You could have been free from that old woman if you had left well enough alone!"

Determined, Wendy screams out to all of the people, "Look at what you have done to your children! Look what has been done to you! Your childhood was stolen! You have no fire inside you! You're nothing more than zombies! You don't live, you simply exist!"

Luke shakes his head, "But we are safe! We have no crime, no sin!"

Wendy watches as they take Mark into the water in spite of his struggling. Frantic to save him, Wendy screams out again, "Wait! You do have a sinner in your midst! Mary knew and she has been lying to you all of these years!"

Hoping Mark will understand one day why Sharon and Wendy didn't tell him, she explains, "Sharon, the woman who raised Mark, told me Mary begged the nurse to take one of the twins! The nurse was a cousin of Sharon's and knew how desperately she wanted a child of her own. The nurse and Mary were able to pull it off without John ever knowing!"

Luke looks at her shocked, "You lie!"

Wendy shouts her theory out, "What if Mary did know? What if it was her way to save one of her children from this cult?"

Everyone gasps at the thought. Suddenly the old woman in the river speaks up, "Yes! She did know! How dare you deceive me! Who do you think you are to have slowly taken my youth away from me over the years! You broke our arrangement!"

Mary stands strong and holds her head up defiantly, "Yes! I did know! Back on the day that I was baptized there was a great storm during the baptism. As I came out of the water lightning hit the inlet. I believe it allowed a tiny spark of essence to remain inside of me."

Mary sighs, "My parents knew and hid it. They disciplined me over and over to keep that spark dim. When I traveled outside of town with my husband, how I envied how everyone lived! How the children played! None of you can feel remorse, I can!"

Mary looks over at Luke apologetically, "You have no idea how hard it was to choose which one of you was going to actually live!"

The old lady shakes her head in disbelief. A long screeching sound comes out as she points to Mary. In turn, Mary soon matches the old lady's scream with her own!

Wendy watches in horror as the top of Mary's head begins to melt. A long agonizing death for Mary as she literally melts into the spot she is standing. The gooey remains of her trickle down into the inlet.

The entire town watches the trickle, mesmerized into a sense of obedience. As soon as Mary's remains hit the water, bubbles race towards the old woman. The bubbles envelope her and then disappear. Standing in the water now is a middle age woman.

Knowing Mark's essence will give her even more youth, the woman motions for them to bring Mark next. Wendy cries out but finds herself surrounded by the obedient followers. There is no way they are going to allow her to interfere with tradition!

Wendy is not sure if Mark is in shock or there is something in the water that subdues him, but suddenly he stops struggling. Mark allows the woman to baptize him.

Wendy holds her breath the minute he goes under the water. Several minutes pass and Wendy's lungs burn. She can no longer handle it and gasps for air. A few more minutes pass. Surely her poor Mark has drowned by now!

Finally, the old woman raises Mark up. Instead of gasping for air like you would think, he calmly wades out of the water towards Wendy.

Bubbles envelope the middle age woman again. Now standing in the inlet is a beautiful young woman and yet, not as young as she had been before.

Wendy is surprised no one is holding her any longer. They simply let her go. Wendy runs to Mark and hugs him tightly, but she quickly realizes he is not the same.

Wendy looks over at the young woman in the inlet and notices her disdain. Apparently, she is not as young as she would like to be.

Wendy knows there has to be an answer to all of this, but what? This is obviously an outside force they are dealing with! Like anything else that can't be explained, these people use religion to justify it. She wonders though, if religion was the base of the original pact perhaps it could be its undoing as well? Before knowing fully what she is doing, Wendy calls out, "Wait! You must baptize me too!"

The young woman shakes her head, "You are not a descendant of this town!"

Wendy, knowing the town thinks they are married, blurts out, "By extension I am! I am married to him!"

Before the beautiful woman can answer, Wendy tempts her, "Who knows how much more beauty and youth could be added to you from my essence?"

The woman admires her reflection in the water but hesitates, "What will you gain from it?"

Wendy puts a hand up to Mark's face and lovingly caresses it, "I will be like him and I will remain with him."

The woman agrees, "Come forward."

Wendy wades out to her while Mark simply stands there watching. Totally complacent, Mark does not even try to stop her.

Wendy holds her breath as the woman plunges her under the water. She finds herself unable to resist as she is held at the bottom of the inlet by an unworldly force. Her lungs burn until she can no longer handle it. She gasps under the water only to have the water painfully enter her lungs! An awful feeling of despair comes over her as she feels herself dying. Before the darkness can consume her though, Wendy frantically screams out into the water, "Know the truth!"

Suddenly the water around her becomes angry bubbles! The bubbles push her to the top, as if to cleanse itself of a lie. Unlike Mark, when Wendy breaks the surface she quickly gasps for air.

Coughing and sputtering, it is difficult for Wendy to stand; however, seeing the confusion on the woman's face suddenly makes her strong. Determined, she calms herself and stands defiantly, now breathing in the precious air effortlessly.

The woman's face turns from confusion to fear as she sees the bubbles that saved Wendy advance towards her. She screams out, "What have you done?"

Seeing all of the town's people staring at her, Wendy speaks up for everyone to hear, "Mark and I are not married, we lied! I took a chance that perhaps a lie would not be a good pretense to be baptized on!"

Wendy smiles smugly as she watches the bubbles get closer to the woman, "I also realized that for this mumbo jumbo to work it somehow must be based on sin."

Wendy looks a little confused, "Although I'm not sure how you got away with being vain all these years. Perhaps the essence of man's sin before it could develop was an easy tradeoff for whatever agreed to your original pact?"

Wendy looks at them as she shakes her head, "Unfortunately, as with most pacts, only one benefits the most while the others lose so much!"

Wendy tries to make sense of the current situation, "Perhaps being an outsider who lied and her being greedy was the deal breaker?"

The bubbles rise up more furiously and encompass the beautiful woman. Her screams can surely be heard from miles away. Once the bubbles fade away, no longer is there a beautiful woman; only a skeleton barely held together. A slight wind picks up, breaking the skeleton apart and turning it into ash! Before the ashes can become absorbed by the water, the wind blows the ash upward and towards the town people.

As the ash falls down over the town people, they all act as if they are waking from a deep sleep. Suddenly, the children are skipping and running around playing! The adults laugh out loud as they hug each other warmly. The air fills with the beautiful sounds of happiness.

Mark runs into the water to Wendy and picks her up, laughing, "You did it! You not only saved me, you saved the whole town!"

Clumsily, they walk out of the water onto the shore. There waiting for them is Luke. He looks concerned, "What about all the sin that can be done now?"

Wendy tries to reassure him, "Luke honey, without the bad you can never truly appreciate the good! Look around you and enjoy the happiness here now."

Wendy sighs, "Sure, there's bound to be some dark times once in a while. However, the happiness, the children laughing and playing, all of this is not appreciated as much when you have nothing to compare it to!"

Mark puts an arm around his brother, "She's right Luke. This is all sweeter when the dark times do come. You look back on moments like this and it is what helps us get through the bad things."

Luke sadly looks over to where their mother had been. "I only wish mother had been here to see her dream finally come true!"

Wendy looks around as she feels the slight breeze that carried the ashes over the town people, "I believe Luke, she is the one that kept the ashes from going back into the water! I truly believe your mother is the one who gave back what was taken!"

White Noise Stories Continued

Lauren's warm feeling after listening to the touching story is short lived when a grumpy Roxy mumbles, "I'm hungry!"

Lauren shakes her head as she turns the radio off, "More like 'hangry' if you ask me!"

While Roxy fumbles around to sit up, Lauren is able to stop her phone from recording and quietly puts it back in her pocket.

Now fully awake, Roxy looks around, "Where are we?"

Lauren shrugs her shoulders, "Pretty much in the middle of nowhere."

Roxy looks disappointed, "Meaning nowhere has nowhere to eat?"

Lauren sees an exit sign coming up. "You are in luck! There's an exit in five miles with food. Maybe not food we are used to, but food none the less!"

Roxy is excited, "Yea! I could go for some local flavor right about now!"

Lauren laughs, "Well, remember out here the restrooms are few and far between!"

Roxy nods, "I got it! Oh, look! A café named Route 66, let's go there! We need to stop more at these little tourist traps!"

Lauren follows the signs and agrees, "Not a problem. Now that we are no longer on a time limit, wherever you want to go, my dear!"

Roxy and Lauren settle into a booth and order their lunch. Roxy quickly signs them in on Facebook.

Bored watching Roxy on her phone, Lauren decides to check hers. Surprised, Lauren sees a message from an old school mate. "Hey Roxy, listen to this. Robby, an old school friend of mine, has been following the posts you have been tagging me in."

Lauren looks up, "Apparently, he is in the area! He wants to know if we want to meet up with him."

Roxy is confused, "He lives around here?"

Lauren shakes her head, "No, he's a truck driver. He's on down time right now at a station not too far from here! What do you think?"

Roxy smiles, "Sure, why not? It would be stupid to pass right by and not say hi!"

Excited, Lauren quickly texts Robby back, "Cool! I told him after lunch we'll meet up with him! What are the odds that I would know someone all the way out here?"

Roxy laughs, "Small world! So, who is this guy?"

Lauren thinks back, "A boy I used to sit with on the school bus. He was older but he always looked out for me!"

Suddenly Lauren becomes a little bitter as she thinks back, "I never liked the school bus. Except for Robby, no one would ever let me sit with them. None of my friends lived in the area so I was easy prey."

Roxy is surprised, "And here I thought you were loved by all!"

Lauren sighs, "Nah, we had cliques just like any school! No one from my clique rode my bus. If not for Robby, it would have been a lot worse!"

Roxy understands, "Kids can be cruel!"

Lauren agrees, "They can, but I suppose it just prepares you for what the real world has to offer! Bullying has been around forever. I sort of hate the idea that everyone thinks it's new."

Roxy smiles, "There does seem to be a movement out there to put everyone in a bubble. You know, the whole 'participation awards' crap!"

Lauren shakes her head, "Would you believe I read the other day they are beginning to play soccer without a ball? It's because they don't want the kids that can't play well to feel bad!"

Roxy is shocked, "By pretending there is a ball? Wow!"

Lauren laughs, "Crazy, right?"

The waitress brings their food. Too excited at the thought of seeing Robby, Lauren finds it hard to eat. Fortunately, Roxy has no problem devouring everything and before they know it they are back on the road heading towards Robby's exit!

Lauren pulls up beside the big rig Robby had described to her. She quickly gets out of the car as she sees Robby stepping down from the rig. "Hey, stranger! How cool is this?"

Robby smiles as he gives her a big hug, "Very cool! Although I didn't think it was going to happen since you weren't checking your phone!"

Lauren blushes, "I know! I am terrible about that, but thanks to Roxy's passion for her phone, sometimes it motivates me to check mine!"

Lauren points to Roxy, "By the way, Robby this is Roxy. Roxy this is Robby."

Roxy shakes Robby's hand, "Nice to meet you."

Robby nods, "I don't envy you being on a road trip with this one! Must be quite an experience!"

Roxy laughs, "That it is!"

Lauren rolls her eyes as she looks at Robby, "Oh please! This one here is the trouble maker! I'm not sure how poor Beth puts up with him! How are things at home?"

Robby shrugs his shoulders, "A struggle, but it wouldn't be life if it wasn't, now would it?"

Robby looks over at Lauren's car, "I must say, I am loving your car!"

Lauren sighs, "Quit teasing me! It's not that bad! Anyway, it's kind of sentimental, it was my grandmother's."

Robby smiles, "You know I gotta tease you! Hey, I want you two to go into the truck stop with me. You will not believe the stuff they have in there!"

Now it is Lauren's turn to tease back, "Sure there is! You just want to be seen with two girls!"

Robby chuckles, "Well, that may be true too! You know, I do have a reputation to uphold around here!"

Robby wasn't kidding about all of the stuff the truck stop had to sell! It was a tourist's dream haven! Roxy quickly wanders off as Robby and Lauren shop together.

Lauren admires the jewelry, "I guess there is no excuse for you not bringing Beth back all sorts of cool things!"

Robby nods, "Yea, it's nice here, but further west there are even better stops! About two exits away there is a really cool knife shop you might like to stop and see!"

Lauren looks a little unsure, "I don't know, two girls traveling alone going to a knife shop? To be honest, we wouldn't have stopped here if it weren't for you!"

Robby agrees, "I understand, but that's why I'm telling you where to go! Trust me, these are places you will want to go to. Not only do they have cool things but they'll be safe for the two of you!"

Encouraged, Lauren asks, "Alright, what's another one?"

Robby looks at the jewelry, "If jewelry is what you are interested in, two more exits after the knife store is a tourist pull off with teepees out front."

Lauren smiles, "Sounds like a plan! I can't believe I am standing here talking to you! It's so nice to see you! You know, I was able to see Teresa and Jodi while coming out here!"

Robby shakes his head, "I could feel a storm a coming, just didn't know it was you!"

Lauren laughs, "This is exactly what I needed! Unfortunately, I had some things I was dealing with back home. It seems like seeing my old friends has somehow rejuvenated me!"

Robby doesn't want to pry but has to ask, "Don't you get that with Roxy?"

Lauren thinks about it and has to be honest, "No, but it's different. All of us grew up together! I think when you form friendships when you are older it's naturally harder!"

Robby is not so sure, "A friend is a friend! All I am saying is there may be a reason there isn't that strong connection with her like you have with us!"

Lauren is surprised at how many of her friends don't seem to like Roxy! She looks around making sure Roxy can't hear, "I hear you Robby, but you can't go through life not taking chances either!"

Robby agrees, "You are right! I'll say no more. I want to buy you something little, if you will let me?"

Lauren blushes, "Oh Robby, you don't need to!"

Robby takes her over to a small section and points, "Pick one out. They are not expensive and I think you should have one!"

Lauren looks at the little car chimes Robby is pointing at. As she tries to decide which one she wants she admits, "I have to say, this surprises me!"

Now it is Robby's turn to blush, "I know! I'm a bit more sentimental than you may think! Someone gave me one for the rig when my dad passed. It gives me comfort during the long drives. Wind chimes are meant to keep evil spirits away, but it is also a way for loved ones to soothe your soul."

Lauren is surprised at his tenderness. She chooses a moon and sun, thinking about the story she heard earlier. She can't help but chuckle as she picks it up, "I like this one! Reminds me of a story I heard where the sun is our father and the moon is our mother. What child would not want something that represents their parents?"

Robby takes it from her and goes to the cash register, "Guess I'm not the only sentimental one!"

Roxy comes up with an arm full of items, "Look at the cool things I found!"

Lauren smiles, "Robby, does she have anything we will find better or cheaper somewhere else?"

Robby takes a quick look, "Nope, she's good!"

Roxy looks confused so Lauren explains, "Robby told me about two more places we'll want to stop at along the way!"

Roxy is excited, "If they are anything like this place, I can't wait!"

Robby laughs, "They are better!"

After completing their purchases they returned to the car. Lauren proudly puts the wind chimes on her rear view mirror. Roxy doesn't hide her disdain, "Great! More noise in the car! I wonder how quick we'll be taking that down?"

Lauren shakes her head, "No time soon! It was Robby's idea and I love it!"

Roxy mumbles a halfhearted apology, "Of course! I'm sorry, Robby. I didn't know."

Robby looks over at Roxy and can't help but tease her, "No problem, I guess there's no accounting for taste!"

Lauren laughs as she goes over to give Robby a goodbye hug, "There's my Robby! You be safe out there and thanks so much for reaching out! I loved seeing you! Tell Beth I said hi!"

Roxy merely gets in the car and shouts out, "Yea, nice meeting you Robby!"

Both Lauren and Robby are surprised Roxy isn't friendlier. As they hug, Robby whispers, "I think you are the one that needs to be careful!"

Lauren whispers back, "I'll be fine!"

Although Robby's warning did not resonate with Lauren, once she was back on the road and Roxy was fast asleep, she begins to doubt herself on her decision to move out here with Roxy.

Of course, so far she has had a good time. But then again, she has to be honest with herself; the good times seem to be with her old friends! With Roxy most of the time it is forced! Lauren is realizing that, more often than not, she is the one who compromises so they will have a good time!

Lauren sighs, looking at the signs on the road. Robby said the knife shop was only two exits away but out here the distance in between exits was unbelievable!

Lauren turns the radio on and is surprised to hear a story already in progress! Quickly, she pulls her phone out and starts recording.

Strangely, as the story is being told, the little wind chime Robby had bought for her gently sways back and forth, tinkling almost in unison with the voice on the radio.

Recluse

Arnie shuffles home from work which is within walking distance. A car drives by honking and filled with teenagers calling him names. Arnie takes a mental note of the license plate. Either the driver or the parent will get their just due for making fun of him!

Arnie's life has been a hard one. Abandoned at birth, bullied at school, and now even as an adult he is not accepted. All those teachers, counselors, even ministers had been wrong! It was not just a passing phase, it was a life sentence!

As Arnie turns at the corner he is surprised to see Paige waiting for him. Sweat instantly rises up on him. He tries desperately to calm his racing heart. Clearing his throat, he tries to sound casual, "Hi Paige, what are you doing here?"

A mousey looking girl who has known her fair share of abuse timidly answers, "George wanted me to bring over the schedule so you could review it."

Feeling important, Arnie stands a little taller. "Thank you, I'll be sure to review it tonight!"

As Arnie reaches for the folder, Paige lets go too soon and the papers fall to the sidewalk. They both bend quickly down to retrieve them. As they do, another car drives by full of kids laughing and yelling out, "Look at the losers!"

Arnie sees how hurt Paige is and immediately assures her as he memorizes their license plate, "Don't worry, they'll get theirs!"

Paige adjusts her glasses, "It's ok, you get used to it."

Arnie, not one for conversation, has to ask, "Really, how?"

Surprised, Paige shrugs her slumped shoulders, "I guess by ignoring it."

Arnie sighs, "I would rather remove myself completely from it!"

Paige agrees, "I guess it would be easier to be a recluse, unfortunately we have to work!"

Arnie knows Paige is new to the company. "You'll like working for George. If you feel uncomfortable, he understands. Plus, he does not tolerate bullies. In fact, I think he likes hiring people like us because he knows we're good workers. I feel very fortunate to be working for him!"

Paige smiles, "That is very nice of you. Did you know he is my uncle?"

Now it is Arnie's turn to be surprised, "No, I had no idea!"

Paige assures him, "It's ok, he likes you too. In fact, I think that is why he sent me over here." She blushes as she looks down at the ground, "I think he may be trying to play matchmaker."

The pit in Arnie's stomach tightens, "I thought it was not allowed to... uh..." Arnie searches for the right word but can only come up with, "you know, if you work at the same place?"

Paige is now bright red, "I don't think it is a rule."

Arnie's hesitates a minute. Although his mind is screaming no, he finds himself asking, "Would you like to come inside for some fresh lemonade? I made it this morning before I left for work."

Paige stumbles, "That sounds nice."

They go inside the small dark house. Arnie senses Paige's fear. "I'm sorry, I like to keep the place dark. It's my retreat from the outside."

Paige follows Arnie into the kitchen. Although the house is dark and a little creepy, the kitchen is very clean. Beginning to relax, Paige has a seat at the kitchen table, "Do you live alone?"

Arnie gets two glasses out, "I do. I've lived alone since I was nineteen."

Paige is curious, "Was this your parents' house?"

Arnie retrieves the lemonade out of the fridge, "It was my adoptive parents' house. They died in a car crash not too long ago."

Paige softens her voice, "I am sorry, that must have been tough on you!"

Arnie pours the lemonade and shrugs his shoulders, "Not really, I guess they never understood me. As bad as it sounds, their death was sort of a relief."

Paige understands, "I like your honesty. What about your real parents, did you ever try finding them?"

A dark mood comes over Arnie, "I did, right before my adoptive parents died. Unfortunately, my real parents are dead too."

Paige sighs, "That's rough. Did you at least find out what you wanted to know about your real parents?"

Arnie gives her a glass and then has a seat across from her. He is surprised at how easy it is to talk to her. "I guess, I think it helped me understand more of who I am. However, my adoptive parents took my research like some sort of betrayal."

Paige takes a sip of the lemonade. Surprised at how good it is she can't help but blurt out, "Oh my gosh! This is good!"

Arnie laughs, "Thank you!"

Paige wipes at her mouth, "I get it though. If you were having trouble connecting with your adopted parents, it stands to reason you would want to find out more about your past!"

Arnie takes a nice long drink before answering, "Exactly! My adoptive parents felt like they had to shelter me but I was of age, I had a right to know!"

Paige wonders, "What did you find out?"

Arnie is not sure he should tell her, and yet, it is so nice to talk to someone. Plus, there is always the alternative if the conversation does not turn out the way Arnie wants it to. "It was much darker than I had ever dreamed it could be!"

Paige finds herself looking deeply into Arnie's sad eyes. A protectiveness comes over her and she whispers, "You can trust me."

Strangely enough Arnie felt as if he could trust her, "I guess they found me abandoned in an old house."

Paige does not understand, "Who is they?"

Arnie hesitates, "The police. I was only a baby."

So many questions come to Paige's mind she is not sure which to ask first, "Where were your parents?"

Arnie is hesitant, "My father was in jail. As for my mother, she had overdosed in the other room."

Shocked, Paige quickly puts her hand on top of Arnie's to comfort him, "I am so sorry!"

Arnie is surprised he did not yank his hand away from Paige's touch, in fact, he is enjoying the contact. "I'm afraid it gets much worse."

Before Arnie can finish, out of the corner of his eye he sees a spider timidly making its way across the kitchen floor. Amazingly, at lightning speed it takes itself up off the floor and onto the kitchen table. Curious about how Paige will react, he holds his breath.

Paige notices the spider but calmly sits at the table, looking at the spider hesitantly advancing towards her, "Oh my goodness, look! Isn't that a brown recluse?"

Arnie nods as he takes his hand out from under Paige's and pretends he is about to smash it, "Yea, they are common in our area."

Paige stops him, "Oh no, please don't kill it! Can we just put it outside? I'm sure it means us no harm!"

Just then the spider turns and starts crawling away. Arnie watches as the spider quickly leaves the table and disappears. Paige apologizes, "I'm sorry! I know you are probably a little worried now that it's on the loose. It means you no harm. Did you know they only bite if they are squeezed in an area like a shoe or glove?"

Arnie can't believe what just transpired, "I do, though I never figured you would know! I have to say your reaction is not like most girls!"

Paige giggles a little, "Or most boys! Some people are so terrified of spiders they will practically kill to get away from one!"

Arnie can't help but smile, "Why yes, they will!"

Paige returns to their earlier conversation, "Please, tell me more about where they found you."

Arnie's earlier concern about telling Paige has now been completely erased, "I was a newborn that had many of the same drugs in me that had killed my mother."

Paige shakes her head in disgust, "I'm sorry, but how could she use drugs while pregnant! I know this is harsh, but good riddance!"

Arnie has to admit, "I agree. When they found me they also discovered the house was infested with brown recluse spiders."

Paige looks concerned, "How odd, I didn't think they nested like that."

Arnie nods, "They do. Anyway, when they found me I had bites all over me. Technically, I should not be alive today!"

Paige agrees, "Yes, usually young children and older people with failing immune systems succumb to a brown spider bite."

Paige thinks about it, "It was the drugs in your system that saved you, wasn't it?"

Arnie shakes his head, "No, more like the other way around. It was like the spiders knew I was dying due to malnutrition and the drugs. The bites not only neutralized the drugs, they fed me through their poison."

Paige is astonished, "Amazing! So often you hear of the animal kingdom protecting a child."

Arnie smiles, "They did." He can't help but mumble again, "And still do."

Something clicks in Paige's mind and she lowers her voice, "How many?"

Arnie is not sure what Paige means, "How many what?"

Paige lowers her voice, "You know, incidents! Obviously, you still have a connection with them and they are still protecting you!"

Arnie laughs, "I can't believe we are having this conversation! You really want to know?"

Paige smiles really wide, "Yes, please! Let me guess, your father was mysteriously bitten while in jail and died. No other inmates were bitten and they never found the spider."

Arnie sighs, "Yea, funny how it worked out to be right around the same time I found out he was my mom's dealer too!"

Paige nods, "What are some of the other 'incidents'?"

Arnie thinks about all the incidents that he knows of, "I don't always know who they get and it hardly is ever them biting someone, unless they have to. Like you said earlier, most people practically kill to get away from a spider and it's usually themselves!"

Arnie starts to list some, "A few as easy as falling down the stairs. One was when a nasty teacher at school pulled the chain on her lamp and the spider scared her so much she tried using the lamp to smash it, only to electrocute herself."

Paige guesses another one, "A spider in the car scaring the driver so much they swerved and crashed. Perhaps, like your adoptive parents?"

Arnie has to ask, "Why are you so accepting of all of this?"

A sinister smile comes over Paige, "Look over your shoulder."

Arnie gasps as he sees a snake slithering towards him. He gulps, "Am I going to be ok?"

Paige laughs, "Oh yea, he's been there the whole time. There's another one by the back door."

Paige explains, "I was a toddler when I fell into a big nest of snakes. By all rights, I should have died too! However, they kept me alive. They took care of me and are still taking care of me."

Arnie can't believe his luck! He now knows he has found his soul mate! What fun they will have seeking revenge on all their bullies out there without ever having to be accountable!

White Noise Stories Continued

Lauren begins to see billboards for the big knife store Robby had told her about. She turns her phone off and then the radio since she needs to wake Roxy up for their next stop. She can't help thinking how ironic it was for the latest story on the radio to be about bullies! Especially since Roxy and her had been talking about the same thing at lunch!

Roxy, sensing something is going on, wakes up and asks, "Are we getting close?"

Lauren nods, "Yea, it's just a few miles ahead. I think we should get gas there too. These exits seem to be getting farther and farther apart. I don't want to take any risks!"

Roxy agrees, "I hear you! We're making good time though, even with stopping at the casino!"

Lauren smiles, "Yea, I don't see us spending as much time at the next stops. I am pretty tired and am looking forward to the hotel bed tonight!"

Roxy sympathizes, "You poor thing, you must be exhausted! I'm hoping the place I booked us for tonight is not too much of a dump!"

Lauren is surprised, "I'm sure it's not. So far the hotels you picked have been great!"

Roxy sighs, "That's because you had both of your friends tells us where to go! Unfortunately, this hotel is out in the middle of nowhere."

Lauren is curious, "Why did you choose it?"

Roxy answers, "Remember how I told you I wanted us to see the solar eclipse?"

Lauren nods, "That's tomorrow, right?"

Roxy smiles, "Yup! However, where I want to take you to see the solar eclipse is in the middle of nowhere! The hotel we're going to is the closest one I could find and it's not a name brand."

Lauren pulls into a gas station, "I'm sure it will be fine! I want to fill up before we shop." Afterwards, she drives across the street and pulls into the parking lot of the knife shop.

They both get out of the car, a little cautious. Roxy has to ask, "Are you sure Robby knows what he is talking about when it comes to this place?"

Lauren looks around, "He was right the last time!"

Lauren and Roxy go into the store and are instantly surprised at how impressive the store is! Roxy whispers, "I don't even know where to begin!"

Rows upon rows of knives in glass compartments fill the store! A big burly guy asks in a gruff voice, "Are you two looking for anything in particular?"

Lauren is not intimated, "My friend Robby, a truck driver, recommended we come here."

The burly guy smiles, "Most of our business is repeat business and word of mouth. Nice to have you here. My name is Pete."

Lauren smiles, "I'm Lauren and that's Roxy."

Roxy was already clear across the store and barely looked up when Lauren introduced them. Pete sort of rolls his eyes, "Must be from the East Coast?"

Lauren nods, flushing with embarrassment, "That obvious, uh? Actually, I'm from the Mid-West but we are moving to California from Jersey."

Pete can't help but laugh, "Trading one evil for another? You, young lady, should return home! You'll be much happier!"

Before Lauren can answer an older looking Chinese woman comes out from the back. "Petey, leave the poor girl alone! You're embarrassing her!"

The old lady reaches her hand out to Lauren, "Hi Lauren, I'm Lin. Welcome to my shop!"

Looking like a fragile woman, Lauren is surprised at how strong Lin's handshake is. Lin, noticing her surprise, laughs, "Never judge a book by its cover, dear!"

Lauren blushes but laughs, "I guess not! I wouldn't want to mess with you in a dark alley!"

Lin, proud of herself, stands a bit taller, "Got that right! Do you carry?"

Lauren looks a little confused, "Carry? Oh, you mean do I have a knife on me? Oh, no! I guess in the back of my mind I always thought if I had one it would be taken away from me before I could even use it!"

Lin looks frustrated, "Nonsense! They must get to knife first and before they do, a lot of damage can be done from you!"

Lauren looks down at the knives and changes the subject, "Perhaps I will get one for my father."

Lin warns, "Never give knife as gift! It will sever the relationship you have. If you insist, give knife with coin and make the person give you coin immediately back. This will ensure lasting relationship!"

Lauren is intrigued, "I have never heard of that! I guess giving knives for a wedding present is not such a good idea?"

Lin is serious, "No, never! Here, come with me! I show you knife good for you!"

Lauren smiles at Pete, "Well Pete, I guess Roxy is all yours!"

Pete chuckles, "Only when she summons me. Have fun!"

Lin goes behind a case and unlocks it. She pulls out a plain small knife and hands it to Lauren. Nervous, Lauren doesn't hold onto it hard enough and drops it, "Oh! I'm so sorry! Did I hurt it? I'll pay for it if I did!"

Lin looks down at the knife and shakes her head, "No, it's ok, you can't hurt it! Though it does mean a man is coming."

Lauren doesn't quite understand her, "A man?"

Lin leans over, picks up the knife and places it on the counter. "Yea, yea! If spoon drop, child is coming. If fork drop, woman is coming. If knife drop, man is coming!"

Lauren is curious, "Are there any more interesting facts about knives?"

Lin smiles, "In China we put knives under the bed to keep away evil spirits!"

Lin looks down at the knife on the counter with a troubled expression, "This knife called to me for you. It is a steel knife. Steel knives are known to protect you from curses and demons!"

Lauren suddenly feels vulnerable, "Demons? I'm not sure there is much call for that now a days, is there?"

Lin is not amused, "Pick it up and tell me it does not feel like a fit for you!"

Before Lauren can pick it up, Roxy interrupts, "Don't tell me you are thinking of buying that one! There are way prettier ones over on the other side!"

Lin scoffs, "Beauty is no protection! Go on, pick it up Lauren and see how it feels!"

Lauren reluctantly picks up the knife and is instantly surprised at how nicely it fits in her hand. "That's crazy, it's like the knife was made for my hand! You're really good. I never thought I'd be comfortable with a knife but this one does feel right!"

Frustrated, Roxy takes the knife from Lauren, "Why would you ever need this?"

Before Lin can object Roxy closes the blade and hands it back to Lin, "Here you go."

Lin shakes her head, "You should never close a knife that someone else has opened! It is bad luck!"

Annoyed, Roxy snaps, "Sorry! Lauren, we should be going! Are you ready?"

Lauren can't believe how rude Roxy is being, "Why don't you go ahead to the car. I'll be there after I look around some more!"

Roxy sighs and shuffles off, "Whatever!"

Lin smiles at Lauren, "Good for you! Here, I want to show you a few things before we finish the sale!"

Roxy sits miserably in the hot car as she waits for Lauren. The little wind chime that Robby had bought for Lauren tinkles almost mockingly at her. She glares at it, "Oh shut up!"

Lauren finally comes out of the store proudly carrying a leather box. Once she is in the car, she reaches over to the glove box, "We'll keep the knife in here, just in case we need it!"

Roxy looks over at her in disbelief, "I can't believe you bought into that crap! You, my dear, have been tourist sucker punched! Buying into the idea of needing a knife, really?"

Lauren has had enough of Roxy and her attitude, "What's the big deal? I liked it and I bought it! I didn't stop you from buying any of those stupid souvenirs you bought!"

Roxy knows Lauren has a point but won't let it go, "I didn't buy a weapon for God's sake!"

Lauren rolls her eyes, "Oh please! It's only a weapon when it's used as one! The knife sitting in my glove box is not going to hurt anyone! Oh wait! Maybe it will go off and hurt someone! Do you hear how ridiculous that sounds?"

Roxy sits quietly, refusing to answer her. Frustrated, Lauren has to ask, "And what was your problem in there? You were so rude to those people!"

Roxy glares over at her, "I'm sorry, I'm not a country bumpkin that has to talk to every stranger I meet!"

Pissed off, Lauren retaliates, "And I'm no spoiled princess that always has to have her way!"

Roxy grabs for her headphones, "Before we both continue to say things we'll regret later, I think it's time for a time out!" She puts her headphones on without giving Lauren a chance to respond.

Lauren doesn't care, she got to say what she wanted!

Several miles pass before Lauren realizes Roxy has fallen asleep, as usual. She turns the radio on and is happy to find a station with yet another story.

Shuttering

Shuttering

Rena rushes around trying to figure out four outfits. Four outfits! This is crazy! She is not even sure she has four full outfits that are clean for God's sake! Why did she ever agree to this silly idea?

Her girlfriend, Amy, had talked her into getting her picture taken professionally at the mall. Rena had been filling out job applications since graduation and found some of them wanted actual pictures for her profile.

Not liking the idea that her new job may be based on how she looks, Rena quickly realized she had no choice. Amy, being the sweetheart that she is, believes the Glam Shot in the mall is the perfect solution to Rena's dilemma. Not only will they tap into her "inner beauty" but also be able to give her tips on how to bring that "inner beauty" out and possibly keep it out.

What a crock, thinks Rena. It's basically Amy's way of telling her she needs to start wearing makeup. She glances in the mirror at her plain face. While all of her friends in school had worn makeup, she had not due to her parents' strict religion. Even after going to college and being free of the damn restraints of that religion, Rena had not succumbed to the evils of vanity. And really, had it hurt her? Granted, she did not have a boyfriend, but she had been top in her class.

Trying to get back to the task at hand, Rena lists in her mind what the store had told her. Four outfits: one professional, one casual, one different than she normally wears, and one sexy.

The last two on the list were throwing her. Weren't they the same, at least for her anyway? Rena sighs as she gets farther back in her closet. Wait a minute, here's that sweater Amy let her borrow when she spilled her drink all over hers that night at a party.

Rena blushes at the memory. It was one of the few times she had let Amy talk her into going to a frat party. Man, had she felt like a fish out of water! A guy bumped into her causing her to spill her drink all over herself. Fortunately, Amy had bought a new sweater that day and let her borrow it.

Rena looks at the sweater. It definitely was something she would not normally wear. The color is all wrong and the neck line is way too low, but if she remembers correctly, the guy that bumped into her did give her his number after seeing her wearing it. She never had the courage to call but it did happen. She shrugs her shoulders and throws it on the pile of clothes to take with her. At least it was clean.

Rena glances over at the clock in frustration. She has to get going or she'll be late! Coming to the end of her closet she finds an old sexy Halloween costume a friend of hers gave to her for a high school graduation present. It was meant as a joke. Little Red Riding Hood making her escape to the big bad ole college. Sighing, Rena grabs it along with the other clothes and rushes to the car.

Fortunately there is no traffic and she makes it on time for the appointment. Out of breath, she enters the shop. A highly energetic woman approaches her, "You must be Rena. I'm Jasmine but everyone calls me Jaz. Here, let me help you with your stuff."

Jaz takes a couple of items from Rena and heads towards the back, "Follow me to where the magic happens!"

Rena smiles and begins to relax. Maybe Amy was right, this might be fun. Rena hangs her clothes with the ones Jaz took and then takes a seat where Jaz wants her.

Surrounded by mirrors, Rena begins to feel a little uncomfortable but Jaz is not about to let her. Running her hands through Rena's hair Jaz admires it, "Your hair is such a beautiful color! Don't tell me it's natural!"

Rena blushes, "It is."

Jaz shakes her head, "Girl, you're making me hate you already! How would you like me to style it?"

Rena shrugs her shoulders, "I don't know. My friend Amy said you would figure that out for me."

Jaz literally squeals with excitement, "Awesome! I am back in love with you all over again! It is so much easier to create when the subject allows me to."

Rena smiles, "Create away, I am nothing but a blank canvas."

Jaz starts getting her makeup out, every once in a while glancing at Rena's eyes and complexion. "That makes it easier for me. You have no idea how many princesses I get in here who are so difficult to work with!"

Rena sighs, "Not a problem for me. Since I don't wear makeup, I guess I can't be too critical of your work."

Jaz is curious, "If you don't mind me asking, why don't you?"

Rena thinks about it, "Growing up my parents didn't allow it due to religion, you know, the whole vanity thing."

Jaz rolls her eyes, "Makeup only enhances what God gave us!"

Rena quickly agrees, "Oh, I know. I'm not part of that religion anymore, but the time I would have been most interested in learning how to put makeup on, I missed out."

Jaz completely understands, "I see. Well, if you are up to learning today I will explain. You will see how easy it is, what colors to use, and what to buy if you want to try it at home."

Rena finds herself curious, "I think I would like that."

Jaz is excited, "That, my dear, is the hardest step! Being open to suggestions. This is going to be so much fun!"

For the next hour Jaz works on Rena, explaining as she worked how to use all the makeup. Once the makeup is finished, Jaz styles Rena's hair giving her suggestions along the way.

When they are finished, Rena is not only amazed at how she looks, she actually feels confident she can pull the look off herself at home! She can't wait to go shopping for makeup afterwards!

Jaz has her grab her clothes and follows her into another room, "Alright my dear, from here Rick will be taking care of you."

Rena looks a little disappointed, "You won't be taking my pictures?"

Jaz sighs, "Normally I would, but Rick does not know how to do hair and makeup and we are overbooked. You'll be fine, he's a pro!"

Rena looks around feeling uncomfortable, "If you say so, thank you Jaz."

Jaz winks at her as she turns to leave, "You will be fine and I'm right outside this door. I'll sneak in and check on you during the shoot."

Rena is not sure what to do with herself after Jaz leaves. She looks around at the small confined room. It was far from impressive. Some props lay on the floor, curtains half hung, big lighting stands and a fan. How in the world are they going to make any of this look good?

Having a sudden thought, Rena looks around again. Where was she supposed to change? Right here in the middle of the room? She sighs heavily, what outfit is she even supposed to put on first? She tries to think logically. Probably the professional pictures first. After all, that was the whole reason she is here. Best to get those out of the way first while she looks her best.

Rena quickly changes, terrified Rick would come in at the most inconvenient time. Just as she is putting her last shoe on, there is a knock at the door with a man asking if he can come in.

Rena nervously replies, "Yes."

An elderly man walks in, "My name is Rick and I will be taking your pictures today."

Rena smiles shyly, "Hi, I'm Rena."

Rick takes a long look at her and nods, "Ok Rena, what is our objective today?"

Rena likes that Rick is being professional and begins to relax, "I need to have some photos for some of the job applications I am filling out. They want some sort of profile pictures."

Rick nods, "I see, not a problem." He quietly changes the curtains behind her and pulls out a wooden stool, "Have a seat."

Rena is a little disappointed at the simplicity. "It's kind of frustrating to think someone may hire me only because they like the look."

Rick waits until she is seated, "I couldn't agree with you more! Today's society is much too absorbed in the outer beauty verses the inner glow."

Rick begins to give her instructions such as chin down, eyes towards me, drop your shoulder a little more. Rena finds herself in the most uncomfortable positions. How in the world are these pictures going to turn out looking nice? Before she knows it, her first set is done and Rick leaves the room for her to change.

The next set goes the same with different curtains and props. Again, Rick leaves the room for her to change. Getting into the swing of things Rena figures the next set should be the same; however, as Rick does this shoot his whole manner starts to change.

Rena finds herself explaining how the sweater is her friend's and not something she normally wears. This time, Rick concentrates on difficult and provocative poses. It almost feels like he is begrudgingly auditioning her. Finally he leaves for her last change.

Rena looks at the sexy Halloween costume and wonders, if Rick didn't approve of the sweater what the hell is he going to think of this?

Rena finds herself becoming a little defiant. Why should she care what he thinks? It was his dumb photo studio that told her to bring in a sexy outfit! She thinks back to all the photos on the wall when you first walk in. For Pete's sake, at least she will be semi covered! Half the girls out there barely had bra and panties on!

Rena finishes getting dressed and waits for Rick to come back. Instead, it is Jaz knocking at the door. She comes in and takes one look at Rena and gushes, "Oh my gosh, look at you! That is sexy as hell on you! You look fabulous!"

Rena is not convinced, "Are you sure? I have a feeling Rick is not going to approve!"

Jaz rolls her eyes, "Don't worry about him, he's an old fuddy-duddy! It may not seem like it, but he's working his magic on you! I've taken a peek at the photos he's already down loaded and they are absolutely gorgeous!"

Rena looks around the confined room, "Really? I don't see how!"

Jaz laughs, "I know, right? But you have to remember, it's not so much about what you see but what the camera sees. Don't sweat it. Believe it or not the most important thing is the lighting and this little room is perfect for it!"

Jaz reaches out to fix her hair, "I want you to have fun with this. It's not about Rick, it's about the camera. The camera loves you! When you see the pictures you'll see what I mean. Meanwhile, have fun with it. Don't let the big bad wolf Rick get ya!"

Beginning to feel better Rena laughs, "You're right! We only live once, right?"

Rick walks in holding a glass of water and looks at the two girls, "My ears are burning. You two wouldn't be talking about me, now would you?"

Jaz heads towards the door, "My girl here is a little worried you may not like what she's wearing. I told her it's not you who decides but the camera. And anyway, there's nothing wrong with stepping out of your element every once in a while!"

Rick nods, "You're right."

Rick hands Rena a glass of water, "Here, I thought you may be thirsty." After being under the hot lights, Rena gulps the water down.

If Rena thought she was uncomfortable with the last shoot, this shoot was far more intense! Granted, being in the tiny costume made her feel uncomfortable, but Rick moving her and touching her 'all in the spirit of getting the right shot' didn't seem right. He almost seems like a different person, treating her rough because of the way she is dressed. It bordered on being perverted!

Rena decides she has had enough! As Rick comes over to handle her again she shakes her head, "No, I think we've done enough for the day!"

Rick steps back, "I'm sorry, I meant no offense. I was just trying to get you in the right frame of mind. Let me do one last shot and we'll be done. Your look of defiance right now will be perfect, I promise!"

Rena sighs, "Ok, one more."

Rena watches Rick change cameras and is curious, "Why are you using a different camera?"

Rick looks annoyed, "Because even with the advanced technology we have, sometimes an old school still provides us a better capture of your light. It's all about the shutter."

Rena does not think any more about it as he takes her picture with the camera. Although, when the session is done, she feels a bit strange. She feels a little off, not even sure how to explain it. The session must have worn her out more than she thought.

Getting dressed in her regular clothes, Rena heads out to the lobby to view her photos. Jaz was right, the photos were amazing! Never in a million years would she have thought such magic would occur from being in a cramped little room! Of course modern technology had a lot to do with it, creating backgrounds she had no idea they were going to use. In fact, one of her in the red riding costume has a cool forest background with magical looking stardust kicking up around her.

Rena can't believe it is actually her in the photos! She had to admit even the uncomfortable poses paid off. However, her excitement quickly dwindles as the manager starts going over the pricing. No way was she going to be able to afford any more than the one professional picture she needed!

Cliff, the manager, feels bad as he watches Rena look long-ingly at the one of her in the forest. He decides what the hell and quickly thinks of an idea, "Rena, if you allow us to use one of your pictures for advertising I can give you a print for free. Any picture you want to choose."

Rena is grateful, "Really? That's so nice of you! I really like the one in the woods!"

Cliff smiles as he finishes the paperwork, "Of course! These should be ready for pickup next Thursday."

Rena excitedly answers, "I can't wait!"

Rena leaves the shop and heads right over to buy makeup before she changes her mind. Meanwhile, Amy calls, "How did the shoot go?"

Rena juggles the phone as she continues to shop for her makeup, "Great! Would you believe I'm actually over here buy-ing makeup? Jaz was sweet enough to help me figure it all out."

Amy is shocked, "You're kidding me? All the years of trying to give you a makeover and now suddenly it's ok! What the hell, girlfriend?"

Rena laughs, "I guess it's all about timing. I realized maybe I should start taking better care of myself. It is still because of you that all this has happened!"

Amy feels better, "Well good! Now what do you say to taking it a step further? Let's go out tonight and celebrate your new look. I can't wait to see you!"

Rena is hesitant, "I don't know, that shoot really took it out of me! I'm exhausted!"

Amy sympathizes, "I know, but you don't want to waste that new look. Let's go celebrate! I promise once we are out you'll get energized!"

Rena glances over at a mirror in the makeup aisle and has to admit she does like the new look. What harm would there be in showing it off? "Sure Amy, let's do it!"

Rena and Amy go out that night and Rena ends up having one of the most memorable nights she has ever had! In fact, she even meets a guy! And this time, the guy asks for her number and calls her that night!

Yes, Rena enjoyed her new look the next couple of days. And yet, today it will all be tested by her mother's visit. Nervously, she checks her apartment one last time before letting her mother in. Her mother had a way of making her feel guilty even when she had done nothing wrong. Although, today will be different since she has makeup on!

Rena answers the door pleasantly, "Hi Mom, come on in."

Her mother, with her ever present frown locked into place, sighs, "I'll be glad when you get a real home! Those stairs are a pain!"

Rena nods, "Yes Mom, I know."

Her mother is barely through the doorway when she looks at her sternly, "Rena Ann, is that makeup you are wearing?"

Rena closes the door and goes to the kitchen, "Yes it is. I have tea water boiling, would you like some?"

Her mother puts her bag on the couch and has a seat at the kitchen table, "Dear, how many times have we told you about vanity? It's a very slippery slope!"

Rena gets the tea cups out, "Mom, it's not a big deal. You can barely tell I have any on. That's what I like about it. Jaz taught me the right colors and how not to overdo it."

Her mother looks at her critically, "Why do it at all then?"

Rena brings their tea over and sits at the table, "I used to think that too but then I realized what Jaz said was right. It's a way for me to pamper myself, build up my self-confidence and, believe it or not, it takes stress away. I find myself getting up earlier to do it and while I'm doing it I'm concentrating on me which gives me "me time." Afterwards, I look forward to the day and am not in such a rush."

Curious, her mother asks, "Who is this Jaz person you keep talking about?"

Rena smiles, "It is the girl at Glam Shot who did my hair and makeup for my photos."

Rena's phone rings before her mother can retaliate with another nasty comment. Rena blushes as she sees it is Joe calling. She quickly hits the ignore button. Now is not the time to bring him up too!

However, her mother is no fool, "You see? A slippery slope! You already have boys calling you that you are ashamed to talk to in front of your mother!"

Rena has had enough, "Yes Mom, I met a very nice boy the other night. His name is Joe. It is new. I still don't even know what to say when you're not around, let alone when you are sitting right across from me!"

Her mother merely shakes her head and takes a sip of tea disapprovingly. Rena realizes it is time to pull out her secret weapon. She reaches over to the cabinet and retrieves a picture. "I found this the other day, Mom. I thought it was interesting."

Her mother glances over at the photo as Rena continues, "A picture of you and Daddy before you were married. I do believe you are wearing lipstick!"

Her mother sits there in silence as she drinks her tea. Rena shakes her head, "A 'slippery slope' Mom! If you think about it, that lipstick may have been the reason for you and Daddy's 35 years together!"

Her mother does not back down, "Maybe, but I met and dated your father under Christian fellowship! I bet that is not how you met this Joe!"

Although her and Amy had been to the bar earlier that night, Rena leaves that out and reveals how she did meet Joe, "Believe it or not, I met Joe at the grocery store! He is a dentist."

Her mother is clearly shocked. A bit more humble she asks, "Same age as you?"

Rena smiles, "He's two years older, same as you and Daddy. I think you'd really like him, Mom!"

Her mother smiles, "I'd like to meet him. Maybe next Sunday for dinner, if it's not too soon and would make him uncomfortable?"

Rena replies happily, "I'll throw it past him and see what he says."

Her mother has to admit, "You do look pretty Rena. I want you to be happy, I just worry about you."

Rena appreciates it, "I know this is all so hard on you. I have to give you credit. Even though it's not the lifestyle you and Daddy wanted for me, you still have supported me."

Her mother is torn between religion and her daughter. The one and only thing she disagrees with her religion. One should never have to choose between them.

Even though she has a new boyfriend and a new look, there is something different about her daughter that she can't put her finger on. "Are you sleeping ok? You look tired."

Rena is not surprised that her mother can tell, her mother knows everything. "It's weird. After the photo shoot I haven't felt…" she stumbles for the right word, "whole."

Her mother looks concerned, "Your soul is in danger!"

Rena chuckles, "Oh please Mom, don't start!"

Her mother doesn't back down, "I'm serious Rena! Ever since you stepped away from the church you have weakened your soul. Who is to say, now that it has been weakened, it can't be taken?"

Rena teases, "Wait, I know! My soul was captured when I had my picture taken! You know many cultures believe that could happen!"

Before her mother can reply Rena adds, "Seriously Mom, how could a person survive without their soul?"

Her mother lowers her voice, "There are plenty of soulless people in the world and most don't even realize it!"

A few days after her mother's visit, Rena is on the way to pick up her prints from the Glam Shop. Still not feeling quite herself, she finds herself replaying the conversation she had with her mother.

Something nags at Rena about the topic. Did she seriously think her soul could be captured? Even if it could, is she really entertaining the idea it could be captured by a camera?

Rena thinks back to the day of the photo shoot. Everything had gone well enough, although Rick had made her feel very uncomfortable with the sexy poses. The way he touched and moved her, it was almost as if she was being violated. But she had chalked it up to being part of his job to make her look sexy. Feeling foolish, she had told no one about it.

Suddenly, Rena remembers how odd it was when Rick used a different camera for the last shot. Rena doesn't remember seeing that shot when she previewed the photo shoot. Perhaps it would be a good idea to ask Jaz about it today.

Arriving at the shop, Jaz, being her bright bubbling self, greets Rena, "There's my girl! Look at you all done up! I couldn't have done it better myself!"

Rena blushes, "And I couldn't have done without your expert advice!" She looks around and is surprised to see the shop empty, "Are we alone?"

Jaz nods, "Yes, we had a cancellation and Rick called out."

Rena waits as Jaz gets her prints out for her. Proudly, Jaz shows her a 16 x 20 of her as a sexy Red Riding Hood in the woods. "Isn't this the most beautiful thing you've ever seen?"

Rena admires the portrait, "It really is! It was so nice of Cliff to offer a solution for me to get it."

Jaz looks around and lowers her voice, "He's a great guy! Between you and me, there is no promotion or special. He just wanted to make it so you could have it."

Rena is very appreciative, "Make sure to tell him how happy I am and how much it means to me!"

Rena suddenly becomes serious, "Is there a chance I could look at all of the photos taken?"

Jaz is surprised, "Why, did you want to buy more?"

Rena shakes her head, "No, I just want to see all of the shots that were taken. I think one is missing."

Jaz explains, "When we show you the little slide show of your shots we've already eliminated the ones that were less than perfect. You know, ones with your eyes closed, that sort of thing."

Rena feels a little better, "That must have been the reason I didn't see it. I mean, Rick only took one shot while using the other camera. Perhaps it was bad?"

Jaz looks confused, "What other camera?"

Rena begins to get butterflies in her stomach, "The one he used at the end. He said sometimes old school technology captures the best light."

Jaz's eyes begin to get big, "He's not allowed to use other cameras! It's against protocol!"

Rena worries about the implications, "So, what do you think we should do?"

Jaz picks up the phone, "I'm calling Cliff and see what he thinks!"

Rena anxiously waits for Jaz to get off the phone. She tries to listen but Jaz goes in the back for privacy. Finally she returns with a solemn look, "I'm sorry Rena, I'm not allowed to say any more. Cliff says the company will do their own investigation."

Rena nods as she takes her prints, "Ok Jaz, thank you."

As soon as Rena gets in the car she calls Amy and explains what happened. She even tells her how uncomfortable it was during the sexy photo shoots.

Amy is concerned. How Rick handled her was unacceptable! And using a separate camera at the end was plain creepy! Fortunately, her father, Charles, is a captain over at the police station. Amy convinces Rena to go directly to her father's office and tell him what she told her.

The rest of the afternoon became a whirlwind. Rena filed a complaint while Charles ran down information on Rick. His profile was becoming increasingly alarming, a man who never stayed in one area too long and worked for several photographers throughout his life.

Charles knew Glam Shot would be investigating to protect themselves and it was only a matter of time before Rick would be tipped off and could become a flight risk.

With Rena's statement they are able to get a warrant for Rick's arrest. Since a camera was involved, they obtained a search warrant too. At his residence they found a spare bedroom that was used as a photo gallery of sorts. Hundreds of pictures lined the walls and Rena's was one of them. An investigation was quickly begun.

Several days pass before they are able to track down any of the women on the walls. Meanwhile, Rena had to be hospitalized due to a mysterious illness.

Charles worked frantically to connect the dots. One by one, the girls they tracked down were already dead. It looked as if Rick was a serial killer and a very good one!

Each girl so far had died mysteriously without any real tie to one another; other than being a picture on Rick's wall. Realizing there may not be much time, Charles takes the picture of Rena to the hospital. He shows the picture to barely conscious Rena to make sure it was the pose she thought Rick took with his own camera.

Rena is shocked to see the most vibrant, beautiful picture of her in the Red Riding Hood costume. Although it was a little out of focus, it was still amazing! A little ashamed, but strangely proud, Rena simply nods.

Realizing Rena may be a little embarrassed by the picture, Charles decides to leave it with her. He steps out to talk to the doctors about the investigation. Since there is a possibility Rick had done something to Rena, the doctors decide to run some tests to see if she was poisoned.

One of the tests was due to talking to Amy to see if Rena had mentioned anything odd about the photo shoot. Amy remembered Rena mentioned the water at the Glam Shot smelled strange, like bitter almond. This quickly led the doctors to test for cyanide poisoning. Only certain people with a specific genetic trait can detect cyanide by smell and apparently Rena happened to be one. The test confirmed that she had been poisoned.

Upon hearing this, Charles does more research on cyanide and finds out cyanide is a photographic fixer in a wet plate collodion process. Potassium cyanide, KCN, dissolves silver where it has not been made insolvable by the developer. This reveals and stabilizes the image, making it no longer sensitive to light. Most photographers prefer less toxic fixers for developing but it is still used. Rick had several gallons of it in his house.

To cover all the bases, the police test the water at the Glam Shot to make sure it was not an accidental poisoning. It came back clean.

While Rena is being treated for cyanide poisoning, Rena's mother informs the police Rena had complained to her about smelling a bitter almond smell on dates with the new guy, Joe. This led Charles to find out more about Joe. Lo and behold, Joe is none other than the son of Rick. It becomes obvious that Rena meeting Joe by a chance encounter at the grocery store was not accidental! Charles quickly locates Joe and brings him in.

Strangely enough, both father and son confess and had an unusual story that started with the purchase of an old camera. The father had purchased the camera from EBay after his wife died several years back. Upon receiving the camera, both father and son had an unusual dream that night. The dream revealed the camera's history.

It all began when a father took pictures of peoples' departed loved ones. A time when people wanted a memento to remember the ones they lost. It became a dark family business that surrounded itself in death. No different than family operated funeral homes. The father had modified his camera several times so that it could capture the best lighting.

He was good at what he did. Using props and lighting allowed the father's photos to be beautiful keepsakes for those in mourning. To this day, some of the photos the father took are so good it is very hard to distinguish between the dead and the living.

However, what started out as a way of helping people with their grief turned into a darker passion for his son. Spending day after day arranging dead people for the perfect shot for his father traumatized the son. He became obsessed with capturing more than an image. The son wanted to capture their actual soul before the person died, allowing loved ones to remain with one another throughout time.

The son had heard tales of tribes being terrified of having their picture taken. They believed their souls were captured in the camera. This led the son into a dark path of research. He wanted to see if he could make his father's camera capture souls.

Knowing his father was obsessed with lighting, the son presented the idea to his father. Would capturing the soul be the ultimate picture? After all, does not the soul have its own light? Being an artist in his own right, the father became intrigued.

However, no matter how much the father modified the camera he did not know how to capture the soul. And, for that matter, if they had captured the soul how would they know?

Then one fateful day, the mother, Eleonore, became gravely ill and her death was imminent. The father, in immense grief, prayed fervently for his precious wife to be spared. As days went by and his wife's condition deteriorated, he knew his prayers to God were going unanswered.

The father then found himself praying to anyone or anything who would listen to his pleas to spare her life. One night both he and his son had the same dream. In the dream, a visitor told them they were very close to realizing their quest. The visitor would reveal the answer in exchange for the camera to capture Eleonore's soul.

The deal seemed perfect; it was exactly what the father and son wanted! Plus, they would have the knowledge to be able to capture souls, giving dying souls a chance to be with their loved ones. In the father's grief and the son's madness, they readily agreed. After all, it was nothing more than a dream, was it not?

The next day, the father took a different approach to their problem. He started using a special solution to develop his photos. He reasoned that if they did capture a soul perhaps he needed to stabilize it in the process of developing the picture!

Meanwhile, the son wondered if the solution they were using to process the picture should also be administered to the person before the picture is taken.

The ideas seem to go hand in hand. Should they proceed? Was it merely coincidence they came up with these ideas the day after their dream?

Seeing their precious Eleonore slipping away gave them no choice. Both father and son agreed to use the camera and the solution on her before her death.

The picture was amazing! None of the pictures the father had taken throughout his life came close to the beauty of this one picture! However, as beautiful as the picture was, it was strangely out of focus! Plus, after the picture was taken, poor Eleonore did not die quickly. It was a slow and agonizing death.

The father once again prayed out to anyone or thing who would listen, to ease her pain. The visitor from the dream before appears, assuring them everything would be fine if they gave her more of the solution.

Each time the developing solution was given to Eleonore the picture strangely seemed to come more into focus! The father and son realized that they were, in fact, capturing her soul! Eleonore's magnificent picture would be a way for her to be with them after death!

However, just as the picture was to come into full focus and Eleonore was taking her final breath, a fire broke out and quickly enveloped the house. Fearing for their own lives, the father and son flee while still hanging onto their precious camera, leaving Eleonore and her picture to burn.

The visitor in their dream had not lied. The camera did indeed capture poor Eleonore's soul, trapping it deep inside. Because the picture was destroyed in the fire, there was no release for her from the camera. Bitter, Eleonore haunted the camera.

The camera took over the father and son's minds, forcing them to try their methods on young healthy women in hopes that Eleonore could somehow trade places with them. But it was to no avail.

As for the beautiful pictures taken with the young women's souls captured, they were to be saved until the visitor could come and collect them at his convenience.

Eventually the father and son were captured for their crimes of poisoning the poor women. Once they were away from the camera, they confessed that the visitor and the camera were what made them do it.

Insanity was no defense at the time so the father and son were hung. The camera used for their photos was mysteriously gone, only to find its way into another father and son scenario furthering Eleonore's own quest of having her soul released and the visitor obtaining more young women's souls!

Rick explained that he had to have the camera with him at all times. When the camera found a woman it wanted, it forced him to take a picture of her.

His son and he had tried resisting the wishes of the camera several times, only to be tormented day and night until they finally would succumb.

After hearing the ridiculous confessions from Rick and Joe, Charles returns to the hospital. He finds his daughter Amy sitting anxiously by Rena and her stern mother pacing the room.

Unfortunately, Rena has slipped into a coma. The doctors are at a loss. Amy explains to her father that they have treated Rena for cyanide poisoning and her body seems to be responding; however, for some reason they seem to be losing her.

Charles tries to explain as much as he can about the father and son's testimony. Shrugging his shoulders in defeat he finishes up, "As far as I can tell these guys are using a cursed camera as a way of explaining their serial killings. A sanity plea for sure!"

Marilyn, Rena's Mother, is not so sure. Suddenly her attention is focused on the night stand by Rena's bed. Disgustedly she goes over and picks up the photo of Rena in her Halloween costume.

Looking at the sordid picture, Marilyn softly quotes Isaiah 4:4, "When the Lord has washed away the filth of the daughters of Zion and purged the bloodshed of Jerusalem from her midst, by the spirit of judgment and the spirit of burning."

Out of nowhere Marilyn asks, "Do any of you have a lighter?"

Charles pulls his out and gives it to her without thinking. Marilyn promptly sets the photo on fire. Shocked, Amy and Charles yell out, "You can't do that in here!"

Marilyn calmly takes the burning photo into the bathroom and drops it into the sink. As she does she mumbles, "Only in fire can the soul be cleansed!"

As the photo burns they suddenly hear a scream! Frightened, they realize the scream is coming from Rena in the bed and they all rush to her side!

With eyes wide open Rena finally stops screaming. Tears course down her face as she looks at her mom, "Thank you!" She stumbles for the right words to describe how she feels. She can only come up with, "I feel whole again!"

After making sure that Rena is going to be alright, Charles offers to take his daughter home. As they ride in the car, Amy asks, "Did you notice that as soon as the photo stopped burning, Rena stopped screaming?"

Charles concentrates on the road in front of him but solemnly answers, "Yes, I did."

Amy needs to know, "Do you have the photos of the other women?"

Charles nods, "I do. I have the originals in the back seat and the precinct has copies."

Amy wonders, "If those photos were destroyed would it really matter to the investigation since there are copies?"

Charles sighs, "I suppose not. Evidence tends to get lost from time to time."

Charles sees a sign and smiles, "How about there?"

Amy smiles, "Yes, why not?"

Charles pulls into the local park. Amy and Charles take the photos with them to a small secluded fire pit. Charles asks, "How do you want to do this, one at a time or all together?"

Amy thinks about it, "How about one at a time, out of respect?"

Charles agrees, "Ok, here we go."

Charles places a photo of a deceased girl into the fire pit. When he lights it both Charles and Amy are shocked as a scream comes from the photo!

Terrified, neither knows what they should do. Should they put it out or let it burn? While they try to decide, the scream turns into a satisfied sigh and they realize the soul has been released.

After releasing all of the souls, emotionally exhausted, Charles and Amy return to the car. Once inside Charles pulls out his phone. Amy is curious, "What are you doing?"

Charles answers as he waits for the phone to ring, "Releasing the souls is one thing, but now we have to make sure that damn camera is destroyed!"

"Hello? This is Captain Merrick. I need to check out an item in the evidence room. Could you pull it for me before I get there? It's the camera listed in the investigation of Rick and Joe Morgan."

Charles listens intently, "What? Who? What authority did he have?"

Disgusted, Charles hangs up the phone. Amy anxiously asks, "What's the matter, Dad?"

Charles looks over at her, "The camera was checked out earlier today. They discovered afterwards the guy who picked it up had fake papers and used a bogus identity. Now, no one knows where the camera is!"

Charles shakes his head, "That means the camera can end up in the hands of another father and son team! It will go on capturing souls of unsuspected women while Eleonore continues to try and release her own soul!"

Chills come over Amy, "And God knows, what happens to the souls that are captured and are eventually obtained by the visitor?"

White Noise Stories Continued

This time it is Roxy leaning over to turn the radio off. "Isn't this the exit Robby told us about? You know, the one with the teepees? I can already see them, cool!"

Lauren shakes her head a little as if she is in a daze, "Uh? Oh yea, I guess it is!"

Roxy looks over at her concerned, "Are you ok?"

Lauren rubs her eyes, "Yea, I'm just really tired. Some of those stories can really lull you into another place."

Roxy pulls her bag out to freshen her makeup. Lauren is curious, "Did you hear that last story? Pretty bizarre if you ask me!"

Roxy shakes her head as she mumbles, "No, same old white noise crap as usual!"

Lauren is furious! Raising her voice, "You can't tell me you did not hear that story on the radio when you turned it off!"

Shocked, Roxy looks wide eyed at her as she reaches for the radio, "No, I didn't and I'll prove it to you! Here!"

The radio comes on full blast with nothing but white noise! Startled, Lauren blames Roxy, "You must have hit the tuning button when you turned it on! It's easy to do."

Roxy sighs as she turns the annoying noise off, "Honey, it's ok! I've come to realize it's not a big deal! Actually, I've been giving it a lot of thought."

Roxy finishes freshening up as she speaks, "I think that white noise sort of lulls you into a hypnotic state! While in that state your mind sort of dreams up little stories to pass the time!"

Lauren is not buying it. She defiantly pulls out her phone, "I forgot to tape the last story, but I did the previous ones! Listen for yourself!"

Roxy takes the phone from her and finds what Lauren was talking about. She hits the play button and nothing but loud annoying white noise comes from the recordings!

Tears stream down Lauren's face! She can clearly hear the white noise and not the stories she thought she had heard! Roxy asks, "Didn't you ever wonder why you never heard the beginning of the stories? Never heard a DJ cutting in for commercials or even the radio call signs?"

Lauren can barely see the road, her eyes filled with tears, "I'm going crazy, aren't I?"

Roxy pats her on the knee, "I wouldn't say that, in fact, I think maybe you've tapped into something very creative!"

Lauren is in disbelief, "How can that be? The voices are different! The stories are unique! How could I even come up with these stories about things I have never heard of and things I know nothing about?"

The enormity hits Lauren hard, "Why have you even let me drive? Aren't you afraid I may be too far gone to function normally?"

Roxy sighs, "Honestly, I never really thought about it! I haven't been exactly with it this trip either! What with these damn pills knocking me out every time!"

Lauren looks at Roxy and simultaneously they begin to laugh. Lauren shakes her head, "My, aren't we a fine pair for road travel!"

Roxy dabs her eyes trying not to ruin her make up as she laughs, "I know, right?"

Lauren pulls off at the exit and parks in front of a huge teepee, "What are we going to do?"

Roxy checks herself one last time in the mirror, "Let me ask you, how do you feel?"

Lauren tries to evaluate herself, "Tired, but that is natural from all of the driving!"

Roxy persists, "How do you feel when you are listening to the stories?"

Lauren thinks about it, "A little anxious. Curious about where the story will take me. I seem to function ok during the stories. I mean, I usually know where our exits are and I find myself checking the gas while listening."

Lauren sighs, "Honestly though, I can't see it being me coming up with these stories!"

Roxy shrugs her shoulders, "I don't know. What if it's your tooth fillings or something like that picking up a strange signal?"

Chills suddenly come over Lauren as she whispers, "Like in the apartment!"

Roxy shakes her head, "No! Not like the apartment!" She hesitates and then goes on, "If it is, at least this time you are handling it much better! You are eating and you are not consumed with it!"

Lauren is appreciative, "Thank you, Roxy. I'm sorry, here I was going to prove you wrong by recording these stories and you were the one who was right all along!"

Roxy looks down, "I know Jodi tried to warn you about me. I know I'm not the easiest to get along with but I do care about you! I would never put you in harm's way! I trust you! I must or we wouldn't be here!"

Lauren reaches over and gives her a big hug, "And I care about you! I promise that if I feel at all out of control I will tell you!"

Roxy breaks the hug happily, "I believe you! Anyway, we're close to stopping for the day!"

Lauren looks confused, "Are you serious? I thought we had a couple hours to go yet!"

Roxy blushes, "I forgot about the time changes! We have an extra three hours baby! Our hotel should be in the next town!"

Lauren is excited, "Get out of here! Oh, a hot bath sounds good right about now!"

Roxy gets out of the car, "This place looks cool! Maybe we can find some snacks to take to the hotel with us!"

Lauren, feeling better, nods, "Might not be a bad idea, especially if the hotel is in the middle of nowhere!"

Lauren and Roxy walk past the teepees, admiring them as they go. When they enter the gift shop it is hard for their eyes to adjust from coming out of the bright hot sun into a dark cool building! Lauren clumsily walks right into a man, "Oh! I'm sorry! I didn't see you! I'm still a little blind from the sun outside!"

The man smiles pleasantly, "We get that all the time! In fact, I stand by the door just so beautiful women will bump into me!"

Lauren blushes, "Oh please! That line must be used and abused around here!"

Another man steps around the counter sizing Roxy up, "Not as much as my brother and I would like, that's for sure! Anything we can help you ladies with?"

Roxy instantly enjoys the flirting game, "I'm sure we could think of something, right Lauren?"

The man Lauren bumped into smiles, "Lauren is it? I'm Kevin and that is my brother Ken."

Lauren can't resist teasing, "Let me guess, your mother is named Karen?"

Kevin laughs, "Yup, and our poor dad is Carl but with a C."

Lauren loves how easy it is to interact with Kevin, "Close enough, right?"

Kevin nods, "That it is! Come on in. I feel like my brother and I are intruding! Nothing worse than pushy salesmen!"

Ken and Roxy go one way as Kevin and Lauren go another. All of them liked how the chance pairings worked out. Kevin has to ask, "Moving or vacationing?"

Lauren smiles, "Moving to Long Beach in California."

Kevin is surprised, "I know right where it is! In fact, I grew up there!"

Lauren is shocked, "Really? How did you end up here?"

Kevin looks around, "My uncle passed away and willed this store to my brother and I. We visited here many summers."

Lauren replies pleasantly, "That's sweet. I'm sure your uncle would be proud that you are keeping it in the family!"

Kevin agrees, "Yea, it may not have been what either my brother or I had planned on doing with our lives, but we've been here for over two years and we love it!"

Lauren smiles, "Good for you!" She adds, "You were highly recommended to me by my friend Robby! He's a truck driver. We were able to meet up with him during his down time a couple stops back. He told us about the knife store and here for jewelry."

Kevin walks around the counter and pulls out a tray of jewelry, "Did you get anything at the knife store?"

Lauren looks down a little embarrassed, "Yea, I did. Roxy said I was tourist sucker punched!"

Kevin shakes his head, "Nonsense! I think a girl should be armed now a days! I bet Lin took real good care of you!"

Lauren is surprised, "Actually, she did! She picked out the perfect knife for me! I couldn't resist! I take it you know her?"

Kevin laughs, "Oh yea, we all live in the same town! It's the next exit."

Lauren has butterflies in her stomach, "Really? That's where we will be staying tonight! Roxy chose that town so we could see the solar eclipse in the canyon tomorrow."

Kevin looks a bit concerned, "The canyon? I don't know if it's such a good idea for you two to go there alone!"

Lauren offers, "Maybe you and your brother would like to go with us?"

Kevin thinks about it, "I suppose we could get our nephew to watch the shop for a couple hours."

Lauren is excited, "That would be nice!"

Roxy comes walking up with Ken. Ken wonders, "If you two have no plans tonight why don't you let us take you to dinner? Not that there are many choices. In fact, we'd probably bump into you again there considering it is the only restaurant in the town!"

Both Lauren and Roxy readily agree. Lauren speaks up, "Ok, but you have to give us a chance to clean up and rest. It's been a long trip!"

Kevin agrees, "Not a problem! We don't close for a couple hours anyway."

After hanging out for a while the girls finally leave. On the way to the hotel they talk excitedly about Kevin and Ken.

Once in the hotel Lauren lets Roxy have the bathroom first. Excited, Lauren plans out her outfit for the evening very carefully.

Lauren blushes as she thinks about Kevin. What was it about him? Her heart races just by thinking about him! She had never quite believed in love at first sight but damn! After meeting Kevin, she may become a believer! She tries to calm herself. She realizes that looks can be a big factor in a relationship but she can't help but feel like Kevin and she already have a deeper connection!

How crazy would it be for her to have just met her soul mate? Lauren has had her share of boyfriends, some even serious. However, none of them gave her the feeling she has with Kevin and she just met him! She chides herself, even if they were soul mates, how in the world could they make a long distance relationship work? Although, Kevin did say Long Beach was only five hours away. Close enough that he visited here on the weekends while he lived in Long Beach. Lauren lies on the bed thinking; maybe it wouldn't be that hard.

Fearing she will fall asleep and knowing how easy it is for Roxy to get lost in the bathroom, Lauren reaches over and sets the clock radio to go off in an hour. It's a good thing because within minutes she is fast asleep!

Skin Walker

Skin Walker

As DJ gets his gear ready, Eric has to ask again, "Are you sure you want to do this, man? I'm not saying you're not capable, I just don't know if it's worth the risk!"

DJ looks determined, "I'm telling you that cattle was everything to my grandfather! Justice needs to be done!"

Eric is not sure, "Why can't we hike in?"

DJ sighs, "I told you the damn thing keeps returning to the reservation and we're not allowed on the reservation! I can parachute in but it has to look like an accident. After I am on the reservation I can track and kill the predator before they can catch me!"

Eric looks nervously over at the plane, "Alan is going to be so pissed when you do this! He'll never let you jump again!"

DJ nods, "I know and I know he can get into a lot of trouble over this, which is why it is so important for you to do your part! You have to make it seem like an accident to everyone! You can never tell anyone of the real plan!"

Eric picks up his gear, "I'll never forgive myself if something happens to you!"

DJ smiles, "You know I'm the best jumper around! I am also the best tracker and shooter! What could possibly go wrong?"

As they walk towards the plane, Eric answers, "Gee, I don't know. How about the whole concept of tracking and killing an unknown monster?"

Butterflies start forming in DJ's belly at the thought of it, "Dude, we have heard about Skin Walkers all our lives! This attack on my grandfather's cattle is a classic scenario for them!"

Eric doesn't back down, "We have only heard one story that was told to us as kids to warn us of the dangers on the reservation! Other than that, we have yet to get one Native American to even speak about them to us first hand!"

DJ has to admit that is true, "That makes me even more convinced they exist! Every time we ask, you can clearly see fear wash over them. Then there's the YouTube video!"

Eric shakes his head, "You and that damn video! It's all you talk about! Sure, it's creepy and it's hard to explain but it is also the only so called evidence out there in all of the internet!"

DJ pats his helmet where his camera is attached, "Until now! Think about it! I might be able to kill two birds with one stone! Not only track down and kill the predator for revenge but get video proving that Skin Walkers do exist! This could make us famous!"

Eric laughs, "Or, it could simply be a coyote which you yourself said is what the tracks by the cattle looked like!"

DJ sighs, "Yea, but I also said the tracks just stopped and a strange set of bird tracks were there too! It looked almost as if the coyote changed into a bird and flew away!"

Eric rolls his eyes, "Wishful thinking on your part! You've always wanted there to be a Skin Walker, which is crazy when you think about it! Why in the world would you want something out there that powerful?"

DJ shrugs his shoulders, "It would explain a lot of the disappearances around here! The tribe can hide behind the fact that anyone that comes on the reservation is at their own risk but I think there is something more! What if the tribe is protecting the Skin Walker? Or, maybe they are being forced to protect it? Maybe they somehow worship this thing and have convinced themselves it can't be killed because it's a God or something to them?"

Eric sighs, "Or, maybe some things should remain unknown?"

DJ shakes his head, "In this day and age, nothing should be unknown! Not with our technology! Maybe the old ways are not the answer anymore. Maybe it's time to expose it for what it is, study it and learn more about it."

Eric is not so sure, "Aren't your plans to go in there and kill it? How much are you going to learn from something that is dead?"

DJ shrugs his shoulders, "If I do kill it and there are more of them, it'll prove to them the tables have turned! Man is no longer bound by fear and religion! They will come to fear us!"

DJ looks determined, "You can't tell me, if I either video tape it or even bring it back dead, this place won't be covered by people wanting to do research on it! This could be the thing this town needs to avoid eventually becoming a ghost town!"

Eric knows there is no changing DJ's mind, plus he can't help but get caught up in his enthusiasm, "Alright, let's get this over with! You jump and look around a couple hours, then get your butt over to our meeting spot before dark! My hands will be full with search and recovery for your dumb ass but Tia is going to meet you there!"

DJ feels guilty for involving Tia, "I really didn't mean for Tia to get involved! I know how protective you are."

Eric sighs, "Dude, she's had a crush on you since I first brought your scrawny ass home! I just wish you two would acknowledge the damn feelings and get on with it!"

DJ blushes, "I'm not the problem. You know all too well her desire to leave this place and never look back! Unfortunately, I am part of this place and I have no desire to leave."

Eric shrugs his shoulders, "Maybe you will be the only thing that will keep her here! You won't know unless you give it a try!"

DJ and Eric board the plane. DJ thinks about what Eric said. Unlike Eric, he appreciates Tia's desire to break free. He's seen that same desire in some of the horses he's broken. Sure, they can be tamed but it always breaks his heart when he catches the horse gazing longingly out at the valley where their freedom was. He doesn't have the heart to give Tia that same look.

The jump goes off perfectly. DJ makes it look like he mis-heard Eric and jumped before the intended mark. He does a couple of planned moves in the air to not only make him fall faster but to also fall closer to where he thinks he wants to land.

Finally, it is time to open the shoot. As DJ falls effortlessly he can't help but admire the beauty around him. When he jumps he feels small and unimportant in the huge sky. A quietness comes over him, almost a spiritual-ness, and in those few moments DJ feels completely alone in the world. Which is ok, for he is one with himself.

Fresh with a burst of adrenaline and a clear mind, DJ lands a bit rougher than he had planned. He quickly gathers up his gear and packs it away. As he does, a hawk flies overhead silently watching.

Finished packing, DJ gets his bearings. The animal that killed his grandfather's cattle had an unusual set of prints making it very easy to identify. He chose this area because it is not too far from the line separating the reservation and his grandparents' property.

One would think it would have been easier just to cross the reservation line from his grandparents' property to do the tracking! However, his grandfather recently crossed the reservation line for water his cattle desperately needed due to the drought and the tribe had forewarned him! The next time any animal or person was found on their reservation, they would report him!

Before, the water had always flowed freely from the reservation onto his grandfather's property, but with the drought the water stopped flowing and his grandfather had no choice but to take the cattle farther out. He simply opened the fence up and let the cattle find the water themselves knowing they would come home for the feed. He thought it would be no big deal because it was only temporary. When a decent rain comes the water would flow freely again and they would repair the fence. No harm, no foul, it was just water.

It worked and more than likely no one would have known, but unfortunately DJ's grandfather had to report the attack on his cattle. With the cattle going onto the reservation, it was thought the cattle attracted a predator that followed the cattle home and slaughtered them.

DJ and his grandfather thought differently. They felt it was punishment for the cattle going onto the reservation. DJ had not told Eric, but his grandfather and DJ were concerned the cattle would not be the only price that would have to be paid! We're not talking about the fines. Sure, the laws protecting the reservation were strict and the fines were steep. However, before those laws were made there was an original pact.

DJ's grandfather had raised him after his parents died in a car crash. His grandfather was very old school and taught him the old ways.

His grandparents' property had been in the family a long time, even before the reservation had been set up. There had been a pact between the family and the tribe long before any laws. The pact was simple enough; each would keep off the other's land. If they did not, there would be consequences! For the most part the pact had been respected.

Now and then curious boys throughout his family's generations wandered onto the reservation and disappeared. It was their own fault since they were not allowed on the reservation.

Back in the early 1900's another drought as bad as this one had happened. It too caused his ancestor's to allow their cattle onto the reservation. The cattle had not only been slaughtered, the family living on the property had been slaughtered as well! The attack on the family was done at a much later time. It was a vicious attack done outside and inside the house which made an animal attack highly improbable but there was no evidence to prove otherwise.

Relatives that took possession of the property after the horrible massacre mended the fence and handed down a tale of the Skin Walker to try and deter any wayward curious boys from going on the reservation. A tale of what little was told to them by the tribe which was the Skin Walker would rip off your skin and then walk around in it simply for fun!

His grandfather and he never knew whether the Skin Walker tale was just a made up boogey man to keep the peace or not. All of the people from the tribe they ever had interaction with, when asked about the Skin Walker, refused to talk about it.

DJ had always wanted to go onto the reservation and track down the Skin Walker but his grandfather had done well instilling great fear and respect in him. He could never bring himself to disobey his grandfather or the pact.

Now that the family may truly be at risk, DJ's grandfather and he realized maybe they needed to be proactive! Perhaps they needed to hunt down the predator who slaughtered their cattle before it comes after them! DJ jumped at the chance, he would finally be able to quench his own curiosity! Using his parachuting hobby seemed like the perfect excuse. No law or pact could fault him for an innocent accident! The plan seemed perfect.

DJ sets off towards his grandparents' property, since if he actually had a parachuting accident it would be the logical thing for him to do. Tia picking him up saves him time on making it back to his grandparents' house. Time he can use now to track.

DJ is surprised to discover the same tracks he found by the cattle are not too far from where he landed. A slight chill comes over him. It's almost as if the animal is taunting him, knows he is coming for it! He smiles as he turns his camera on, perfectly fine by him! This only proves it is not an animal but a creative, thinking monster!

He is prepared. He pats the revolver in his holster. The thing about vermin was you had to show them who was the true intellectual and there are consequences from our side of the pact as well! If not, suddenly you get lower on the food chain! Next time may not be just the livestock. Their very lives might be at stake and they were not going to live in fear! In addition, who is to say one day Skin Walkers will not leave the reservation of their own accord? Branch out and see how easy it would be to take over the world if they truly can take your skin, wear it and possibly even deceive others!

DJ tracks the footprints for several hours, becoming increasingly discouraged. This animal may be smarter than he first thought. Although, it stands to reason that if there is not that much known about them they must be good at hiding!

DJ reviews in his mind what he does know about them. A Skin Walker is a type of harmful witch who has the ability to turn into, possess, or even disguise themselves as an animal, usually with the intent to harm livestock or people. The tribe does not discuss them with outsiders simply because the outsiders may in fact be a Skin Walker in disguise!

He looks at his watch disgustedly. It is already time for him to start making his way over to where Tia is if he is going to make it before nightfall. All of this and it was for nothing!

As he begins to make his way back DJ picks up a new trail of tracks. The tracks seem to magically appear out of nowhere! In fact, right next to the unusual tracks is what looks like a set of bird tracks! This is the exact set of tracks that were near the slaughtered cattle! DJ should feel excited, but if anything, he feels cautious. Obviously, the Skin Walker is playing with him.

DJ gets his gun out of his holster. Better safe than sorry! Sure enough, ahead of him is a scraggly looking coyote staring at him. The shots from his gun violently wake up the mesa. Birds of all kind fly suddenly into the sky and small prey quickly take cover.

Not too far away Tia sits in the truck waiting for DJ to get there. She had already spoken to Eric. Apparently, this whole plan may actually work! The airplane pilot agreed with Eric in his statement that it was all a big misunderstanding. The only reason DJ jumped was because he thought Eric gave him the ok.

Eric is with the others doing a search and rescue. Of course, he is taking them farther away from where DJ actually landed. He is also assuring the native people if DJ did land on their land, it was no fault of his own and he would immediately make his way off the reservation!

Tia smiles as she looks in the rear view mirror while she freshens her lipstick. The idea of being alone with DJ always gets her going, even if he does have crazy notions about stupid myths such as the Skin Walkers. As she finishes, she notices a figure limping closer to her in the rear view mirror. Her heart begins to beat a little faster, it is after dark and being in the canyon alone can be terrifying! Her fear is instantly replaced with excitement when she realizes it must be DJ!

Tia hops out of the truck and runs up to him. "Hey stranger, nice to see you still in one piece!"

DJ looks her up and down, "Are you my ride?"

Tia blushes, "Maybe. Did you get the bad ole Skin Walker?"

DJ puts his gear in the back of the truck, "Come to find out it was nothing more than an old coyote!"

Tia is not surprised, "I figured as much. Did you at least get video of the kill?"

DJ looks confused, "Video? What are you talking about?"

Tia playfully taps his hat, "Did you forget you had your camera on?"

DJ takes his hat off and looks at the little camera, "A light is blinking."

Tia nods, "Looks like you have been taping all along. Do you think you got anything good on it?"

DJ looks perplexed, "Maybe. How am I going to check it?"

Tia is a bit surprised, "No different than any other time. You just plug it into your computer in your room, then for the next several hours you'll spend time editing, cropping and deleting what you don't like."

Tia is curious, "What happened out there? You seem a bit off."

DJ gets in the truck carefully, "Sorry, it's been a long day."

As Tia drives she notices DJ rubbing his leg, "Everything ok? I noticed you limping when you came up. Did you land hard today?"

DJ nods, "Yea, I did. Where are you taking me?"

Tia answers, "Back to your grandparents' house. That was the plan, right?"

DJ smiles, "Yes, that is perfect!"

Tia gets to DJ's grandparents' house quicker than she wanted, "Do you need help with your gear?"

DJ gets out of the truck as he answers, "Nah, I got it. You go on home."

Disappointed, Tia sighs, "Ok, feel better!"

After Tia leaves she calls Eric, "Hey Eric, I just left DJ over at his grandparents' house."

Eric sounds relieved, "Nice! Everyone is on board with it all being a misunderstanding. They won't think twice about DJ ending up at his grandparents. No one saw you, did they?"

Tia shakes her head, "I don't think so. We passed no one on the road and we came up the back side so none of the neighbors would have seen us. I'm taking the same way back just in case."

Eric hopes not, "Ok, I'd like to keep you out of this. After I tell everyone here he's safe I plan on going over there to talk to him."

Eric is curious, "Did he get what he wanted?"

Tia sighs, "Yes and no. It ended up being a normal old coyote, which he shot. However, you can tell something more is up. DJ was real distant on the way home and I think he may have landed hard. He was limping and rubbing his leg."

Eric thinks about it, "Stands to reason. If it was nothing more than a coyote then he is disappointed. This whole Skin Walker theory was a bust. Added to the fact that he may have had a crappy landing, would not have made for a great day! I wouldn't take it personally."

Tia agrees, "You're right! Call me in the morning and let me know what you find out."

Eric nods, "Will do."

Tia gets a call from Eric in the morning but it is nothing like she had planned on! He is calling from the police station! He proceeds to tell her what happened the night before.

Eric had gone over to DJ's grandparents. As he pulled into the driveway there were dead livestock scattered everywhere! Never had he seen such a gruesome sight! He took his shot gun with him to go in the house, fearing the worst. Whatever had been done outside paled in comparison to inside the house!

There didn't seem to be a spot where blood had not splattered. Chunks of skin, intestines, and what looks like brains is scattered throughout the house. Eric is not sure if the remains in the house are human but he has a sickening feeling they are! The house is deathly quiet. He calls 911 and tells them what he sees. As he does, he thinks he hears a noise upstairs.

Eric tells the operator to hold on, he is armed and he is going upstairs to check on a noise. The operator tells him to wait until the police get there but he ignores the advice. It could be someone that needs his help!

As Eric reaches the stairs he notices the remains of an arm, the hand still gripping a shotgun. An arm he can only assume belonged to DJ's grandfather!

Slowly, Eric goes upstairs with his gun aimed. Fear has been replaced with an urgent need to find his friend DJ! He quietly walks down a hallway towards a room where he hears noise.

Even upstairs the floor way is littered with body parts. A torn nightgown makes him realize this must be what is left of DJ's grandmother.

Over and over in his mind he pleads, "Please let DJ be ok, please!"

Eric steps carefully so he won't slip on all of the blood! He makes it to the room where the door is open and steps in. DJ is standing in front of the computer covered in blood! Eric can't tell if it is DJ's blood or not. Relieved, he cries out, "Dude, are you ok?"

DJ ignores him as he continues with what he was doing. Eric hesitantly takes a step forward, noticing a bullet wound in DJ's leg.

All kinds of questions come into Eric's mind. Did DJ come home to this mess? Why is DJ covered in blood? Did he get shot by someone else or did his grandfather shoot him?

Being in shock himself, Eric simply says, "Oh my God! DJ, you have been shot! Don't worry, I've already called 911!"

DJ finally gets the camera hooked up to the computer and plays the video he had taken earlier in the day.

Eric looks at the images on the TV as he whispers, "What is that?"

DJ is holding a small remote. As he deletes the images off the camera he replies, "Nothing to worry about now, am I right?"

Fear washes over Eric as he looks at his friend in disbelief, "No Sir, nothing to worry about!"

Before any more can be said, the police show up.

Eric leaves out the last part and simply tells Tia they took DJ to the hospital while they brought him to the station for questioning. As Eric explained everything to Tia on the phone, he sounded like he was still in shock.

Listening carefully the entire time, Tia is already in the truck and on her way over to the station. Not only does she need to be there for her brother but she has to make sure DJ is ok!

After being cleared, Tia and Eric go back to her truck in silence. Once in the truck Eric stresses for Tia not to get involved! How DJ got to his grandparents' house will not change the outcome! He explains that the investigation is leaning to where they think DJ is the one responsible for the mayhem!

Tia is now in shock herself, "How? How is this all possible?"

Eric shrugs his shoulders, "I don't know. Something must have happened to him when he was on the reservation. I'm just thankful he didn't snap while he was with you!"

Tia is still confused, "Or when you found him!"

Eric becomes quiet. Realizing he has been through enough, Tia drops him at his house without pressuring him to know more.

With her head whirling, Tia finds herself going back to the place she picked DJ up last night. She parks and sits there trying to make sense of it all.

Back in town, DJ gazes out his window, a hospital window to be exact, and as a precaution he is handcuffed to the bed. He is looking towards the same area Tia is looking at.

After a few moments Tia notices a large circle of buzzards hovering over something in the distance. Chills sweep over her. She tries to reason it is nothing more than the buzzards waiting for an animal to die; however, she finds herself compelled to find out more. She grabs the shotgun off the rack in the cab of the truck and decides to take a look.

She walks quite a ways from the truck, ever watchful of her surroundings. The buzzards see her coming and reluctantly perch nearby. Tia sees a crumpled figure lying on the ground and realizes it is a person.

Quickly, she shoots the gun up in the air to scare any predators and runs up to the poor person on the ground. At first glance, Tia is confused as she tries to figure out what is wrong with the person! They are naked and completely covered in blood. On closer inspection she realizes all of their skin had been removed! Tia cautiously whispers, "Are you ok?"

A voice harshly whispers out, "Tia, please help me!"

Tia is in shock, it is DJ! How is that possible? Tia squats down and whispers, "Oh my God! DJ, is that you? What happened?"

Barely able to talk, DJ answers, "The Skin Walker got me!" Just then a huge bird flies over, its cawing sounds like laughter.

Back in the hospital, the nurse had come in to check on DJ only to find an empty room, handcuffs on the bed, and an open window. The most disturbing thing was a pile of goo and skin left under the window.

To this day no one knows for sure what happened. How could DJ be where Tia found him, when he was handcuffed to a bed in the hospital? Unfortunately, when Tia found DJ his words to her were his last.

Only Eric knows the real truth. What he saw on that video would explain it all. DJ had run into a Skin Walker, even shot it.

On the video, DJ had shot the coyote in the leg and it had dropped. He had cautiously approached the injured animal only for it to transform right in front of the camera's eye.

The coyote became nothing more than a husk. What slowly rose out of the coyote was a form of blood, muscles and meat! Something that looks like all of us, animals included, on the inside.

Being in shock, DJ was not able to get another shot off before the monster came at him! The camera had shown only blurred images of what happened next.

Eric played those images over and over in his mind throughout his life. His take was that the monster had been injured by DJ's gun. When it rose up out of the coyote it somehow paralyzed DJ. It took its time taking his clothes off and then it slowly took his skin off as well.

Wearing DJ's skin and his clothes, still hurt from DJ's gunshot to the leg, it limped out and came across Tia. Unknowingly, Tia took it to the house where it finished its revenge. When Eric found it, it was removing any trace of its existence from the camera.

Eric had been warned not to tell what he had seen. Fearful of his own life as well as the ones around him, he respected its wishes.

One day Eric happened to have a conversation with one of the tribesmen about Skin Walkers. He was told that if a Skin Walker is injured it will take whatever host is around. Once it is healed it will shed that host's skin. That would explain the skin left at the hospital and the injury to DJ's leg was not from what happened at the house! It was from when DJ had shot the coyote on the reservation!

Eric had to ask the tribesman, "Why would your tribe protect such a thing on your reservation?"

Surprised, the tribesman had answered, "We don't protect it, we protect you! Our ancestors were able to contain it to a certain area by boundaries. Once those boundaries are broken, it can do as it pleases."

"We must keep the boundaries in place so it is not tempted. It is not aware of what is outside the boundaries or, for that matter, how powerful it is. Small children and adults unwelcome in its home are easy prey in its familiar surroundings. However, in an unknown environment it may be unsure. Like us, fear keeps it in check!"

Eric realized rules made by the tribe were for a reason. Rules that needed to be respected. Secrecy is not a thing to be taken lightly. What you don't know, may in the end be what protects you!

DJ's curiosity not only put him at risk but his grandparents as well. If the boundaries had been mended they would have been safe!

As modern technology encroaches on the unnatural, don't be surprised if the unnatural not only defends itself but, in turn, overcomes its own fear! Which in the end should make us all more fearful!

White Noise Stories Continued

Lauren feels someone nudging her awake. She slowly opens her eyes. Concerned, Roxy asks, "Are you ok?"

Lauren sits up confused, "Yea, I think so. Why?"

Roxy sighs as she motions to the clock radio, "When I came out of the bathroom the radio was on!"

Lauren looks at the time, "Yea, I set it to go off in an hour. I must have fallen asleep. I'm sorry, I didn't hear it go off!"

Roxy looks at her intently, "Did you have any unusual dreams?"

Lauren is surprised, "Yea, I did. How did you know?"

Roxy lowers her voice, "Because when I came into the room white noise was playing through the clock radio!"

Lauren is visibly upset, "What am I going to do, Roxy?"

Roxy tries to dismiss it, "You are going to forget all about this white noise crap! Anyway, when you think about it, what's the big deal? They are just stories and they are not hurting you!"

Before Lauren can reply, Roxy continues, "The bathroom is all yours! Go pamper yourself and make yourself gorgeous for your new man, Kevin!"

The mere mention of Kevin's name sends butterflies flooding into Lauren's stomach, "You're right! Tonight is going to be so much fun!"

Roxy teases, "Look at you, all hot and bothered! I don't think I have ever seen you this way!"

Lauren blushes and quickly gets out of bed, "Honestly, I don't think I have ever felt this way!"

Lauren heads to the bathroom, "I hope you didn't take all the hot water, I am so looking forward to a soapy bath!"

Ken and Kevin show up at the hotel on time and take the girls to the only restaurant in town. Conversation was easy and the dinner was over before they knew it.

None of them wanted the night to end so they discussed ideas to keep the night going. Ken and Roxy decide to go to a movie while Kevin and Lauren opt for some time alone exploring the town.

After a nice stroll through town, Kevin and Lauren find themselves on a bench overlooking the mesa. Kevin senses Lauren is troubled, "Is there something wrong?"

Lauren thinks back to the story she heard earlier, "The reservation is out there, correct?"

Kevin nods, "Yes, it is."

Lauren wonders, "Do you know much about them?"

Kevin shakes his head, "No, they keep to themselves. Even though my uncle had good relationships with them in acquiring their jewelry for the store, he knew very little about them."

Lauren lowers her voice, "Have you ever heard of a Skin Walker?"

Surprised, Kevin answers, "I have but I am surprised you have!"

Lauren anxiously asks, "What do you know about them?"

Kevin tries to remember, "Not much. Basically a story told to us as kids to keep us off the reservation! Something like a shape shifter who could steal your skin if you were not careful!"

Lauren persists, "Have you ever heard of an actual attack?"

Kevin gets quiet, "Ken has a friend, Eric. One time when he was drunk Eric swore his best friend was killed by one! He parachuted onto the reservation and they found him without his skin. Personally, I think it was nothing more than the buzzards. They can do crazy things to a body!"

Lauren knows she will sound crazy but feels she can be honest, "I heard a story about that and the jumper was called DJ, right?"

Kevin answers hesitantly, "Yes, where did you hear the story?"

Tears quickly fill Lauren's eyes, "Through white noise, believe it or not! Before I explain I have to say, I don't know why, but I feel like I have a real connection with you!"

Kevin reaches over and tenderly holds her hand, "I feel the same. Honestly, I've never had such a strong connection with someone so fast! Please, don't think this is a pick up line. I just can't explain it!"

Lauren looks deep into his eyes, "I don't because I've been trying to explain it to myself ever since I met you! I think, am I crazy enough to believe in love at first sight or maybe even finding your true soul mate?"

Kevin lifts his hand from hers and pushes her hair back, "Then I think maybe we both are crazy!"

Kevin leans in and kisses her. Lauren returns the kiss passionately. Breathless, they break away, both knowing instantly what they had suspected is true!

Kevin is unsure what to do next, "Now what?"

Lauren looks down, "Before we go further, I need to tell you what I am dealing with and then you can decide." Without letting him answer, Lauren proceeds to tell him all about what happened to her in her apartment. Then she tells him what she has heard through the radio during their road trip.

While talking, Lauren watches Kevin's reaction and is pleased to see she has his full attention and his face shows no signs of doubt! Finally, she finishes up telling him the latest story about the Skin Walker.

They sit there in silence for a moment as Kevin tries to figure out a way to convince her that he believes her completely, "I feel bad for you! I can't even imagine! However, I do appreciate you being honest with me! If anything, you telling me gives it even more credence!"

Lauren is surprised, "What do you mean?"

Kevin tries to explain, "How could you have come up with all these stories you have told me on your own? For that matter, why would you? What would you have to gain from it? That in itself proves it must be true!"

Lauren whispers, "You don't think I'm crazy? Or going crazy?"

Kevin thinks about it, "I can certainly see how it could make you go crazy! But no, I think it truly is happening to you! For some reason you have a connection with white noise. Souls are able to tell you their stories through the white noise!"

Hearing it put out there in the open, Lauren begins to feel hope, "Do you really believe in souls, ghosts or whatever I could be dealing with?"

After a moment to gather his thoughts, Kevin replies, "My mother used to say we are made up of energy. Her way of stopping me from being afraid of ghosts was to have me believe that perhaps a ghost was nothing more than a fingerprint of energy. A residue of the energy we had while alive, you might say."

Kevin ponders, "Perhaps that energy is picked up by white noise? Don't they use white noise sometimes to communicate with ghosts?"

Lauren becomes excited, "They do!"

Kevin offers, "Then maybe that is all this is! You are more sensitive than most people and can actually hear the stories that the rest of us can't!"

Kevin has to know, "Did the stories ever try to hurt you?"

Lauren tries to think back, "In the apartment things are still a haze, but I think for the most part, no. The only thing is, maybe if I wasn't listening they would try to make sure I did. Or, at least my subconscious may have taken over and tried to make sure I was listening!"

Suddenly Lauren remembers and chills come over her, "Although, the last story in the apartment I did get too involved! It was like the soul tried to have me take their place! That was when I became terrified and thought there were masked demons that live among us!"

Lauren tries to explain, "Demons in the form of family, friends and strangers. All trying to do their part in weakening our soul so it can be taken!"

Kevin remembers the Mermac Caverns story she had told him, "Then the souls would be placed in others waiting for a soul?"

Lauren looks at him wide eyed in disbelief, "That can't be real, can it?"

Kevin looks out over at the mesa and stares up at the immense sky full of stars, "Who am I to say? Our universe is only a small piece of the puzzle! Perhaps, there are other universes or parallel universes desiring something we have? Something we know nothing about and take for granted?"

Kevin notices Lauren is becoming chilled from the desert night, "Would you like to go back to my place? It'll be warmer there and we can speculate about our existence in comfort."

Lauren cuddles up, "I would like that, but honestly, I think I'm done theorizing! I think getting to know one another sounds like a better idea!"

Kevin smiles, "Now we're talking!"

Trail Of Terror

Trail of Terror

Dan and Alan sit at the bar trying to map out their next hike. "I'm telling you dude, this is the place we need to see!" He points to the location on the map, "Between Chuar and Temple Buttes."

Alan is surprised, "You seriously want to go to 'Crash Canyon'?"

The area is nicknamed 'Crash Canyon' due to two airplanes crashing into one another back in 1956, killing 128 people.

Dan answers, "Not Crash Canyon, what's located next to it!"

Alan takes a swig of his beer, "And what is next to Crash Canyon?"

Dan explains, "A sacred Hopi site called Sipapu, a gateway to the underworld. Supposedly it's where the Hopi emerged and where the dead can come back."

Alan rolls his eyes, "And why do we need to see a gateway to the underworld?"

Dan smiles, "Because every vacation we go on, we always have to do a local horror tour!"

Alan sighs, "And each and every one of them has been lame! C'mon dude, we always get burned on stuff like this, you know how cheesy it gets. Take Salem for God's sake! I thought that would have been cool but we quickly realized how lame it was!"

Dan has to agree, "You're right, it was awful. I'll give you that but this is going to be different!"

Alan is curious, "How?"

Dan replies, "There is no tour!"

Alan is confused, "Why is there no tour?"

Dan shrugs his shoulders, "Because no one will do one! I called all over and they all refused!"

Alan is becoming intrigued, "Why, is it a dangerous trail?"

Dan sighs, "All I can gather on the internet is the locals refuse due to the gateway crap. Apparently several hikers through the years have gone missing while going on the trail. Their bodies were never found."

Alan wonders, "Maybe this trail is out of our league? We are novice hikers at best!"

Dan is not concerned, "The terrain doesn't seem to be the problem. The speculation is that the hikers simply got lost. You know with me that is never an issue!"

Alan has to admit, "You're right, I have never known you to get lost. It's uncanny, must be all those years of being a Boy Scout nerd."

Dan chuckles, "Hey! Don't be a hater! The scout master said it was a natural talent! I was a human compass! They used to make a game of trying to get me lost and I never did!"

Alan pats his friend on the back, "Then I am with the right hiking buddy, just don't lose me! I get lost in a one stalk corn maze!"

An older man sitting down from them at the bar has been listening to their conversation. He waits until the bartender goes in the back before he speaks up, "I know of the place you two speak of and I can get you there! But, I want no one knowing I helped you! People around here get a little bent out of shape when I help hikers and I have to live here!"

Dan notices no one else is around to hear them but lowers his voice anyway, "We're interested. What do you suggest?"

The older man replies, "Finish up your conversation and drinks. Fifteen minutes after you leave I'll meet up with you in the parking lot across the street."

Dan nods but does not answer him when he sees the bartender come back. Instead, he turns to Alan and points to the map, "I think we can do this ourselves. It looks easy enough, we just need to stay on the trail. We'll leave first thing in the morning and by nightfall we should be close enough to camp."

The bartender comes over shaking his head, "Forgive me for listening in on you two but in good conscience I have to try and warn you. It's not a good place to go and there are so many other beautiful trails around. Try one of them instead."

Dan is now even more intrigued, "We've already done a couple of the other trails and yes, they were beautiful. This time we're not so much into the nature scene as we are into the historical folklore!"

Alan has to agree, "Yea, around here whether it's an easy trail or a winding difficult trail, it all seems to end up looking like the same scenery."

The bartender smiles, "Who is to say this trail will be any different?"

Dan turns the table on him, "You tell us! Why is it so different than the other trails?"

The bartender sighs, "The wildlife seems to be more intense, more aggressive. There are more snakes, scorpions, and coyotes, among other things."

Dan has to know, "The 'other things'… do you believe in them?"

The bartender hesitates before he answers, "I believe some things should be left alone! Respect for the dead is not only morally correct it is for our own safety!"

Alan is curious, "What is your take on the ones who have survived and come back to tell the tale? Are those not the ones who are brave and can give us all more insight on the unknown?"

Dan becomes excited, "Exactly! If you have non-believers go into a situation that makes them believers, does that not help the cause? Their story adds to your conviction!"

The bartender sadly shakes his head, "Their stupidity only adds to the death toll around here! Besides, people who do come back always have conflicting stories. In the end, no one believes any of them!"

Dan laughs aloud, "Nice one! Ok, we get the doom and gloom and can appreciate it. Here's our money for tonight's tab and," Dan reaches in his pocket and pulls out a fifty dollar bill, "it will also cover our next tab two nights from tonight. When we come back we'll have our own stories! I guarantee Alan and I will have the same story and it will be believable!"

The bartender reluctantly takes the money and gives them one last piece of advice, "Think of it as the Bermuda Triangle out there. It is easy to get turned around so make sure you take note of your landmarks!"

Alan stands up with Dan as they get ready to leave, "Not a problem, I have the human compass here! See you day after tomorrow!"

The bartender resignedly watches them leave. The only people he'll be seeing will be the police! Damn kids, oh how he hates filling out those incessant police reports!

In the parking lot across the street, fifteen minutes pass as Alan and Dan patiently wait for the old man in the bar to show up. Getting cold, Alan wonders, "You think this guy is going to show up? And if he does, do you think he'll mug us?"

Dan teases, "Nah, not here. Bet he'll wait until we're alone with him on the trail!"

Alan becomes concerned, "Dude! That's not funny, it could happen! Especially since no one knows he's meeting with us!"

Just then the older man seems to appear out of nowhere. Once he is standing in front of them he nods, "My name is Jerry. Sorry for all the cloak and dagger but I'm sure it adds to your adventure!"

Dan answers, "I'm Dan and this here is Alan. Actually, I've been thinking how you and that bartender have a nice set up! You whisper to us while he's gone, then he comes back spouting all sorts of doom and gloom. Let's cut to the chase. We were already sold on going on the trail so there's no sense in having all the theatrics."

Jerry laughs, "You two think you have it all figured out."

Alan nods, "We've been going on a trip every year together for ten years. We've seen and survived it all."

Dan agrees, "We're not naïve. Let's just say if we get into an uncomfortable situation we're confident we can get out of it!"

Jerry sighs, "Hate to burst your bubble but ole Nate, the bartender, was being sincere back at the bar. Surprises me he still even tries after all this time."

Dan rolls his eyes, "And how many are we talking about that have gone missing?"

Jerry looks out towards the canyon, "No one really knows. Not all of them advertise their idea of going on the trail like you two!"

Alan looks concerned, "Then how do you know the missing ended up on this trail?"

Jerry shrugs his shoulders, "Speculation, I suppose. Anyway, I can get you close enough to the gateway for you to find it."

Dan is curious, "Why not all the way?"

Jerry hesitates, "It's something you should experience on your own."

Alan needs to know, "How much?"

Jerry smiles, "No charge."

Dan is suspicious, "Why not?"

Jerry answers honestly, "Unlike the others, I'm proud of the gateway. The more people see it the more people will believe. Believing in something is pretty uncommon now a days."

Dan and Alan both begin to get excited, "There's really something unexplained out there?"

Jerry nods, "Unexplained for you two right now, but hopefully afterwards you will have your answers."

Jerry feels he has to warn them, "Nate was right about the wildlife though, for some reason it is fiercer on this trail than any others! I know what to look out for, know what snakes to be cautious of, and how to avoid the coyotes."

Dan teases, "And what about 'the other' that Nate mentioned?"

Jerry gets serious, "I'll let you deal with them! I've already had my interaction!"

Dan wants to know, "What happened?"

Jerry shakes his head, "Be time enough for all of that during the hike tomorrow. We have a deal?"

Before answering Alan asks, "No offense, but are you up for hiking?"

Jerry sighs, "Boy, I can still walk circles around you when it comes to that canyon. Lived here all my life. The thing you need to worry about is, will you be able to keep up with me?"

Dan interrupts, "Ok, then it's settled. We're going! What time and where?"

Jerry instructs them where to meet him in the morning and then leaves. Dan and Alan quickly go to a local store to get the supplies they will need. Back in the hotel they gather up all their gear.

After their incident in a hostel in Europe, both Alan and Dan are very careful tourists. Both are packing guns and have been trained in self-defense. Never again would they be victims.

At the crack of dawn the three of them head out. None of them are in the mood to talk this early in the morning. After getting pretty far into the trail they stop for lunch. The old man has hardly any supplies on him. Surprised, Alan and Dan offer to share their lunch with him. Jerry politely refuses, "When I go out on this trail it's sort of a sabbatical for me. I fast so I can be more aware."

Not wanting to overstep his boundaries but curious to know, Dan asks, "Have you always lived here?"

Jerry shields his eyes from the harsh sun as he answers, "No, after school I went in the army. Wasn't until I got out that I came back."

Alan offers, "Being a veteran is not too glamorous these days."

Jerry agrees, "True, but it's not why I went in." He looks around as he continues, "I believe in our country. Nowhere in the world do they have the freedom we have. We're damn lucky! You don't join the services for fame or glory. You join, not only to keep your own freedom, but help others keep theirs!"

Dan is impressed, "That is very noble. Is that one of the reasons you help tourists look for the gateway?"

Jerry nods, "It is. And sure the locals believe they are protecting you, but really they are protecting their secret."

Alan is a little surprised, "Secret? Are you saying the locals have experienced the gateway?"

Jerry smiles, "Experience it? Hell, it's a rite of passage! Sons and daughters, after graduation they all come up to camp on the trail."

Dan is curious, "Aren't they worried they'll get lost too?"

Jerry shakes his head, "Nah, everyone that goes out has already been taught how to read the landmarks."

Alan nods, "Ole Nate told us to make sure we read the landmarks."

Jerry looks out at the canyon as a hawk flies in the air, "He meant differently than you think. Landmarks, you would think, would be a certain rock or cliff that doesn't move."

Dan is confused, "What other landmarks are there?"

Jerry looks directly up at the hawk, "The way the hawk tilts his wing. The way a lizard casts its shadow. Does the coyote walk forward or back up?"

Dan shakes his head, "You can't be serious! I'll take moss growing a certain way on a rock or the sun's shadow, but the behavior of animals as landmarks? That's baloney!"

Jerry understands, "On a normal trail I'd agree with you, but this trail is a lot like the Bermuda Triangle. I've seen whole mesas shift and change! It's why it is so easy to get lost. It's also why bodies are never found. Some are under the mesas themselves!"

Alan is not buying into it, "Nice ghost story, without the ghosts!"

Dan is anxious to know, "What about the ghosts? Are they real?"

Jerry looks disgusted, "If you don't believe me about the landmarks, why would you believe me about the ghosts?"

Jerry gets up and looks forward, "We best be going. The next bend will start the beginning of the trail and some days it's worse than others! Let's hope for a good day."

Dan and Alan gather their things and start to follow Jerry but Dan wants to keep talking, "Did the locals learn their ways from the Native Americans?"

Jerry smiles, "No, they tend to keep to themselves. I suppose we learned from our own mistakes."

As they turn the bend, Jerry follows a smaller trail that goes to the left. Dan looks around seeking clues to keep his bearings. Not even a half mile down the trail a coiled snake lies in their path.

Jerry stops and thumps his walking stick several times on the ground. The snake slowly slithers off. Alan teases, "What? No magic words too?"

Jerry chuckles, "Not yet, and usually it's not magic words but prayers to God."

Dan does not look impressed, "I would have done the same thing. The vibration caused the snake to leave."

Jerry smiles, "Got ourselves a live Boy Scout with us today, do we?"

Dan blushes, "Hey, say what you want but I learned a lot of things that will help save me in the wild!"

Jerry grumbles, "That's what I thought when I joined the army! They taught me how to shoot a gun, surely I could survive being a soldier. But instincts are not taught, either you have them or you don't! No matter what, always trust your instinct!"

Dan agrees, "You're right. There were times when all logic pointed to something else but sticking to my instinct is what saved me."

Alan speaks up, "Saved 'us'! We were on a back packing excursion in Europe, right out of college. Come to find out we were staying in a hostel where tourists were known to go missing."

Dan adds, "Of course at the time we didn't know it."

Alan's hands begin to sweat from just thinking about it. "They kidnapped us and took us to a remote place where we saw others being tortured."

Jerry, intrigued, stops and turns to ask, "How did you get away?"

Alan looks gratefully over at Dan, "His instincts helped us! They had a pretty girl that looked sweet and innocent who offered to be our torturer. Later we found out she was far more sadistic than any of the male torturers!"

Dan nods, "At the time it felt like the logical thing to pick the girl. But my instinct told me to request the largest, nastiest looking one to take us both. The kidnappers agreed."

Alan sighs, "I was terrified, too afraid to even speak! However, I trusted Dan. Trusted him with my life actually. How many can say that?"

Alan thinks back, "This beast of a man shoves us into this room filled with bloody torture devices. In the corner were chunks of human remains!"

Jerry can't believe the horror these poor kids must have gone through, "I would have never thought this of you two!"

Dan shrugs, "It's not something we're proud of. It was our stupidity and ignorance that put us in that situation."

Alan admits, "Although, surviving that ordeal did teach us to be more prepared and not so naive."

Jerry has to wonder, "And yet, here you are with a stranger out on a trail in the middle of nowhere."

Dan laughs, "Yea, you would think we would be more cautious. However, the ordeal also gave us a thirst we can't seem to quench."

Alan agrees, "We never felt more alive than during that vacation. Every vacation since then has been lame. I think we've been searching to find ourselves, if that makes sense?"

Jerry can't help but smile at the irony. If they only knew. Curious, Jerry asks, "How did you survive?"

Chills come back over Alan as he thinks about it, "The beast of a man said if we screamed and acted like we were being tortured he would get us out."

Dan grimaces as he finishes the story, "The screaming was easy; however, covering ourselves with the chunks of flesh and blood from other victims was way more difficult! He then wheeled us out and dumped us in a pit of decomposing bodies."

Alan proudly pats Dan on the back, "Even though we had no clue where we were, Dan got us back to civilization! We even waited to get back into the main city before we contacted our embassy and told them everything."

Dan smiles, "Again my instinct kicked in. I did not trust the local police!"

Jerry smiles, "Smart boy!"

Dan nods, "They tracked down the location and was able to save three hostages that were still there. The beast of a man provided evidence and was protected. Come to find out he was nothing more than someone who had been kidnapped and tortured himself."

Alan adds, "They thought they had broken him but somehow he held on to his humanity."

Jerry turns to continue on the path, shaking his head, "Never can assume anything about strangers!"

Dan feels that maybe now Jerry will share his story, "What about you and your story? It's only fair we hear it now."

Jerry agrees, "Fair enough. Like I said, I've only gone to the gateway once. I was with fellow graduates looking for the meaning of life."

Before he can continue a large group of scorpions block the path. The three men stand in disbelief as the scorpions suddenly circle them. Dan blurts out, "What the hell? Scorpions are nocturnal!"

Alan agrees, shaking in disbelief, "These are far larger than they supposed to be! They look like freaking lobsters, for God sake!"

Jerry adds calmly, "Did you know that scorpions are perceived as an embodiment of evil and yet a protective force that counters evil?"

Dan shakes his head, "All I know is, this isn't normal! They shouldn't be this size! And they definitely shouldn't be working together to attack us! Hell, they shouldn't even be here in the middle of the day!"

Jerry casually pulls a mirror out of his pocket, "Be thankful it is daylight! Can you imagine coming up against these things at night?" He positions the mirror to catch the bright sun, reflecting the sun's rays down onto different scorpions. Suddenly the scorpions turn on each other, viciously attacking.

Not bothering to stay and watch, the three men carefully step over the fighting scorpions. No one says a word until they are further down the path. A little ways after the next bend Dan finally speaks up. "Ok, I understand that scorpions are sensitive to light, thus the harsh rays of sunlight would hurt their eyes! However, why did they attack each other?"

Alan, still trembling, can't help but wonder, "And why did you select only certain scorpions to focus the beam on?"

Jerry sighs, "Because it is as I said, scorpions can be evil but also be a protective force that counters evil. Scorpions don't travel in large packs. They themselves were not even aware of the evil among them; they were just in a group. Once the light was shone on them, they could see the evil."

Alan can't resist chuckling, "A bit cryptic. Almost sounds like religion, don't you think?"

Dan is still in shock, "They would have attacked us, even though it is against their nature!"

Jerry looks around at the vast canyon, "You will find this path is filled with such dangers! Two or even more dimensions fighting over one area."

Alan nervously looks around, "What contains it to this particular area? If we can walk in, why can't they walk out?"

Jerry answers, "Because walking out is the hardest thing to do!"

Dan thinks it is time for Jerry to tell them what they are really in for, "Ok, let's cut the bullshit. Jerry, what happened to you when you were here and will it happen to us?"

Jerry nods, "Yes, it always happens." He stops and looks at the two anxious men, "I would love to give you the option of going back now. Just leave and never think about this place again. But I can't, we've already come too far!"

Jerry explains, "We walked through the first doorway when we passed the snake. The scorpions were simply another turn in the path. Unfortunately, we can't go back the way we came because the journey is not over."

Dan does not understand, "There is a different path that takes us home?"

Jerry sighs, "Yes, different but the same. We have to finish this journey before we can get to the journey of coming back."

Alan shakes his head in disbelief, "Dan, I'm really tired of this mystic crap! Let's just leave now. I'm getting a really bad vibe and I just don't think it's worth the risk!"

Dan agrees, "I think you are right! Sorry Jerry, but we're going back, with or without you!"

Jerry smiles, "Ok, go ahead and try."

Dan and Alan take the challenge, turn and start back the way they came. Carefully following the path, they get to the last bend only to find a wall of rock directly in their path! They look at each other in disbelief as they look straight up at a mesa looming over them! Alan cries out, "How can this be?"

Dan is shocked, "This can't be here!"

Jerry clears his throat behind them, "You two should be careful. As I said, hikers have been known to be swallowed up by mesas around here!"

Dan and Alan quickly step back and get next to Jerry. Jerry turns and continues on the path in front of them. "We need to make up some time to get to the safe zone for camping tonight."

A little relieved, Dan says, "At least there is a safe zone for camping! That is good to know!"

Alan asks nervously, "Wait! Jerry, at the beginning you told us you would only take us close to the gateway! You're not going to leave us are you? How will we be able to get back? I mean, I give Dan a lot of credit for knowing directions, but not when freaking mesas appear out of nowhere!"

Dan agrees, "He's right, man. You can't leave us out here! Screw the gateway, just take us home!"

Jerry sighs, "You two don't get it, do you? You have to see the gateway before you can go back home!"

Dan argues, "Then how will you get back home?"

Jerry mumbles, "Once seen, you can't un see it."

The three men walk in silence. Dan and Alan are filled with adrenaline; not sure what to expect next but anxiously aware.

Suddenly Dan stops, "Listen! Do you hear that?"

Alan strains to hear, "Hissing! Oh my God, hissing all around us!" He looks frantically around, "But where?"

Jerry looks cautiously around and finally is able to focus his eyes to see through the illusion, "Snakes are all around us, they are the color of the rocks!"

Dan finally sees what Jerry sees, "Oh my God! He's right! There's so many of them!"

Alan is the last to see them, but when he does it's like all the rocks beside them are in motion! Alan pleads with Jerry, "Please tell me you have some sort of cool trick to get rid of these things!"

Jerry looks concerned, "I do, but it may not be enough! Get close to me and hopefully we can get through this!"

Jerry takes a canteen that is tied to his waist and starts sprinkling the contents in front of him. To Dan's surprise it is sulfur. "That's right! Sulfur will repel them. Now that's what you call being prepared!"

Alan is not so sure since he is the last one in their little line and there is no sulfur behind him. The snakes seem to realize he may be their only prey and seem to be gathering towards him!

Jerry looks back at Alan and sternly yells out, "Alan, don't look in their eyes! Soon you will be stepping on some of the sulfur I have on the trail. Keep walking slowly with your eyes focused forward!"

Easy for him to say, the path is clear in front of Jerry and Dan. Behind Alan there no longer is a path! Only a mass movement of snakes moving towards him! How in the world is a sprinkling of sulfur going to keep all of them at bay?

Alan finds himself stopped in the path, no longer following Dan and Jerry. The sound and movement of the snakes seemed to have hypnotized him into a paralyzed state! So much so, he actually finds himself moving towards the snakes and away from the sulfur!

Jerry yells to Dan, "You need to break the hypnosis your friend is in! Shock him back into reality! Say something that will kick him into action!"

Dan thinks back and quickly yells at Alan, "Alan! If you don't move those chunks of meat all over you is what is going to be left of you! Now move, damn it!"

A flashback comes over Alan as he remembers being in the pit with all those dead bodies. He had frozen up there too. Shock had consumed him and he was ready to give up, but Dan had not let him. Dan's yell shocked him with the very fear Alan was afraid of and it worked!

Alan shakes his head a little and looks over at Dan and Jerry only a few feet away in what seems to be a safe zone. Unfortunately, the snakes had advanced enough that they were now in front of Alan as well as behind! Taking a big breath he musters up all of his strength and jumps over the snakes that are blocking his path! In midair several strike at him but fortunately his pants and boots block them.

Alan lands safely and is about to run ahead when Dan quickly grabs him. "Hold up, we're safe here for now. For some reason the snakes are not crossing that threshold. We need to gather our strength and wits before we run off!"

Alan looks around the little area they are in and has to ask, "Another safe zone? What are these exactly?"

Jerry shrugs his shoulders, "I suppose remnants of our world. Dimension plateaus or whatever the hell you want to call them."

Dan looks over at Alan, concerned, "Hey buddy, you doing ok?"

Alan's eyes are wide with fright as they dart back and forth, ever watchful of the swarming snakes behind them. "As well as can be expected I suppose!"

Dan slaps him on the back confidently, "That's my man! We can do this! Jerry definitely seems to know what he is doing! We just need to pay careful attention and before you know it, this will all be over!"

Jerry looks a bit nervous himself, "Nice that you have so much confidence in me but, as I mentioned before, some days are better than others! Unfortunately, this is not a good day! I have never seen them in such numbers, the scorpions or the snakes. It makes me worry about what is to come!"

Alan is tired of the mystery, "What is to come, Jerry? Don't you think we should be a little bit more prepared than before? It may make it easier on all of us."

Jerry agrees, "You're right. Next will be the hawks and then the coyotes. After that we'll camp. During the night you will hear and see some crazy shit! At first morning light you will walk a little further down the trail and see the gate. Then you will come back to camp and we will make our way towards home."

Alan laughs, a little too hysterically for Dan's liking, "Oh, is that all? Geez, easy peasey! Right, Danny boy?"

Knowing no other way, Dan nods, "Ok, now that we know what to expect let's get on with it!"

Jerry agrees, "It probably is best to go when our adrenaline is high! Unfortunately, there are no cute little tricks for the next turns in the path. Just luck of the draw on who will get hurt and who won't."

Before Alan can ask him what he means by that Jerry is up and walking at a fast pace. Dan and Alan have a hard time keeping up with the old man but they are not about to lose sight of him!

The next attack is by the hawks. Dan knows it is very rare for hawks to attack humans. Hawks will only attack if threatened or during mating season. However, Dan had never heard of what they had to deal with! Hawk after hawk dive bombed them as they tried to make it further down the trail. At one point a hawk took a big chunk out of Dan's neck. He screamed in agony, held his hand over the wound, and kept running with the other two!

Finally they make it to another safe zone. Alan is quick to get the supplies out they need to dress Dan's wounds. The hawk had come close to Dan's jugular, too close!

Exhausted and not sure how they will make it past the coyotes ahead, they all press on. A vicious looking pack of coyotes is waiting for them!

This time though, Alan and Dan are the ones prepared! Guns already drawn, they fire their way through the pack. None of the bullets seemed to do any damage but it is enough of a distraction to get them through unscathed.

Relieved to see Jerry setting up camp, Dan and Alan have barely enough strength to do the same. Once a fire is made, the three of them begin to relax; enjoying the heat and safety of the fire along with the bounty of the food they had brought. After eating, the men find themselves staring into the fire. Dan needs to know, "What is in store for us next, Jerry?"

Jerry looks around and lowers his voice, "You will see soon enough."

Just then a slight breeze picks up and both Dan and Alan hear people talking. Too terrified to move, Alan whispers, "Do you hear them?"

Dan nods as he slowly pulls out his gun, "I don't think I have any more ammo, do you?"

Alan shakes his head in fear, "No, I ran out too!"

Jerry shakes his head, "No weapons needed for what you're about to see. As with the snakes, make no eye contact. Let them be and they'll be on their way."

Shadowy people walk right by their camp. Although dark around the campsite, the dancing flames of their fire reveals glimpses of the people when they pass by the light. The shadows cast them as normal people but the light of the fire tells a different story. Horrific images of how each one died.

Most were burned beyond recognition. Others had missing limbs, some were mere torsos! While in the light, their missing parts were no longer shadows that gave an illusion of normalcy. The light casted them for what they really were, bloody and gory! Even Hollywood would have a hard time portraying the true horror that was being displayed as a death parade in front of Alan and Dan!

Careful not to look any of them in the eye, Alan and Dan could not look away. Obviously, some of the victims were from the two airplanes that crashed back in 1956. Others were more modern day. Hikers it seemed. Alan cringes as he sees one that had snakes still slithering around him constantly striking at the poor man's body. That could have easily been him!

The death parade continues but seems to take on an even older era of demise. All the way from the Old West to Native Americans. Each one's cause of death worn like a costume.

The death parade goes on throughout the night. Time passes quickly and Alan and Dan are shocked to see that the morning light is about to break. Just as Dan is about to ask Jerry when they should leave to see the gateway, the answer presents itself in a most unusual way.

At the end of the long parade, Dan and Alan see themselves! Without being told, they quickly get up and follow their shadowy selves. Jerry simply sits by the fire and waits.

They follow the death parade up the path onto a strange mesa. A halo glows dimly on top as the parade disappears into it. Dan and Alan run after their shadowy selves!

Once they are on top of the mesa they see the halo is actually the gateway! Never had they seen something so beautiful and yet so terrifying!

Before they reach the gateway their shadowy selves turn to them as if they are ready to talk. Alan and Dan approach them timidly. When they are close enough, their shadowy selves reach out and touch them. Once they are touched, each one is trapped in a vacuum with their shadowy selves. A private interaction that can only be seen by themselves.

Dan is the first one to come back to the fire where Jerry is waiting. Anxiously he asks, "Is Alan here?"

Jerry shakes his head, "No, but he will be, don't worry. Did you find what you were looking for?"

Dan nods, "I did! When you see death it puts life in a different perspective!"

Jerry smiles, "That it does, and look, there is Alan!"

Dan is immediately relieved and runs over to Alan, "We did it!"

Alan still looks concerned, "We still need to make it back!"

Jerry starts gathering his things, "Don't worry, I'll get you back. The key is to concentrate on going right. Everything from this dimension is left, as in left behind. They can never get out because they always turn left."

Sure enough, Jerry leads them through several split trails, always turning to the right. In Dan's logical mind it makes no sense since eventually would they not go in a circle? However, instinct tells him Jerry is right and that is all he needs to know! Fortunately, instinct wins and by the end of the day Dan and Alan find themselves back in town!

You would think Alan and Dan would simply want to go back to the safety of the hotel after their horrific ordeal! On the contrary, it was quite the opposite! The two of them wanted to celebrate! Back to the bar they went.

Nate, the bartender, is surprised to see them. "Look at what the cat dragged in! You two did make it, good for you!" He places two glasses of beer in front of them to celebrate.

Dan has to be honest, "If it hadn't of been for Jerry, I'm afraid we would not be here to tell the tale!"

Nate looks confused, "Jerry?"

Dan looks around for Jerry, "Yea, Jerry. He was our tour guide!" He looks over at Alan, "Tell him about Jerry, the old veteran who was our tour guide."

Before Alan can answer, Nate looks at Dan in disbelief, "You wouldn't be talking about Jerry Peterson, would you?"

Dan thinks about it, "He never gave us his last name but sure, I guess that was him."

Nate shakes his head, "Nah, it couldn't have been! Ole Jerry died a few years back while taking some hikers up the same trail!"

Dan looks at him in disbelief, then looks over at Alan for back up, "Tell him, Alan."

Alan shrugs his shoulders as he picks up his beer, "Not sure what you're talking about it. We conquered that path all on our own!"

Full terror sweeps over Dan, not because he thought a dead man was their tour guide and could possibly be going mad, but because Alan picked up his beer with his left hand! Alan is right handed! The realization hits poor Dan that this Alan sitting beside him is not the same Alan!

What if Jerry had not been a guide for them after all? What if Jerry had been a guide for what was left on the mesa instead? Only taking Dan and Alan up there so he could bring down a replacement?

Dan suddenly remembers what the bartender had said about anyone that made it back. Their stories were always conflicting, therefore making it hard for anyone to believe them! No one is ever going to believe Dan's story!

Dan tries to make sense of it all. Frustrated, he tries to remember the interaction with his own shadowy self. He doesn't remember much, other than feeling a great sense of accomplishment. Dan no longer had to look for an answer because he had the answer. Life may be hard but it was worth living and that is all that matters!

Had Alan thought differently? Or was it even simpler than that? Perhaps Alan had simply gotten lost. Without Dan by his side, maybe Alan had lost his way. A great sense of sadness washes over Dan. Alan had told Dan he had no sense of direction!

When one finally confronts oneself, how hard is it to know what direction to go? Perhaps if that direction is too hard it is easier to let someone else do the journey!

White Noise Stories Continued

Kevin rolls over cursing, "Damn! I am so sorry! I forgot to turn my alarm off!"

He looks over at Lauren sleeping in his bed and is surprised the alarm didn't wake her! Clumsily, he tries to turn it off by reaching over her.

Strange, usually his normal radio station plays when the alarm goes off; however, for some reason today there is nothing but white noise! Realizing what that means, Kevin quickly nudges Lauren to wake her up. "Lauren, are you ok?"

Not knowing where she is, Lauren wakes up with a start. Seeing Kevin beside her, she instantly blushes, "Yea, I'm fine!"

Curious, Kevin asks, "Did you have any strange dreams?"

Lauren nods, "I did, why?"

Kevin sighs, "Because when the alarm went off, white noise came through instead of music. But I don't see how it could have been enough time for you to dream anything from it!"

Lauren disagrees, "You would be surprised! Time seems to be irrelevant!"

Lauren proceeds to tell him about the dream she had. Kevin listens intently. When she is finished all Kevin can say is, "It's crazy how detailed your dreams are!"

Lauren, feeling a little vulnerable, pulls the sheets up. "I'm sorry, you must be second guessing yourself right about now!"

Kevin smiles, "Not at all! In fact, I feel very close to you! Protective! And yet, I can't help but wonder if we could maybe get to know each other more?"

Lauren blushes, "After last night, what more is there to learn?"

Kevin shrugs his shoulders, "I'm not sure, but I think it'll be fun trying to find out!"

After they were done exploring more avenues, Lauren's phone rings. It is Roxy. "Hi Roxy! Sorry I didn't come home last night! Everything go ok for you?"

Roxy giggles, "As good as it went for you, I'm sure! Ken took your place here at the hotel!"

Lauren laughs, "Then it was a good night for the both of us!"

Roxy smiles, "That it was! Hey, why don't we meet up at the restaurant for an early lunch? Then we can head out to where I want to see the solar eclipse!"

Lauren nods, "Sounds like a plan. We'll see you there!"

Kevin moans, "Couldn't we just stay here the whole day?"

"I would love that but I promised Roxy I would do this with her! Honestly, it sounds kind of fun! Seeing a solar eclipse that only happens every so often and now getting to see it with you will make it even more special!"

Kevin becomes very serious as he looks intently at her, "How is it possible that I am falling in love with you so quickly?"

Lauren sighs, "I don't know, but I love you too!"

Floating on cloud nine, Lauren can't wait to see Roxy at the restaurant! The two of them quickly excuse themselves so they can finally talk alone in the bathroom.

Roxy is shocked to hear Lauren talking about love. "Honey! For God sake, it's only been one day! There's no way you can truly be in love!"

Lauren looks a little disappointed, "What about you and Ken, didn't you feel a connection?"

Roxy shrugs her shoulders, "He was alright but I see it as being nothing more than a one night stand! I'm fine with that, we are on vacation!"

Lauren suddenly feels bad, "I'm sorry, I can't explain it! Kevin and I have this deep connection! I'm not the only one that thinks it, he feels the same way!"

Roxy rolls her eyes, "Oh please! There has to be something wrong with a guy that tells you he loves you after only one day!"

Lauren becomes defiant, "That's not true! People talk about love at first sight all the time! Plus, who knows, maybe he is my soul mate."

Roxy sighs, "I'm sorry, you're right. Maybe I'm a little jealous. Yea, Ken and I had a good time but it doesn't seem like anything near what you and Kevin have!"

Lauren thinks back about how she felt for Jodi when she found Jady. She was happy for her friend, not jealous! It's sad that Roxy could not be the same!

Lauren smiles, "Well, no matter what, it seems like we all have fun together! Let's just enjoy what the day will bring to us and not worry about the other stuff!"

Roxy happily agrees, "You're right! Who knows, this afternoon when I take my glasses off after watching the solar eclipse maybe I will see Ken as my soul mate too!"

Lauren highly doubts it. Something like what she and Kevin have, you instantly know! However, Lauren is not about to ruin Roxy's day so she simply smiles.

The couples set out in different cars. Lauren drives with Kevin in her car, while Roxy rides with Ken in his Jeep. Lauren had suggested that it would be safer to have two cars where they were going. In reality, it is simply a way for Kevin and Lauren to spend more time alone!

Lauren is curious, "What did Ken think about Roxy?"

Kevin is a little hesitant, "He had a good time with her."

Lauren lets him off the hook, "Yea, Roxy did too. However, she admitted there didn't seem to be much of a connection."

Kevin sighs in relief, "I am so glad to hear that! To be honest, Ken definitely thinks there is no connection!"

Lauren sighs, "That's too bad, but if it isn't there you can't force it!"

Kevin reaches over to hold her hand, "There has been nothing forced about our relationship! It's like I've known you all my life! You are so easy to talk to and this all seems so right!"

Lauren blushes happily, "I couldn't agree more!"

Kevin looks out the window a little concerned, "I'm not sure we should be going to see the solar eclipse though!"

Lauren is surprised, "Why not?"

Kevin is a little embarrassed, "For some reason, something my grandmother told me has been nagging at me all morning!"

Lauren presses him, "What did she say?"

Kevin tries to remember, "You have to understand my grandfather met her overseas and brought her over here. However, she kept her ties with her religion, Hinduism."

Lauren is surprised, "How fascinating! I have heard it is the oldest living religion in the world!"

Kevin smiles, "It is! She always tried to make sure Ken and I understood her roots. Neither Ken nor I are religious, but we always respected her heritage!"

Lauren understands, "I'm sure she had some interesting stories for you!"

Kevin thinks back fondly, "She did! One of them was about eclipses! I think she called them grahanam or something like that."

Kevin is surprised at how easy the story is coming back to him, "She said the word meant planetary possession. Eclipses can torment not only gods, but also humans!"

Kevin tries to explain, "On specific occasions eclipses over-shadow karma and destinies, creating chaos and suffering in human lives!"

Kevin chuckles a little, "She would say 'like the eclipses, sinful karma brings temporary darkness into the lives of people and eclipses their peace and happiness until the light of good fortune shines on them again' a mouthful I know!"

Lauren is intrigued, "How fascinating! Is there more?"

Kevin nods, "As a celestial phenomenon, an eclipse can represent the conflict between good and evil, darkness and light, or gods and demons!"

Lauren cringes when Kevin speaks of demons. Suddenly the memory of the lobby at her apartment complex comes crashing down on her. She now can remember looking out at the people in the lobby and clearly seeing the demons in their midst!

Kevin continues, "Something to do with other shadowy planets that have a score to settle with the Sun and the Moon. I think you telling me that story about Mermac Caverns made me remember all this stuff!"

Kevin thinks about it more, "I remember her saying there was a reason we could predict eclipses so precisely! It was our fear that motivated us!"

Kevin looks over at Lauren anxiously, "Her story was a lot like the Mermac Caverns! However, in her story there were two dark planets portrayed as demons!"

Kevin can't believe the similarities, "The conflict was traced to the churning of the oceans, during which the two demons tried to drink the elixir of immortality."

Kevin finishes, "Before they could drink it the Sun and the Moon noticed it and informed another god who cut off their heads. But get this, a few drops did enter their bodies and so they partially survived and became part of the planetary system!"

Lauren is in disbelief, "How crazy is it that a story believed clear across the world is similar to a belief here?"

Kevin agrees, "And in this day and age we are still repeating them."

Lauren wonders, "Perhaps with good reason!"

Kevin looks worried, "She always told us to stay inside during an eclipse! That symbolically eclipses are associated with demonic possession! It could also be meant to convey dominance or conquest!"

Lauren looks frightened, "The Mermac Cavern story mentioned that solar eclipse really means souler eclipse. Something we obviously believed in when we first named it, but throughout the years it not only lost its spelling but its meaning as well!"

Lauren feels stupid for not seeing all the signs this entire trip! Now, she sees the signs clearly, "I agree with you! I don't think this is a good idea! Can you call Ken and tell him to turn around? Tell him we've changed our minds!"

Kevin quickly pulls out his phone but then shakes his head. "Damnit! We have no reception out here!"

Lauren watches as Ken pulls off the main road onto a secluded dirt road. "Where is he going?"

Kevin shrugs his shoulders, "I have no idea! I have never been out this way. It's pretty close to the reservation and there isn't any reason for us to go there."

Lauren becomes even more concerned as the road becomes harder to drive on, "I'm not sure my poor grandmother's car can handle four wheel driving!"

Kevin has a bad feeling, "I don't understand why Ken would take us out here! His Jeep can handle this with no problem but he knows we're following them! Why not pull over anywhere around here? The view should pretty much be the same for miles!"

Suddenly Lauren stops, "Maybe if we stop he'll realize it and then come back!"

Both Kevin and Lauren watch as the Jeep's tail lights go farther away. Kevin shakes his head, "No, something is wrong! He should have stopped by now!"

Lauren tries to calm him, "I'm sure it's just Roxy trying to get her way! Once she has something in her mind there is no changing it! More than likely, Roxy has convinced Ken it is not much further and it's a once in a lifetime thing!"

Kevin sighs, "I hope you are right! Do you mind if we continue? I really am worried about my brother!"

Lauren carefully maneuvers the car, "Of course! I hope we are getting too caught up in our ghost stories and everything will be fine!"

Before long Lauren is relieved to see that Ken has finally parked the Jeep. She pulls up alongside of them, quickly scanning the remote area around them.

As her and Kevin get out of the car an unnatural silence envelopes them. Ken slowly gets out of the Jeep with wide eyes, "Careful, she has a gun!"

Shocked, Lauren blurts out, "A gun? What the hell Roxy!"

Roxy comes around the Jeep while keeping the gun on them all, "Damnit girlfriend, you have not made this easy have you? What the hell was that stunt of stopping back there when we are this close?"

Lauren stutters, "Kevin and I decided we didn't want to see the solar eclipse! Since the phone wasn't working, I figured stopping would make you stop!"

Ken looks apologetically at them, "I tried! Then I'll be damned if she didn't pull a gun on me and told me to keep driving! I told her you two may need help, your car is not meant for roads like this, but she wouldn't listen!"

Just as Lauren is about to demand an explanation they all hear a car rumbling down the road towards them. When it comes into view they see it is a big service van! Standing in disbelief, they watch as the van parks and twelve passengers get out as well as the driver. Lauren is horrified to see the driver is none other than Mr. Akeru himself!

Smiling, Mr. Akeru approaches the little group. "Hello Lauren, it is so nice to see you again!"

Mr. Akeru is surprised to see Roxy holding a gun on them. "I see my girl is making sure everything is going as planned! How about we all move towards the intended mark?"

Roxy motions them with her gun, "You heard him, move!"

Lauren, Kevin and Ken hesitantly follow Mr. Akeru to an unusual clearing. From a distance you would not think anything of the area because it blends in evenly with the surrounding areas. However, upon closer inspection, small jagged rocks are cleverly placed in a circle reminding Lauren of a miniature Stonehenge.

Looking up at the sky Mr. Akeru smiles, "Almost time!"

Lauren demands to know, "Time for what?"

Mr. Akeru sighs, "I suppose there is time to explain. You see Lauren, you are very special!"

Mr. Akeru motions the twelve strangers to form a circle around them, "I realized while you were in my apartment complex you were being contacted by souls through your white noise sound machine!" He continued condescendingly, "I'm not sure you remember but I did tell you at one time others had interactions similar to yours. However, none of them held the contact as long as you did! No, for some reason after the souls told you their story they stuck to you! Almost as if you were a magnet!"

Mr. Akeru sighs, "When you left my complex you took thirteen souls with you and that was unacceptable! I have a quota to maintain after all!"

Mr. Akeru sees the confusion on all of their faces and tries to explain, "When a soul dies tragically or even is tied to a tragic event it stays in limbo." He begins pacing in front of them, "During this time we try to obtain those souls for ourselves! There are only certain times can we try and get them to be released to us!"

Lauren is beginning to understand, "The apartment complex is an easy place to keep them maintained!"

Mr. Akeru nods, "It is! We have traps all over the world! Some are apartment complexes, hotels, hospitals, even tourist traps!"

Roxy speaks up, "Out on the open road we realized we could use you to round up even more souls for us before the solar eclipse!"

Lauren is in shock, "You were in on this all along?"

Roxy smiles, "No, I was just a lost soul that was attracted to you before Mr. Akeru. I am like the demons you saw in the lobby. I positioned myself to be in your life so I could chip away at your soul!"

Lauren remembers back when she met Roxy. She had been in a dark place and vulnerable. It all makes sense! She has to ask, "Then why have I never seen you as one, like I did with the ones in the lobby?"

Roxy sighs, "You would have if I had come around during your breakdown! Your breakdown allowed you to see on another level! I had to make sure your mind was healed before I came around again!"

Lauren has to know, "Have you always been like this Roxy?"

Roxy smiles a little, "Let me just say, you really shouldn't play around with mirrors!"

Lauren realizes what Roxy is saying, "Of course! When you and your cousins looked in the mirror something did happen!"

Kevin, remembering everything Lauren had told him, has to ask, "Then there really are demons in our midst trying to get our souls?"

Mr. Akeru laughs, "You can call them whatever you want but, yes! Since the beginning of time here on earth!"

Lauren is curious, "Why are there only twelve strangers here? Shouldn't there be more?"

Mr. Akeru answers, "To further our agenda we only want the darker souls. Souls that have been stripped through the centuries and willing and ready to come to our side."

Lauren sighs, "You have somehow found a way to get past the balance! Tip the scales in your favor!"

Mr. Akeru nods, "Slowly but surely! Yes, we have been able to get more evil souls out into the world, now more than ever!"

Mr. Akeru lists them off, "From the complex I am only interested in six of the souls you took! Sissy, the one who burned her sister in the complex."

Lauren has a flashback of the evil girl who tormented her sister, only to burn her in the end so they would be together forever.

Mr. Akeru goes on, "Then there is Bryan, the abusive boyfriend who was able to transfer his soul into the cadaver parts used for a knee surgery."

Lauren is curious, "Wouldn't he still be tied to the guy who had the knee surgery?"

Mr. Akeru smiles sinisterly, "Hadn't you heard? Unfortunately, there was a murder suicide! The guy with the knee surgery went off on a jealous rage and killed the girlfriend and then himself!"

Lauren feels responsible, "I should have followed through and warned her somehow!"

Roxy laughs, "They would have never believed you! That is the beauty of all this! It is so easy to get away with the old ways because no one believes in them now!"

Mr. Akeru continues with his list, "We want Emma, the girl obsessed with her motorcycle."

Lauren thinks back, "Why would you want her? She was not a bad person, the motorcycle influenced her!"

Mr. Akeru shakes his head, "No, her soul had been chipped away for a long time! It is why she was so easily manipulated by the motorcycle!"

Mr. Akeru chuckles, "Then of course there is Ashley, the serial killer on the quest to understand why she was what she was through her DNA!"

Lauren is becoming frustrated, "It never made sense why I dreamed about people who had not died. Ashley wasn't dead; she was just caught!"

Mr. Akeru is becoming impatient with explaining everything, "Stories you have heard are the ones that stand out in the soul's dreams! They may have lived much longer than the incident they told you about!"

Roxy agrees, "Look at the recluse, he merely told you a story of when he first met his wife!"

Lauren wonders, "Then why wouldn't you have his wife's soul too? She was just as bad as he was!"

Roxy nods, "She was, but she didn't tell you the story! She did not make contact with you!"

Lauren suddenly realizes that Roxy knows all of the stories she heard on the trip, "You could hear the stories when I did?"

Roxy looks bored, "Yes! Whether I liked it or not! I heard what you did because I am in connection with you too!"

Lauren looks back over at Mr. Akeru, "What was the last one from the complex you wanted?"

Mr. Akeru smiles, "Morgan, of course!"

Lauren thinks back, "The twin that trapped her doppelgänger in the mirror?" She shakes her head, "She was not dead either. Her doppelgänger was the only one tied to that complex! I would have heard the story from Madison!"

Mr. Akeru sighs, "Eventually she did die and her soul was trapped along with Madison in the mirrors. Remember time is irrelevant when you're dead!"

Roxy agrees, "Look at the hobo, his story was from long ago!"

Lauren shivers, "Morgan still lost her soul to Madison?"

Mr. Akeru nods, "Of course! It is how the doppelgänger works! Unfortunately, Madison was not able to enjoy her life in place of Morgan's, but now she will!"

Roxy adds, "No different than Anna, the hitcher!"

Lauren quickly counts in her head and realizes there are four left from their road trip, "Two more would probably be the girl that haunted the dime and Mike the mechanic from cell 42?"

Roxy smiles, "Very good! Then that would leave us with our most prized two! The witch who fed her babies under Cry Baby Bridge and the woman down by the river who was able to trap the souls of an entire town for generations."

Lauren is curious, "What about the Mermac Caverns?"

Mr. Akeru laughs out loud, "That, my dear, was some stupid random soul of a tourist who had not been collected yet! Awareness happens while you are in limbo. She was only relaying a story she knew from before!"

Mr. Akeru notices that the solar eclipse is about to begin. "That puts us at a tie! 13 Evil Souls and 13 Souls Lost! A balance necessary for the offering!"

Lauren looks over at the twelve strangers, confused, "Why are there only twelve strangers here then, not thirteen?"

Roxy smiles, "Since I was able to help Mr. Akeru with you, I was given the honor to be the thirteenth!"

Trying to buy time, Lauren wonders, "Why thirteen?"

Roxy quickly explains, "The number 13 is symbolic of rebellion and lawlessness. Thirteen represents all the governments made by man and inspired by Satan, or whatever you want to call it, in outright rebellion against the eternal."

Roxy has to add, "Here's an interesting tidbit for you. In the Bible, Mark 7 speaks of 13 things that defile a person. Adulteries, fornicators, evil thoughts, murder, covetousness, thefts, wickedness, licentiousness, guile, blasphemy, foolishness, pride and an evil eye."

Lauren asks, "Wouldn't you have to get each one of those?"

Roxy smiles, "Nah, fortunately for us it's pick and choose!"

Lauren tries to understand, "The solar eclipse opens a doorway and all souls can pass through?"

Mr. Akeru nods, "It does! However, during the eclipse if we quickly baptize my thirteen friends here with the water Roxy has from the Mermac Caverns we can contain the souls here while the door is open!"

Lauren looks nervously around, "What will happen to us?"

Mr. Akeru shrugs his shoulders, "You are still valuable to us and I will be able to set the fog on your mind once again."

Kevin looks over at his brother, "What about us?"

Mr. Akeru shakes his head, "I wasn't planning on Lauren meeting her soul mate along the way! Unfortunately, you two will have to meet again in another life!"

Realizing they have nothing to lose, Ken yells out as he dives for Roxy, "That is unacceptable!"

The twelve strangers take a step forward to help but Mr. Akeru yells, "No! You must remain in a circle at all cost! The eclipse is almost on us! Quickly hold hands! If the circle is broken you will be sucked in dead or alive since you have no soul!"

Roxy realizes she needs to be part of the circle! She fights not only for her life but for her soul!

The strangers obey and stand locked in a circle. Kevin realizes while his brother is fighting with Roxy, he has to go against Mr. Akeru! As he prepares to attack, a sudden fog comes over his mind, paralyzing him!

Lauren reaches down to her ankle and retrieves the knife she had purchased. She had never told Roxy about the strange incident at the knife shop because of the fight they had gotten into in the car afterwards. Looking back, she is thankful she didn't! Lin had told her she had a strong feeling that Lauren needed to carry the knife with her to protect her against demons!

Lin had set Lauren up with an ankle strap so the knife could be concealed. She almost did not put it on this morning but Kevin had convinced her it was smart to have it on her while in the canyon.

Mr. Akeru tries to put a fog on Lauren's mind too but is unable to. Shocked, he sees the knife Lauren is wielding as the last rays of sunlight glint off the steel blade.

Lin had told her the knife would protect her from demons, it was now time to put that theory to the test! Lauren lunges towards Mr. Akeru and easily plunges the knife into his heart. As he falls to the ground dying, the fog lifts from Kevin's mind.

Kevin rushes over to help Lauren. As he reaches her, a gunshot is heard! Lauren's eyes become big as she realizes what that means!

Roxy screams out, having full control of the gun again, "Step away from him!"

Ken lays motionless at Roxy's feet. It takes everything in Kevin's body not to ignore her and run to his poor brother! Kevin and Lauren both raise their hands and step away from Mr. Akeru.

Mr. Akeru calls out to Roxy, "When the souls are released from Lauren the gateway will be busy taking the dead souls first! You can break the circle then and start pouring the water on all thirteen of you to keep the souls we want!"

Mr. Akeru looks back over at Lauren and Kevin laughing, "The plan will go through and there is not a soul out here to help you!"

Roxy quickly grabs hold and completes the circle. Her partner helps her hold the gun while both of their hands are locked.

The solar eclipse starts and they are all in darkness! Roxy realizes, for her to carry out the ceremony alone she will have to kill both Lauren and Kevin! Trying to focus in the darkness, Roxy fires at Kevin first but misses. Suddenly, a bright light overcomes them all! Roxy is temporarily blinded!

Lauren is in shock as she realizes where the light is coming from! Mr. Akeru was wrong! There was a soul still left that would help them; her grandmother!

Lauren's grandmother smiles as she races her car towards the circle of strangers! Lauren screams out to Kevin, "Kevin, move! Grandma is coming!"

Grandma has her sight on Roxy and she runs the car easily through the circle of strangers! Determined not to break the circle, they try to stand their ground but they are no match against her car! Bodies fly up as the car hits them hard!

Roxy focuses on shooting the gun towards Lauren's grandma! However, you can't kill something that is already dead! Grandma continues to race the car towards Roxy.

Realizing her mistake and now knowing her fate, Roxy fires her gun towards Lauren and Kevin hoping she will seal their fate too! She does, as the car slams into her!

Lauren and Kevin both scream out as they fall to the ground! Blood spills out everywhere! Even in their pain their attention is drawn to what they can only think of as, not so much a doorway, but a tear ripping open the sky! A blackness void of all light opening into the unknown!

Lauren feels a bit of a tug as she sees souls releasing themselves from her and flowing into the opening. Dazed, she cries out, "We must help Grandma! She is still trapped in the car!"

However, as luck would have it, when the car hit Roxy the jarring of the collision had opened the passenger door! Grandma's soul is pulled from the car towards the opening!

Once outside of the car, Grandma resists until Roxy and Mr. Akeru's souls have been taken away first! As the solar eclipse comes to an end, Grandma calls out to Lauren right before she enters the opening, "Thank you for releasing me Lauren! Always look for the signs my dear, they will help you with what is to come. I love you!"

Holding one another, Kevin and Lauren find themselves slowly being enveloped by another darkness. Fighting the unconsciousness that is quickly coming over her, Lauren can't help but wonder about what Grandma had said. What signs could there possibly be to help her live without her soul mate, Kevin?

The following are samples of
Tammy Vreeland's other books:

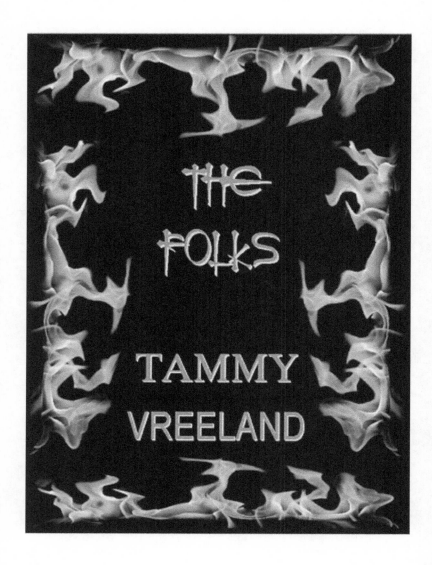

Moving into a new home can become quite stressful. For David, it is the matter of juggling a new job, a mistress and a family at home. For Terry, it is the matter of making her new house into a home and recovering from a nervous breakdown. For Tyler, it is the stress of a five-year-old trying to fit into a new neighborhood with no friends.

A move can be quite difficult on a child, so much so that a way for the child to cope is to have an imaginary friend. This is where *The Folks* come in. You see Tyler not only has one imaginary friend but a whole group of imaginary friends that call themselves *The Folks*. Tyler meets *The Folks* the very first day he moves into his new room.

When Terry, Tyler's mom, finds out about *The Folks* she becomes concerned. Terry's family, friends and even her own therapist tell her that it is a healthy way for Tyler to cope with the move.

However, when accidental deaths begin to occur and Tyler, with his imaginary *Folks*, happens to know more than they should, Terry begins to wonder that perhaps *The Folks* are not so healthy after all!

Tyler, the small boy with the imaginary friends called the Folks, is now grown up. Moving on with his life, he has entered the Coast Guard.

While at Boot Camp, Tyler endures a high fever which brings back flooding memories of the Folks. Memories he's not sure are his own.

Terry, Tyler's mom, ever watchful of the Folk's return, decides to help Tyler get settled in with his new orders. Travis, Tyler's brother, plans on sharing an apartment with Tyler making Tyler's transition even easier.

The two brothers are excited to start their new life in Galveston, Texas. Unfortunately, the island has a dark past of its own. Terry, Tyler and Travis find themselves re-living the past to ensure their future.

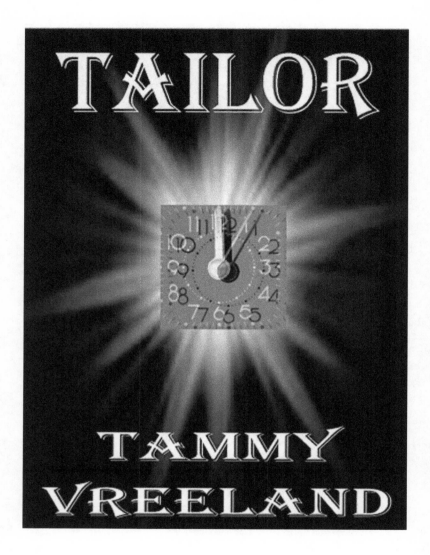

John is a small town reporter who has just been given the chance of a lifetime. The notorious serial killer, Taylor the Tailor, has requested him personally to write her life story. The catch is John has only three days before Taylor is to be electrocuted to interview her.

During those three days John unravels a story like no other. Overwhelmed in just the first interview, John turns to his young assistant Lauren for help. Lauren readily agrees and heads to Taylor's hometown to come up with cold hard facts to help make Taylor's story a credible one.

However, both Lauren and John quickly realize that Taylor's tale may not be that easy to prove. Although both of them are skeptics at heart, they are finding out that Taylor's story is not an easy one to understand or believe. Especially with its supernatural undertones.

John's interviews start off with Taylor's childhood and to his horror John realizes that Taylor had begun to kill as early as the age of four with her first victim being her father. As Taylor grows up her list of victims increases as her skills for being "The Tailor" sharpen.

Tim is Taylor's brother who had been institutionalized at a very young age; upon being released Tim had changed his name so as not to be connected with Taylor in any fashion. Unfortunately, due to Taylor's impending doom, Tim finds himself thrown back into Taylor's world.

Tim and Lauren team up to try and put a stop to Taylor's evil once and for all. Yet, all three of them question why Taylor wants her story to be told now? Is it to seek redemption for all the bad deeds she has done, knowing her time is limited? Maybe, it's to brag to the world how much she got away with and how she did it? Or is it something so much darker that none of them will find out until the third day at the stroke of midnight?

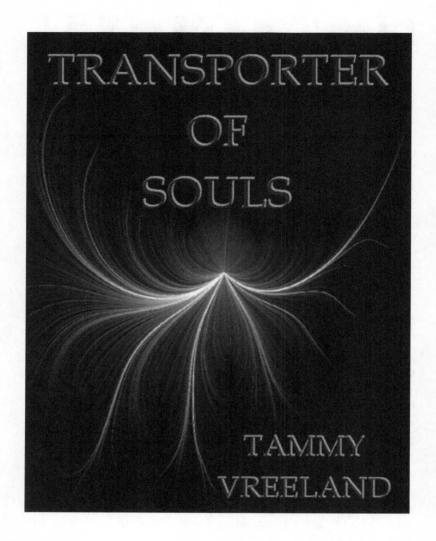

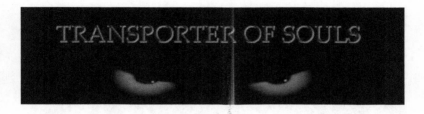

Evan's boss John realizes that Evan has become burned out with Police Towing. The death and destruction that Evan sees on a daily basis has finally taken its toll. Not wanting to lose Evan, John proposes for Evan to start his own business in towing salvage cars.

John assures Evan that he can provide him with enough contacts to start the business up. And strangely enough, the money becomes available to Evan with the unexpected passing of his grandmother.

Now with a new business and a new love interest Evan begins his new life. But soon Evan quickly realizes that the horrors he has encountered at the scene of accidents may not be the end of life as he thought. That maybe souls are still trapped in the ruins of cars they perished in. A curse that began with the very first known automobile accident. A curse that continues to this day. And as with most curses, man has figured a way not to remove it but to profit from it.

CLASS REUNION

Tonya has just received a call from Darla, an old school mate, asking her to come to a class reunion.

Feeling guilty about leaving and never looking back Tonya decides to go.

The reunion is all about catching up with old friends. One friend though, is quite upset with the different paths people chose after graduation.

They feel it is their duty to keep the reputation of the class and school intact. Through the years they had done exactly that.

Now with the reunion coming up, it was the perfect time to deal with many of the classmates in one night.

It's a simple concept, they plan on using the different types of kills Tonya uses in her current horror book "Classmates" to make their own statement.

This will take the suspicion off them and place it on what may simply be a fan of Tonya's making a point.

Only the classmates themselves will know the true identity of the killer, but by then it will be too late!

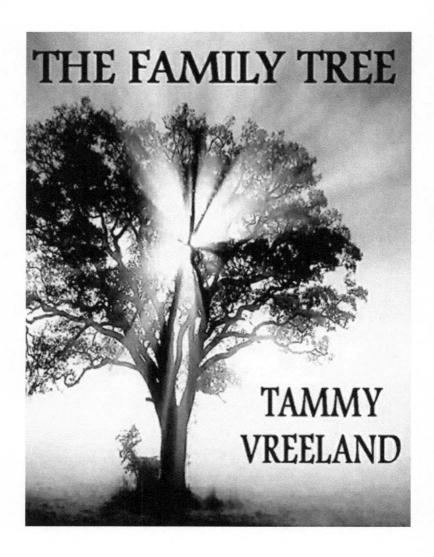

THE FAMILY TREE

Katherine looks down at the book as she lightly runs her fingers over the cover. She can feel the raised insignia of the oak tree with mistletoe in the branches. The title is elegantly written with beautiful penmanship which spells out "The Family Tree".

She timidly opens the book and looks down at the familiar pages in front of her. Tears begin to form in her eyes as she subconsciously rubs her stomach.

Katherine thumbs through the pages. She had always been taught that through her past her future is determined. But, she did not like what her future was to bring.

Why were her ancestors allowed to decide the fate of her unborn twins? Why couldn't she have a choice? Didn't they know what the consequences were? Or were they so blind to the religion, they didn't see it for what it really is?

Again Katherine thinks about the title of the book. Her Family Tree had deep dark roots. Many branches filled the tree but all were tied to one dark secret.

Katherine realizes that she is the one that must cut this tree down. But, how and at what cost? She feels a kick from one of the twins and this gives her hope.

The key had to be the religion. What its origins were, why it was created and how to destroy it. The religion was so old and forgotten that only through tradition had it survived.

Katherine thinks to herself, maybe this generation needed to start a tradition of their own!

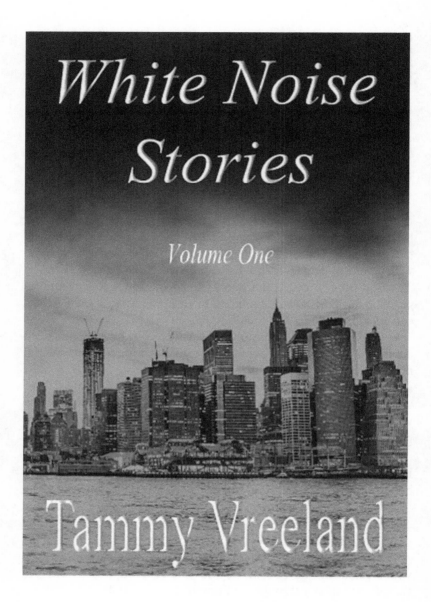

White Noise Stories
Volume One

Lauren finally fulfills her dreams of having her own apartment in the city. However, dreams are a funny thing. They can be your answer but more often than not, a question.

In this case, the apartment is Lauren's answer and yet it brings up the question of how is she going to deal with all of the noise? Whether it be a dog barking, a baby screaming or simply the noise coming up off the street, it is all too much!

Finally, Lauren finds relief when she purchases a sound machine that plays white noise which drowns out all of the noise around her. Perfect! Or, so she thought.

Lauren begins to have strange dreams. Unlike most of her dreams that she cannot remember, these dreams stay with her. Haunt her. Become part of her. Is the white noise giving her access to other people's dreams? People who have died. Can souls dream in death?

Lauren dreams thirteen individual dreams. With each one she finds herself drifting ever closer to the mouth of madness.

Visit me at:

www.tammyvreelandsfanpage.com

****

Also on Facebook:

Tammy Vreeland's Horror Books